LET ME FORGET

(An Ashley Hope Suspense Thriller—Book 5)

Kate Bold

Kate Bold

Bestselling author Kate Bold is author of the ALEXA CHASE SUSPENSE THRILLER series, comprising six books (and counting); the ASHLEY HOPE SUSPENSE THRILLER series, comprising six books (and counting); the CAMILLE GRACE FBI SUSPENSE THRILLER series, comprising eight books (and counting); the HARLEY COLE FBI SUSPENSE THRILLER series, comprising seven books (and counting); and the KAYLIE BROOKS PSYCHOLOGICAL SUSPENSE THRILLER series, comprising five books (and counting).

An avid reader and lifelong fan of the mystery and thriller genres, Kate loves to hear from you, so please feel free to visit www.kateboldauthor.com to learn more and stay in touch.

ISBN: 978-1-0943-8062-9

PROLOGUE

Alden Rayburn jumped in his chair as an explosive blast of thunder rocked the house. The overhead light flickered once and then darkness fell across his study. The power was out. Again. Only this time, rather than it being due to the ancient wiring in the century-old southern colonial, it was the storm that had killed the lights.

Rain pelted the window behind him as he rose from his desk. He'd left his flashlight in the old barn. Braving the icy December downpour, especially this late at night, ranked last on the list of things he wanted to do. But he still had a shoebox full of a client's receipts to go over before their meeting in the morning. He usually didn't schedule business appointments on Sundays, but the client had offered to pay for a round of golf.

Alden thought Grace had stowed a box of candles somewhere in the kitchen. Maybe the pantry. The thought of calling her at her sister's home in Nashville struck him. But it was ten o'clock, and he might wake the kids. He could find the candles on his own.

Easing around the cherry desk that had once belonged to his father, Alden made his way to the door. Obstacles met him in the darkened foyer. Black silhouettes of a ladder, paint cans, brushes, and rollers.

"Restoring the old Taylor mansion will be fun. We can do most of the work ourselves," Grace had said, urging him to purchase the property.

His wife had fantasized about living in the historic home since her childhood. The price for the house that had been updated twenty-five years earlier seemed reasonable, and the sellers had agreed to install a new roof. So, against his better judgement, he'd given in. But the restoration had proven more difficult than just refinishing the hardwood floors, repairing the interior woodwork, and adding a fresh coat of paint to the walls.

They'd discovered hidden termite damage and dry rot, along with a slew of plumbing and electrical problems. He'd already sunk a year's salary into the repairs, and they weren't even half finished.

1

Grace's dream had become Alden's nightmare.

His socked feet rustled the plastic drop cloth lining the floor as he skirted past the ladder. Shuffling through the dining room, he headed toward the kitchen.

Lightning flashed in the window over the sink, followed by a loud clap of thunder.

Alden froze in the doorway—certain he'd heard another noise.

A creaking sound. Like footsteps. The noise seemed to have come from the direction of the rear hallway.

The hairs on the back of his neck bristled.

Was it just the timbers of the old house swaying with the wind?

Tales of restless spirits that haunted the Taylor mansion filled the idle gossip of the Fergus County locals. It was rumored that Zebulon Taylor's wife had poisoned him after learning of his affair with a servant girl. Over the years, several of the locals claimed to have seen his apparition, as well as the spirit of his young lover, prowling the grounds.

But Alden didn't believe in ghosts.

Assuring himself that there was nothing to fear—that it was normal for the old structure to moan and creak in a storm—he stepped into the kitchen. But an eerie feeling still plagued him. He couldn't remember whether he'd locked the door leading out onto the rear porch.

His ears perked for sounds of movement as he crept through the kitchen into the back hallway. The rear door stood closed. His fingers touched the doorknob. It was unlocked. The thumb-turn deadbolt proved unlatched as well.

Securing both locks, he stepped closer to the door, intending to peer out through the glass panes. Icy water seeped through the toes of his socks.

Fear shot through his chest.

Was someone in the house?

Had an intruder opened the back door? Or had the driving wind propelled the rain through a crack in the aging weather stripping?

Alden needed to find the candles. He couldn't work the combination of the gun safe in the master bedroom closet without light. And he wanted the protection of his pistol. Just in case.

Turning away from the door, he stood still and listened. The old house sighed as wind whipped its exterior walls. He thought he heard another creak—footfalls on the floorboards in the adjacent living room.

2

Goosebumps broke out on his arms.

Careful to be as quiet as possible, he hurried back to the kitchen. The hinges squeaked as he edged open the pantry door. In the inky darkness, Alden's hands flew across the shelves, identifying the contents by their shape and size. Boxes of pasta and rice. Canisters he knew held flour, sugar, and cornmeal. Jars of pickles and peanut butter. Canned goods.

Stretching to the top shelf, he reached into an open box. His fingertips slid over cool cylinders of wax. The long-burning emergency candles.

As he grabbed the box, he heard a noise behind him.

Pop!

Pain seared his back.

Every muscle in Alden's body contracted in agony as he crashed to the floor.

CHAPTER ONE

A wave of trepidation hit TBI Special Agent Ashley Hope as she wheeled her shopping cart across the parking lot of Wheldon's Food Market in the Nashville suburb of Briarwood. A familiar eerie sensation swept through her. She'd felt it before—knew what it meant. Someone was watching her.

Tucking errant strands of long, blonde hair behind her ear, she scanned the sea of vehicles and customers crowding the lot, searching for anyone who seemed out of place. No one caught her eye. Still, she knew that he was there. Hiding in the driver's seat of a pickup, an SUV, or maybe a muscle car. Peering at Ashley through the windshield.

Her instincts had never let her down before.

The image of the first note he'd sent—the one he'd stuck beneath her sedan's wiper blade—flashed through her mind.

YOU WILL DIE SOON.

And to let her know that he had the ability to make good on his threat, he'd broken into her apartment while she was away. He'd left another note on her bed pillow. She could still see the capital block-style letters, warning of his intent to strike.

YOUR TIME IS ALMOST UP.

Although she'd investigated, even sent the notes to the TBI lab for analysis, Ashley hadn't been able to uncover the identity of her stalker. She believed the culprit was likely a male cousin of serial killer Ethan Barrett. Ethan hailed from Ashley's rural hometown nestled in the mountains of Laurel County, Tennessee.

As a young teenager, Ashley had fallen in love with Ethan. But after they married, she'd discovered that he had a dark side. A side so evil that it drove him to murder. A judge had granted her a divorce right after handing Ethan a long prison sentence.

Ashley had managed to piece her life back together, earning a master's degree in criminal justice.

But earlier that year, after being denied parole, Ethan had overpowered a guard and escaped. On a rampage, he'd left a trail of

4

bodies behind. And when he'd attempted to murder Ashley, she'd been forced to kill him in self-defense.

The scenes from that night—the horror she'd felt as she'd pulled the trigger of the pistol—haunted her nightmares. And the memory of Ethan's fingers clamped around her neck, choking the life from her body, was one that Ashley would never forget. Killing her ex-husband was not what she'd wanted, but she'd had no other choice.

Now, she suspected Ethan's relatives sought revenge. And like many of the locals in Laurel County, the Barrett clan practiced their own method of law and order. A clandestine vigilante system they termed *mountain justice.*

Picking up her pace, Ashley steered the cart toward her sedan.

As she tapped her key fob that opened the trunk, her eyes swept the vehicles surrounding hers. Everything seemed normal, no one lurking around. She remained on high alert as she loaded the groceries into her car and as she shoved her empty shopping cart into the store's return corral.

The second Ashley slid into the driver's seat of her sedan, she locked the doors. It was only then that she felt somewhat safe. Although armed—her Glock holstered at her side—she still feared that she was a sitting duck. The Barrett clan's reputation nagged at her. Skilled hunters and marksmen, Ethan's cousins possessed the ability to pick her off with a hunting rifle from five hundred yards away.

Ashley's cell phone rang, startling her.

Apprehension grew in her chest. She'd received calls from her stalker before. Threats issued from a staccato, computer-generated voice.

Fishing the phone from her jacket pocket, she glanced at the screen. Relief flooded her body. The call was from her boyfriend, TBI Special Agent Daniel Lansing.

"Hi, Daniel," she answered, forcing a cheery note into her tone.

At this point, she didn't want to alarm him. Not until she actually spotted someone who might be her stalker.

"Hey, sweetheart," he said, his voice like a soothing balm. "Just wanted to let you know that I'll be working until at least six."

Although it was a Sunday, she was lucky to be able to spend the evening with him. Daniel had been assigned to a complicated undercover case that required long hours, even on the weekends.

"Okay, I'll wait until around six-thirty before I start cooking dinner."

Ashley planned to serve his favorite meal: T-bone steak with roasted garlic potatoes and asparagus. They'd recently suffered through a rough patch in their relationship, which she knew was her fault. She'd waited too long to admit that she'd been forced to share a motel room—and a bed—with her male partner during her last TBI assignment. Daniel had found out the hard way—discovering the man's shirt in Ashley's luggage.

Although nothing inappropriate had happened between Ashley and her partner—she'd even slept in her jeans—her omission had hurt Daniel and strained his trust. If she had explained the situation at the onset, although her boyfriend wouldn't have liked it, he would have understood. The trouble in their relationship could have been avoided.

With a busy work schedule of her own, Ashley rarely found the time to cook. Tonight's dinner had been designed as a peace offering. She didn't want to lose Daniel. He'd proven to be the kindest, most thoughtful, and loving man she'd ever dated.

He was smart and funny, possessing the ability to make her laugh with ease. And he'd encouraged her to follow her dreams, setting up her initial job interview with the TBI. Not to mention the fact that he was one of the handsomest men she'd ever laid eyes on, with his dark hair, blue eyes, sexy dimples, and athletic physique.

"I'll get there as soon as I can," Daniel promised.

"Okay. Be careful."

Ending the call, Ashley veered out of Wheldon's parking lot and headed toward her garage apartment, tucked inside one of Briarwood's well-established residential neighborhoods. She checked her rearview mirror as she drove, watching for any vehicles that might be following her.

All seemed clear as she pulled into her concrete driveway and rolled past the main house—a brick Georgian style—that belonged to her landlords. The garage door hummed, rising out of the way. Parking her sedan, Ashley killed the engine.

Before exiting her car, she pivoted in the driver's seat and peered through the rear window. She waited a few seconds, eyeing the street behind her. Satisfied that no one had followed her home, she lowered the garage door and popped open her trunk.

Her arms laden with paper grocery bags, she maneuvered her way out through the garage's side door. A gust of December wind chilled her cheeks as she climbed the open stairs leading up to her apartment.

When she reached the landing, Ashley froze.

The door to her apartment stood ajar.

After the break-in, she'd paid to have the locks changed. And before leaving to go shopping, she'd double-checked the door, making sure it was secure.

The hairs at the back of her neck stood on end.

Ashley eased her grocery bags down onto the floor of the landing. She drew her Glock from its holster. Poised to fire, she nudged the door the rest of the way open with her foot.

The living room was empty. She inched across the threshold. As she crept toward the open dining area, Ashley heard a noise coming from the direction of the bathroom.

Water running.

Was her stalker playing a game? Ashley was certain he—or at least someone—had been watching her at the food market. Her instincts didn't lie.

Did the man have help? Had he sent someone to flood her apartment while she was away?

And more important—was the person still here?

The sound of rushing water stopped. The tap had been shut off.

With her heart hammering in her chest, Ashley skulked through the short hallway toward the bathroom. Glock first, she swung around the door frame.

A man with salt-and-pepper hair stood before her, his eyes wide with fright.

It was Milton Merrick, her landlord.

Ashley had sneaked into the apartment in silence. She'd obviously taken him by surprise.

"I'm sorry if I scared you, Milton, but I thought someone had broken in again," she said, holstering her weapon.

He nodded. "It's always good to have a cop around." He motioned toward the fiberglass tub and shower combo. "I just fixed your shower head."

"That was fast. Thank you."

Only one day had passed since she'd mentioned the leak. She'd never expected Milton to repair it that soon.

"If you have any more problems, let me know."

Ashley followed Milton out of the apartment and onto the landing. After grabbing her groceries, she headed back inside. She glanced at the clock hanging on the wall as she placed the paper bags on the dining table. 10:15 a.m. She decided to go ahead and prepare the steak marinade.

When she reached into the sack that contained the Worcestershire sauce and garlic cloves, she spotted the card she'd purchased for Daniel. Just a little something to help express how much he meant to her.

As she opened the card, a white sheet of paper slipped out and fell to the floor.

A chill raced down Ashley's spine as she unfolded the paper.

THE CLOCK TICKS.

HOW IS SPENCER?

The message had been written by the same hand as the others she'd received. But this time, the stalker appeared to be threatening not only Ashley, but also her father, Spencer Hope.

She remembered leaving her shopping cart unattended for a minute or two while she spoke with Wheldon's butcher. That must have given the stalker the time he'd needed to stick the note inside the card.

Worried for her father's safety, Ashley pulled out her phone and tapped his contact. Spencer was old school. He didn't own a cell—only a landline. The phone rang fifteen times with no answer.

Fear wormed its way into her heart. Had the stalker attacked her father?

The easiest—and most devastating way—to hurt Ashley would be to harm a member of her family.

She knew her brothers, Kyle and Shane, had planned to spend the day hunting deer in Tucker Holler. She tried both of their cell phones but was directed to voicemail each time. The cell service proved spotty in the holler. It might take hours to reach them.

She crammed her perishable groceries into the refrigerator, bags and all.

Ashley needed to make the two-hour drive to her father's home in Laurel County.

And she didn't have a second to waste.

CHAPTER TWO

The sedan's tires kicked up clouds of dust as Ashley sped along the hard-packed dirt driveway that cut into the one-hundred-and-fifty-acre, forested property where her father lived. Frantic to speak with him—desperate to make sure he was safe—she'd been calling his landline every few minutes during the two-hour drive from Briarwood But Spencer had failed to answer.

Ashley had even contacted the phone company, just to confirm the line was in working order. She knew her father had planned to stay home and watch a television sports show followed by a football game. So, why wasn't he answering?

Had the stalker attacked her father during the previous night?

The note stuffed inside Daniel's greeting card hinted that something sinister had happened to Spencer. Family ties ran deep in Laurel County, the mountain blood thick. And the backwoods locals who practiced their own brand of vigilante justice favored harming an enemy's close relative as a form of punishment. They'd drop the victim's body into one of the abandoned wells or old mine shafts that riddled the mountains, knowing the bones would never be found.

Ashley prayed that Spencer was still alive.

As the sedan bounced onto the wooden bridge spanning the creek on the property, a mottled brown and white barred owl swooped down from the twisted branch of a maple tree. The large bird dove straight toward the car. Ashley slammed the brakes, skidding to a stop. The owl's coal-black eyes seemed to lock with hers as it soared across the hood of the sedan, inches from the windshield.

Goosebumps broke out on Ashley's arms.

Barred owls rarely ventured out of their nesting spots in the daytime. Was the sighting a portent of things to come? A bad omen?

Ashley mashed the accelerator, rocketing over the bridge. She feared what she might find ahead. It wasn't just the stalker's veiled threat that worried her. Spencer had suffered a heart attack in the spring. And although he was on the road to recovery, his health still remained a concern.

Images of her father clutching his chest and falling to the living room floor flooded Ashley's mind. He could be lying helpless, mere feet from the phone, unable to answer.

Did the stalker know something she didn't? Was he watching Spencer as well? Had he peered through a window and spied her father's lifeless body inside the house?

With her mind spinning, Ashley increased her speed, driving as fast as she dared up the rutted dirt drive. The forest of dormant oaks and hickories parted, giving way to a large clearing. And the Appalachian farmhouse—built by her great-grandfather from lumber milled on the property—popped into view.

Although her brothers owned trailers located on the land that had been passed down in the Hope family for generations, Spencer lived in the farmhouse alone. And Kyle had told Ashley that he and Shane would be leaving home before dawn, planning to be at Tucker Holler at first light to hunt deer. If their father had fallen ill—or worse—her brothers would have no way of knowing it.

The anxiety in her heart grew as Ashley spotted her father's red pickup parked in front of the house. If his truck was home, he should be as well. Angling her sedan alongside the pickup, she killed the engine.

She scanned the yard as she hopped out of her car. Ashley had expected to be greeted by Spencer's Bluetick hound, Ace. But the dog was nowhere in sight. Maybe he was inside the house. Or maybe …

Pushing the thought that the stalker might have killed Ace out of her mind, she raced up the ancient sandstone walkway toward the house.

As she neared the long front porch, Ashley stopped dead in her tracks.

A sickening sight met her.

A decapitated opossum hung by its tail from a thin rope that had been nailed to the front door. Above the dead animal, a white piece of paper fluttered in the breeze. She bounded up the porch steps and read the note.

ASHLEY IS NEXT.

Her pulse quickened as she pounded on the door.

"Daddy!" she called out. "Are you in there?"

Her fingers flew to the knob. It was locked. Although Ashley had a key, she didn't carry it with her. In her rush to get to Laurel County, she'd forgotten about the key, leaving it behind in her apartment.

Moving to the window on her right, she pressed her face against the glass panes and peeked through the narrow gap between the blind's slats. A Christmas tree adorned with family ornaments—many of which were decades older than Ashley—stood near the window, blocking a good portion of the view. But she didn't think Spencer was inside the living room. At least, he wasn't where she could see him.

The sound of an engine caught her attention.

Ashley whirled around, her gaze shooting down the driveway. Kyle's white pickup broke from the tree line. The sight of her brother's truck stirred a small amount of hope in her soul.

Kyle had a key to their father's house. They could get inside and find out what was wrong. If Spencer was there—if he hadn't been abducted—maybe it wasn't too late to get him medical help. She trotted down the porch steps and dashed toward the driveway.

As the pickup rocked along the dirt drive, easing closer to her, Ashley spotted three people packed in the cab. Her older brother, Kyle, was behind the wheel; her younger brother, Shane, was in the passenger seat; and Spencer was squeezed in the middle.

A sweet sense of relief flooded her heart.

Her father had obviously changed his mind about watching the sports program, opting instead to join her brothers on the deer hunt.

Spencer was safe. For now. But how would he react when faced with the opossum nailed to his door? Would knowing the stalker had left another threat against Ashley's life stress his heart?

She thought about pulling Kyle to the side, having him take the dead animal down before their father had the chance to see it. But then she realized that Spencer needed to be made aware of everything that had happened. He needed to be on guard—ready to protect himself. Just in case he ended up in the stalker's crosshairs.

As the white pickup rolled to a stop, Ace leapt out of the back and loped toward her.

"Hi, boy," she said, scratching the dog's head.

Her brothers' hunt had obviously been successful. A mature twelve-point buck lay in the pickup's bed.

A look of surprise crossed Kyle's face as he swung out of the driver's seat.

He appeared overdue for a haircut, his wheat-blond strands curling up around the sides of his orange hunting cap. Kyle and Ashley had inherited their mother's hair color, while Shane shared the thick, auburn locks of their father. But along with the wisdom time had afforded him, silver now streaked Spencer's head.

"Weren't expecting to see you today, Ash," Kyle said, pulling her into a hug.

His eyes let her know that he was wondering whether something was wrong. She'd told him on the phone that she hoped to spend the day with Daniel.

Shane edged his way around the nose of the truck, his reliance on his cane clearly diminished since the last time she'd seen him. Suffering a spinal injury at the hands of Ethan Barrett, her younger brother had struggled to regain his full mobility. She was amazed by the progress he'd achieved.

At six-foot-three, Shane stood a head taller than his older brother, Kyle, but as he leaned on his cane, the difference between them didn't seem as noticeable.

He gave her a quick peck on the cheek. "Why're you here?" he asked.

Shane wasn't one for practicing the art of tact. Since childhood, he'd always been blunt and to the point.

Instead of answering, Ashley's gaze flew to her father.

She wrapped her arms around his neck, thankful that he hadn't been harmed.

"How's my baby girl a doing?" he asked her, love shining in his blue eyes.

"I'm fine, Daddy," she said, realizing that her words didn't sound very convincing.

Shane pressed again, "What happened?"

Ashley sighed. "My stalker has been here," she stated. "He left another message hanging on Daddy's front door."

Hatred flashed across Shane's face. "I'm gonna kill them lowdown sons of—"

"Shane," Spencer interrupted, his voice strong and firm. "Unless Ashley tells us different, we ain't got no way of knowing who done it."

"It was them Barretts," her younger brother said, conviction in his tone. "And they got it coming."

12

Ashley shot Shane a warning look. "You're not going to do anything to anyone, understand? This will all be handled legally—through the court system—as soon as I get solid evidence pointing to the person who has been following me."

She hoped her younger brother would heed her words and that he wouldn't stir the Barrett clan's ire further, putting his own life in jeopardy.

Kyle asked, "How'd you know they'd been here?"

He obviously realized that she'd suspected her father was in trouble. That worry had spurred her two-hour drive to Laurel County.

"Someone slipped a note into my shopping cart at the grocery store this morning."

"They threaten Daddy?"

Ashley wondered whether she should share the contents of the message, or if she should gloss over the fact that her father's name had been mentioned. The truth won out.

"The note said: '*How is Spencer?*' But that was all. There were no actual threats made against Daddy."

"So, you come running here to check," Kyle stated. "Maybe that's what they wanted."

"Do you think the message was a ploy to lure me back to Laurel County?"

Ashley hadn't considered the idea before, but it made sense. It would be easier for the Barrett clan to attack her on their home turf.

"Damn straight. They're liable to be setting up an ambush. What's the note on Daddy's door say?"

The image of the poor, decapitated opossum flashed through her memory, and her stomach shuddered. Now that she knew her father was out of immediate danger and she could begin to analyze the scene, a question nagged at her. Why had the stalker chosen that particular animal to hang on the door? Did it mean something?

Was the dead animal sending a message by itself?

"Someone killed an opossum," she said. "The note they left says that I'll be the next one to die."

Shane shook his head. "Oh hell, no," he said. "I'm gonna make them Barretts wish they'd never been born."

Spencer put his hand on Shane's arm. "Like Ashley done said, you ain't gonna do nothing. You gotta respect her wishes. Let her handle it like she wants."

13

Ashley suspected that her father shared her fears—that he worried Shane would prove to be the loser in a fight with the Barrett clan.

Shane sighed. "Then I'll come stay with you for a while," he told Ashley. "Till you figure out which one of Ethan's kin done it."

She loved her brother and appreciated his concern, but Ashley didn't really believe it was necessary for Shane to babysit her. After all, she was an experienced TBI agent. She'd been trained to protect herself.

"I'll be fine on my own," she said. "What I need is for you to stay here with Daddy. Why don't you move in with him for a little while?"

Spencer spoke up, "Ain't no reason for Shane to bed down at my place. I got Ace, and I got my partners, Smith and Wesson. They'll do just fine to keep me safe. But I tell ya what we are gonna do. When you get ready to leave, Ashley, we're gonna follow you past the county line. Just to make sure the Barretts ain't lying in wait."

Ashley glanced at the clock on her phone. If she left now, she'd make it back to Briarwood a little after three. And the steaks she planned to cook for her dinner with Daniel needed a few hours to marinate.

"I don't mean to rush off, Daddy," she said, her voice sounding apologetic. "But I really need to head back to Briarwood now."

"I know you got things to do," Spencer said. "You just be careful."

As Ashley slid into the driver's seat of her sedan, a thought struck her. While it seemed likely that the Barrett clan had wanted to lure her to Laurel County, where she'd be easy prey, another possibility tugged at her mind. What if the stalker's true motive had been to ensure Ashley would be away from home for a few hours? What if he'd set up a trap inside her apartment?

A chill raced down her spine.

Ashley hoped that she wouldn't find a surprise waiting for her when she got home.

CHAPTER THREE

Apprehension had nibbled at Ashley during the entire trip home from Laurel County. She'd feared that the stalker had taken advantage of her absence and had broken into her garage apartment again. But when she'd arrived, she'd found the door still locked tight. An inspection of her rooms proved nothing was missing or out of place. And she hadn't discovered any new threatening notes.

At this point, she had no idea why the stalker had lured her to Spencer's house.

But her instincts warned Ashley that there had been a reason.

She'd stopped by Wheldon's Food Market on the way home. Flashing her TBI creds, she'd asked to see the security footage from that morning. But the surveillance cameras in the entire rear section of the store had been down for the past two days. There was no way for her to identify the person who'd slipped the note into her shopping cart

Was it just a coincidence, or did the stalker know the cameras weren't working?

The timer on Ashley's oven beeped, pulling her thoughts back to the present. Dinner was ready.

Hearing a knock on her apartment door, she stripped off her makeshift apron—a kitchen towel fastened to the front of her silk dress with clothespins—lit the candles on the dining table, and rushed into the darkened living room. Although Daniel had called, letting her know that he was on his way, she looked through the door's peephole just to make sure it was him.

Nervous excitement—like that of a giddy teenager—filled Ashley's chest as she caught sight of her boyfriend standing on the landing, a bouquet of roses in one hand and a bottle of wine in the other. Although they'd been dating exclusively for a few months now, it still amazed Ashley how she'd managed to get so lucky. She knew that men like Daniel were few and far between. And she hoped to wow him with her near expert, but seldom used, cooking skills. She unlocked the deadbolt and pulled open the door.

His dimpled smile still possessed the power to make her heart flutter.

Wrapping his arms around her, Daniel met her with a kiss, long and sweet. Dampness from a shower lingered in his thick, dark hair, and his skin carried the mingled scents of soap, bergamot, and sandalwood.

"These are for the chef," he said, presenting her with the deep red blooms.

Ashley returned his smile. "Thank you. They're beautiful."

"Not half as beautiful as you."

The reply was corny and clichéd, but Ashley didn't care. She relished the words.

"Your timing is perfect tonight," she told him. "I just took the roasted potatoes out of the oven."

Daniel followed her inside the apartment. Grabbing a vase from her cupboard, she filled it with water, arranged the flowers inside, and placed them in the center of the dining table.

Although he'd poured them both a glass of merlot, her boyfriend hadn't yet taken a seat.

"What can I do?" he asked.

Although she knew he was referring to helping her in the kitchen, steamy thoughts filled her mind. She felt her face grow warm.

"For now, just sit down, relax, and prepare to stuff yourself."

Ashley carted the platters of food into the open dining area. As she placed the bowl containing the tossed salad onto the table, her cell phone rang.

Although she hated to interrupt the dinner by taking a phone call, Ashley worried something dire could have happened back in Laurel County.

"That could be my father," she told Daniel, knowing he would understand.

He nodded in agreement.

She scooped her phone up from the living room coffee table and checked the screen. It was her TBI partner. Why was he calling her on their evening off?

Still carrying the phone, she returned to the table.

"It's Wyatt," she stated, unsure whether or not she should let the call go to voicemail.

Ashley knew Daniel wasn't a fan of her partner—an agent better known around the bureau for his sexual prowess than for his detective

16

skills. And the fact that she'd been forced to share a motel bed with Wyatt during their last investigation didn't help.

"Go ahead and answer," Daniel said. "It could be important."

She sank into her dining chair, placed the phone on the table, and tapped the speaker icon. Whatever her partner had to say, it would be kept safe with Daniel.

"Hi, Wyatt. What's up?"

"I just got off the phone with Brenda," he said, his voice grave. "We've been handed a new case."

Ashley shot Daniel an apologetic glance. She knew the TBI's hard-nosed deputy director viewed time as their most valuable asset—not to be wasted. Brenda likely expected Wyatt and Ashley to begin working on the new investigation tonight. Now.

Ashley would need to go, leaving Daniel to eat his dinner in her apartment alone.

"Has there been a murder?" she asked.

"It's a missing persons case. A relative of the sheriff over in Fergus County."

A large percentage of the individuals originally classified as missing persons ended up being homicide victims. Ashley realized that their investigation would likely lead to a dead body.

"When do we need to be there?"

Located along the Cumberland Plateau, Fergus County was at least a two-hour drive away from Briarwood.

"Early in the morning," he stated. "I'll pick you up around five-thirty."

She nodded, although she knew that he couldn't see her. "Okay, I'll be ready to go."

"Good. I'll get online tonight and book us a motel room."

Ashley locked eyes with Daniel. The expression that crossed his face let her know that he'd picked up on Wyatt's use of the singular term, *room*.

"Two rooms," Ashley spat out. "We need two motel rooms."

Wyatt hesitated for a moment. "Right," he said, a hint of awkwardness in his tone.

Was his delayed response because he'd meant that he would book a room for each of them and was wondering why she'd freaked out? Or had he planned on them sharing again—as friends? She hoped that it was the former.

17

Ashley sat speechless, trying to figure out what was going on in Wyatt's mind.

"Okay, then," he finally said, breaking the silence. "I'll see you in the morning."

As she ended the call, Ashley noticed Daniel's bottom lip clenched between his teeth. He was obviously pondering Wyatt's motives.

"He was testing you," Daniel said, a note of ire in his voice.

"What do you mean—testing me?"

"He said '*a room*' on purpose, Ashley. He wanted to see if you were open to sleeping with him."

That couldn't be true. Could it? Had Wyatt misinterpreted something she'd said or done? Did he think she wanted a physical relationship with him? By handling the reservations himself, would he claim that they had to stay together again so that he could seduce her? Ashley wasn't so sure.

Even if the situation arose where they were forced to bunk together again, it seemed likely that Wyatt would behave the same as he had before.

"He never tried anything with me the last time we shared a room," she said, thinking out loud.

Ashley wanted to give Wyatt the benefit of the doubt. She'd read him wrong on so many occasions; it had almost wrecked their partnership. And just because he had a reputation as a womanizer didn't mean that he'd decided to hit on her.

Daniel tilted his head. "The last time?"

"The only time. And I don't plan on staying in the same room with him ever again."

Although Daniel had declared more than once that he trusted her, she could tell that he wasn't happy about her trip to Fergus County. But it seemed likely that it wasn't actually Ashley's prior behavior that had raised doubts in his mind. She realized that he might be drawing on feelings from his past.

Ashley reached for Daniel's hand, caressing his fingers. "I promise that you don't have anything to worry about," she said, meeting his gaze. "I'm not Melody."

At the mention of his ex-wife's name, Daniel's face clouded, and he pulled his hand away. He sat back in his chair, putting distance—like a wall—between them.

18

Ashley had obviously said the wrong thing. But it was too late; the words were already out.

Daniel had married Melody, his high school sweetheart, the week after they'd both graduated from college. A year later, he'd caught her in bed with another man.

"The steaks are getting cold," Daniel said, his posture rigid.

He obviously wanted to close the subject.

Ashley realized that if he hadn't been comparing her to Melody before, he definitely was now. She should have kept her mouth shut. Bringing up his past at this moment appeared to have had the same effect as rubbing salt in his wounds.

Melody had been Daniel's first love—someone he'd given his complete trust. And the pain from her betrayal was likely something that he would never forget. Ashley's ex-fiancé, Brett, had cheated on her as well. She knew from her own experience how difficult it must be for Daniel to open his heart again. To allow himself to become vulnerable.

An awkward silence settled over the room as they ate their meal. Ashley wasn't sure what to say. She feared that she would just make matters worse. And Daniel didn't seem interested in conversation. It was as though he'd emotionally shut down, retreating into his own thoughts.

When dinner was finished, he helped her load the dishes into the dishwasher.

"I'm going to head out," he said, dropping the last piece of silverware into the dishwasher's basket. "You need to get a good night's rest before your trip."

A wave of disappointment struck Ashley. She wanted him to stay, but she could tell by his demeanor that he'd made up his mind to leave. And it wasn't because she had to get up early the next morning.

Daniel gave her a quick kiss goodnight. Standing at her apartment door, she watched him trudge down the stairs and slide into his sedan. The fear that he was regretting getting involved with her nudged at Ashley's heart.

Would Daniel decide that she wasn't worth the risk? Was he as committed to making their relationship work as she was?

Or would her trip to Fergus County spell the end of their love affair?

Ashley forced her troubled thoughts from her mind as she closed and locked the door. She had a lot of packing to do before turning in for the night. Hopefully, Daniel would be willing to talk things out in the morning.

CHAPTER FOUR

The frosty morning breeze jostled the bare branches of the oak tree stretching over the end of Ashley's driveway as she wheeled her suitcase toward the rear of Wyatt's black SUV. He popped open the cargo door and stowed her luggage inside. As usual, every strand of his sandy-blond hair remained in place.

Wyatt's tailored sports coat, chinos, and loafers stood in stark contrast to Ashley's multi-pocketed, cargo-style jacket, jeans, and hiking boots. Although her partner always opted for the classic business attire most often worn by the bureau's special agents, the customary look didn't suit Ashley's needs.

Just as comfortable donning a cocktail dress and heels as she was a T-shirt, Ashley's ultra-casual work wardrobe wasn't rooted in a lack of sophistication; it had been well-planned. Her choice in clothing served a key purpose.

Ashley aimed to fit in with the Fergus County locals.

Like her own hometown, Fergus County rested in the heart of Tennessee's majestic mountains. And the locals' attitudes concerning law enforcement likely mirrored the opinions of the people Ashley had been raised around—rural folk saddled with preconceived notions passed down from their ancestors, along with the land on which they lived.

As she pulled her jacket tight around her, blocking out the morning chill, stories she'd heard during her childhood in Laurel County flooded Ashley's mind. Tales of state lawmen who'd ventured into the mountains searching for moonshine stills to dismantle and bootleggers to arrest. Instead, they'd met the grim reaper. Their bodies had never been found. She guessed Fergus County was the home of similar legends.

Even today, a large percentage of the mountain folk considered law enforcement to be the enemy. An arm of the government that threatened their generations-long way of life. This fact had often proven to be an obstacle in investigating crimes in the area. By drawing on her heritage, Ashley had found that she could gain the trust of the rural residents. Winning them over was the first—and most important—step in loosening the locals' lips and obtaining information that could solve a case.

Wyatt slammed the SUV's cargo door shut.

As Ashley slid into the passenger's seat, he handed her a stainless-steel mug, complete with a locking lid.

"Home-brewed coffee," he said, his hazel eyes sparkling.

Wyatt favored a gourmet dark roast with an intense, irresistible flavor. She hoped the caffeine would help shake off some of the grogginess plaguing her. Sleep had evaded her most of the night. She'd lain awake, analyzing her relationship with Daniel. They'd spoken on the phone for a few minutes this morning, but Ashley hadn't broached the prior evening's conversation. The timing had felt off.

"This is exactly what I need right now," Ashley told Wyatt as she accepted the coffee. "Thank you."

Wyatt pressed the button on the SUV's center console, and it flipped open. He pointed to the large, black thermos inside.

"There's plenty for refills," he said. "Just help yourself."

He snapped the console shut and then eyed the rearview camera as he backed out of Ashley's driveway.

Cupping her hands around her mug, she took a sip of the full-bodied brew. The temperature was perfect. The warmth from the liquid spread throughout her body.

"So, tell me what you know so far about the missing person," she said, settling into her seat for the long ride ahead.

"We're looking for a male. Twenty-five years old. He works as a process server for Doak Legal Process."

Upon hearing the nature of the man's occupation, Ashley's stomach sank. Another profession mountain folk hated—almost as much as law enforcement—was that of legal process server. Often viewed as a henchman sent out to do the establishment's dirty work, the server's job carried a high rate of risk in the backwoods.

"Do you know his name?"

"Cole Gowen. He's single, and he's the nephew of the Fergus County sheriff."

Rather than providing Cole with a modicum of protection, the fact that he was related to the local sheriff added another strike against him.

The man had probably gone out to serve a court summons and had been met with a shotgun.

"You do realize that Cole was most likely murdered, right?"

She hated to state the obvious, but Wyatt had grown up in the city. He wasn't accustomed to the mountain clans' views on justice and their lack of respect for the court system.

"Yeah. I'm betting Sheriff Hyland does too."

Ashley agreed. The sheriff's belief that his nephew had succumbed to foul play was likely the reason he'd called the TBI for help. Hyland was probably desperate for answers, and the locals must not be willing to talk.

One thing had always held true: the mountain folk protected their own. Even if one of their clan was guilty of murder.

Staring out the SUV's side window at the sleeping storefronts that lined the downtown streets of Briarwood, Ashley's mind drifted to her own family. She hoped the stalker hadn't decided to pay her father another visit. Although her brothers lived on the same tract of land, they couldn't always be there to watch over him. Both Kyle and Shane worked at their family's automotive repair shop, and of course, they had social lives. There would be long stretches of time when her father would be alone. She just prayed that Ace would alert him if someone tried to sneak onto the property.

As the SUV merged into the interstate traffic, Ashley drained her coffee mug. She glanced at Wyatt. He seemed to be in a much better mood than the last time she'd seen him. The poker face he normally wore had been replaced with a slight smile. She wondered what he was thinking. She hoped that he had good news concerning his seven-year-old daughter. Although Wyatt had never been married, she knew that he held a shared-custody arrangement with the child's mother.

"How have things been going with Kaylee?" she asked.

"Much better. She's finally sleeping through the night again. Not as many bad dreams."

Kaylee had witnessed the death of her best friend—the victim of a hit-and-run driver. And now, the child was terrified she'd lose her father as well. During the last homicide investigation Ashley and Wyatt had been assigned, he'd put his job on the line in order to spend time with Kaylee. To reassure her that everything would be okay.

Wyatt definitely had his faults. He and Ashley had gotten off to a rough start in their partnership, with friction at nearly every turn. He could be stubborn and opinionated. With his usual stone-faced expression, it was often hard for her to know whether he was being serious or if he was making an attempt at humor. There had been a time or two when he'd inadvertently caused her to doubt herself. And she supposed the rumors that he was a Casanova might be true. But from what she'd observed, he was one hell of a dad.

It was his devotion to Kaylee that had led Ashley to see Wyatt in a new light. She'd realized that he wasn't as shallow as she'd once thought. He was intelligent, resourceful, and calm under pressure. And she wanted their partnership to work.

The SUV's tires hummed on the asphalt. Like a lullaby, the steady sound threatened to lure her to sleep. She yawned and stretched. She needed more caffeine.

Ashley and Wyatt both reached for the console's button at the same instant.

His fingers brushed against hers.

Wyatt swung his gaze toward her, and she saw something flicker in his eyes. Longing? Ashley jerked her hand back.

"Sorry," she said, stunned by the near-pining expression that had crossed his face for a spilt second.

Was Daniel right? Did Wyatt plan to seduce her on this trip?

Ashley would have to be blind not to notice her partner's striking features. His thick, sandy hair, his hazel eyes that leaned toward green, and his masculine square jaw. And there had been a moment during their last investigation when he'd removed his shirt—revealing his sculpted chest and shoulders and ripped abs—that had almost stolen her breath away. She had to admit that Wyatt had been well-blessed in the physical sense.

But no matter how attractive she found him, Ashley would never cheat on Daniel.

Not in a million years.

Wyatt opened the console. "You go first," he said, his lips curving into a grin.

Hit by a wave of awkwardness, she pulled out the thermos. After filling her cup, she scooted away from him, pushing her body against the passenger door. Wyatt obviously didn't realize that he'd made her uncomfortable. Touching her hand had seemed to energize him. She thought that she heard a near-inaudible tune as he poured his coffee.

Was he humming to himself?

24

As she hugged the door, the vehicle's cab seemed to close in around Ashley. The space now felt far too small—almost suffocating. She wondered how many miles they had left to drive before they reached the Fergus County town of Arbuckle. She couldn't wait to get out of the SUV.

Ashley wanted to put as much distance as she could between herself and Wyatt.

CHAPTER FIVE

Ashley unbuckled her seatbelt the second the SUV's tires hit the pavement in the parking lot of the Fergus County Sheriff's Department. Her flight instinct had nagged at her for over an hour, urging her to flee as far from Wyatt as she could go. But she couldn't let her uneasiness—or her desire to put distance between them—jeopardize the case. In order for the missing persons investigation to be successful, she'd have to ignore the way Wyatt had responded when their fingers had touched. Pretend it never happened.

Maybe she just needed some fresh air to clear her mind. She should try to analyze the situation objectively. Maybe she'd been mistaken regarding Wyatt's reaction. She'd misread him in the past. It was possible that he felt just as awkward about brushing hands as she did.

As the SUV rolled to a stop, Ashley hopped out of the passenger's seat and took a deep breath. The cold mountain air stung her lungs, but it didn't bother her a bit. In fact, it was exhilarating. She felt like a bird that had just escaped from a cage.

Instead of waiting for Wyatt, she strode up the sidewalk toward the single-story, orange brick building. A burst of heat embraced her as she pulled open the glass door and stepped inside. She spotted the reception desk ahead, just past a grouping of vinyl-upholstered chairs in multiple shades of brown.

She smiled at the young female deputy on duty and pulled out her TBI credentials. "I'm Special Agent Ashley Hope," she said. "My partner and I are supposed to meet with Sheriff Hyland this morning."

Ashley heard the building's front door whoosh open behind her. She glanced back to see Wyatt entering the lobby. He probably wondered why she'd hurried in ahead of him. She couldn't let him know what she'd been thinking. She had to forget the ardent look that had flashed in his eyes and make an effort to ease back into the supportive working relationship they'd enjoyed at the tail end of their last case.

The deputy's brunette ponytail bobbed as she motioned toward a hallway. "He's expecting y'all," she stated. "His office is the second door on the right."

"Thank you."

This time Ashley paused and waited for Wyatt to join her, but she didn't meet his gaze. Instead, she cocked her head to the side— indicating that he should follow—and then headed down the hallway flanked by portraits of esteemed law men, now retired.

The door to Sheriff Hyland's office gaped open.

Hyland stood up from his battered oak desk as Ashley approached the threshold. Tall, thin, and mustached, with flecks of gray peppering his dark hair, he reminded her of a middle-aged Sam Elliott. At first the sheriff appeared puzzled to see her, probably because he mistook her for one of the local townsfolk. But then his eyes landed on the TBI badge in her hand.

"Come on in," he told her. He nodded at Wyatt. "Y'all have a seat."

Hyland motioned toward a sandy-haired deputy standing next to the window, who appeared to be in his mid-twenties, and was almost as tall as Hyland. "This is Deputy Kelton."

Wyatt introduced himself and Ashley.

After shaking hands with the sheriff and Deputy Kelton, Ashley sank into one of the two brown, faux-leather armchairs positioned in front of the desk. Wyatt settled into the other. Kelton grabbed a metal folding chair and scooted it next to the desk.

"Tell us about Cole Gowen," Wyatt said to Hyland.

A haunted look crossed the sheriff's face. "He's my baby sister's only child. And he's been missing since Friday. Now normally, you might think a man his age had just gone off to have a good time. But the evidence here says different."

"What kind of evidence?"

Ashley wondered whether they'd found blood at Cole's last known location.

"Deputy Kelton was patrolling up on Rattler Ridge Friday afternoon. He went to school with Cole, and they're still good friends. He saw Cole's car abandoned on the side of the road and knew something wasn't right. He radioed in at 3:38 p.m. Naturally, I drove right out there. Cole's phone was in the car. His phone records didn't show anything unusual. According to his logbook, he'd delivered a subpoena at three o'clock."

Wyatt asked Kelton, "Did you notice anybody on foot?"

"No, sir," the deputy said. "And there's not a lot of traffic up there that time of day."

A quiet lonely road would make a perfect spot to abduct someone, but why had Cole agreed to pull over? Did he know his kidnapper?

"When did you talk to Cole last?"

"Thursday night. We had a couple of beers over at Treva's Tavern. Played some pool."

Ashley's gaze darted to Kelton's left hand. He wasn't wearing a wedding ring. According to the preliminary information they'd been given, Cole was single as well. Maybe he'd flirted with the wrong woman at the bar.

"Did he do, or say, anything unusual?"

"He acted normal. And he didn't get into any bar fights or anything. We had a pretty quiet night."

"Is Cole dating anyone?"

Wyatt must have been sharing Ashley's thoughts, wondering whether Cole had drawn the ire of a jealous boyfriend at Treva's. At twenty-five years of age, it was possible that Cole liked to play the field.

"Not seriously. He's got an ex-girlfriend, but they broke up over a year ago. They're still on good terms. I don't think she has anything to do with him disappearing."

"Did Cole cozy up to anyone at the bar?"

Kelton shook his head. "I didn't see him talking to any women."

Wyatt shifted his attention back to the sheriff. "I'm assuming you've already interviewed the person Cole served with the subpoena," he stated.

The last person known to have seen Cole had obviously jumped to the top of the suspect list. But evidently, the sheriff either felt the person was innocent, or Hyland hadn't been able to collect sufficient evidence to make an arrest.

"No, he keeps dodging me and my deputies." the sheriff said, a note of frustration in his tone. "His name's Lester Warwick. He's a career criminal—petty theft mostly. But he got himself mixed up with a group that steals cars for a chop shop. He served three years in prison."

"You think Warwick had something to do with Cole's disappearance?"

The leap from theft to murder seemed a little wide but not impossible. Maybe something had happened that had caused Warwick to snap.

Hyland was quick to answer. "Physically, he fits the man responsible."

The sheriff's words surprised Ashley. The expression that crossed Wyatt's face let her know that he'd been taken off guard as well. How did they know Warwick's physical characteristics fit with the person who had abducted Cole? Did they have a witness?

"Have you developed a suspect profile?" Wyatt asked.

Hyland nodded. "Cole's car was found fifteen minutes away from Warwick's place. And Cole didn't drive it there himself."

Maybe the sheriff had security footage from a gas station or some other type of business that showed a blurry image of the suspect.

"How do you know?"

"Cole takes after my side of the family. He looks just like a younger version of me. Six-four. When I checked his car, the first thing I noticed was the driver's seat. It was way too close to the steering wheel. There's no way Cole could have driven that car to the ridge. From the measurements I took, I'd say we're looking for somebody no taller than five-nine."

Ashley knew from her training at the police academy that the average male in the United States stood approximately five feet, nine inches tall. Although they could rule Cole out as the car's driver, narrowing the suspects down by height might prove to be challenging.

"That's good detective work," Wyatt said. "Did you find anything else in the car? Any physical evidence?"

Ashley realized what Wyatt was really asking: *Was there any indication that Cole had been killed in the car?* But considering the sheriff's familial relationship, her partner had obviously chosen to use tact.

"No," Hyland said, shaking his head. "But I'm having the car sent to your lab in Briarwood this morning. Maybe your techs will find something."

The sheriff plucked a manila folder from the corner of his desk and handed it to Wyatt.

"This file's got all of Cole's information in it," he said. "Including a copy of his logbook, pictures of his car, and his cell phone records.

Warwick's information is in there too. Maybe there's something that I overlooked. Something that will help."

The sheriff stood and shook their hands a second time.

Ashley caught a mix of worry and pain in his eyes.

"We'll go visit Warwick right now," Wyatt told him. "Is his place of employment in the file?"

"Yeah, but he won't be there," the sheriff said, stepping out from behind his desk. "He works the night shift. And you probably won't catch him at home either."

Hyland sighed. "I know there's a chance that Cole's already dead. But my sister lost her husband two years ago. It's gonna be mighty hard on her if she has to bury her only child too. I'm holding out hope that you'll find Cole alive."

Ashley heard footsteps click against the tile floor outside the sheriff's office. A tall woman, her dark hair cut in a short bob, appeared in the doorway. Worry clouded her face, and her eyes appeared red and swollen.

"I hope I'm not interrupting," the woman said. "Mary Beth told me to come on back."

Hyland moved toward the woman and draped his arm around her shoulders. "This is my sister, Rosalie."

After the introductions had been made, Rosalie said to Wyatt and Ashley, "I'm counting on the two of you to bring Cole back home to me. Whoever's got him ..." The woman's voice broke, and a sob escaped her lips. "Well, they just need to let him go. Cole's a good son. I don't know what I would do without him."

Compassion filled Wyatt's eyes. "We'll do everything in our power to find Cole."

"Thank you." Tears spilled over Rosalie's cheeks. Pulling a tissue from her purse, she turned away and walked to the window. The woman obviously didn't want them to watch her grieving.

Ashley's heart broke for the sheriff and his sister. She wished she could provide words of comfort, but she knew better than to make promises she might not be able to keep.

Nodding goodbye to Sheriff Hyland, she headed back out into the hallway with Wyatt close behind.

The odds didn't stack in Cole's favor. But it could be possible that he was being held hostage somewhere. After all, Warwick had a history of theft, not violence.

But why would the man kidnap Cole? Could it have something to do with the chop shop ring? Had Cole accidentally stumbled upon something nefarious when he'd delivered the subpoena? Had he seen something he wasn't supposed to see?

Ashley prayed that they could convince Warwick to talk. For Rosalie's sake.

But there was no guarantee they'd be able to find the man. He had successfully evaded the sheriff since Friday. They had to find a way to track Warwick down. Fast.

The clock on Cole's life was ticking.

Ashley rushed across the parking lot and climbed into the SUV.

CHAPTER SIX

The SUV lurched to the side as its front tire hit a rut in the gravel road, banging Ashley's elbow against the passenger door. She shifted her weight in the seat and focused her attention on the aging mobile homes dotting the treed lots of Hidden Springs Trailer Court, nestled in the small community of Yarrow.

Bicycles, swing sets, and children's toys peppered most of the yards. A few hosted holiday decorations—inflatable snowmen, painted wooden sleighs, green wreaths with red bows, and twinkle lights that were not yet lit. Ashley also noticed old rusted-out appliances and tattered furniture. One of the trailers appeared empty, with plywood boards covering the windows.

According to the information in the file the sheriff had given them, Lester Warwick lived at Lot 42 that, from the map on the SUV's navigation system, appeared to be the very last plot in the park.

The twenty-minute ride from Arbuckle had left Ashley feeling awkward once again. Instead of driving in silence—Wyatt's usual habit—he'd pummeled her with questions. And not just about the missing persons case. He'd asked about the wellbeing of her father and brothers and even Spencer's dog, Ace.

Ashley and Wyatt had previously worked two investigations together, and he'd never inquired about her personal life before. In the past, he'd seemed content limiting their conversations to the business at hand. She wondered whether the fact that he'd opened up to her at the end of their last assignment, divulging the information about Kaylee, made him want to strengthen their partnership by becoming friends.

Or was he itching for something more?

She noticed that with all his questions, Wyatt never once mentioned Daniel.

Although Ashley had answered each of Wyatt's queries without hesitation, she'd forced herself not to meet his gaze. She feared what she might see in his eyes. She almost wished he'd never confided his troubles to her. She regretted tearing down the invisible wall that had separated them when they'd first been partnered. Now, it felt necessary to mentally check each of her words before she spoke. Afraid she might say something that would lead him to think she was interested in a physical relationship.

Ashley realized her anxiety level had been lower when she'd thought Wyatt hated her.

As the SUV crawled toward the end of the gravel road, a mailbox marked *42* popped into view on the right. The beige mobile home looked a little newer than those surrounding it, and the lawn appeared tidy—no toys or clutter. There were also no vehicles in the driveway.

According to Warwick's DMV records, the thirty-year-old man owned a green Chevy pickup. His employment information stated that his shift at the poultry processing plant ended at seven-thirty a.m. It was now almost nine. Could he be working overtime?

Wyatt steered the SUV into the driveway and killed the engine.

"Wonder what Warwick's up to," he stated, obviously sharing Ashley's opinion that the trailer was likely empty.

"Maybe Warwick and his chop shop buddies have Cole stashed somewhere and are trying to figure out what to do with him."

"You said that you thought Cole was dead."

Ashley didn't want to admit—not even to herself—what her gut was still telling her. Cole had likely been killed within hours of his abduction. This was one of those times when she prayed her instincts would prove to be wrong and that they'd find Cole alive. Safe.

"I was just trying to think positive—hoping that we'd somehow be able to save him."

"Yeah," Wyatt said, a hint of sadness in his tone. "I know."

Ashley slid out of the passenger's seat and followed Wyatt up the steps of the trailer's wooden front porch. Closed blinds covered the windows, hiding the home's contents from prying eyes. The information in the file listed Warwick's marital status as single. She wondered whether he lived alone.

Her gaze swept across the yard. On the other side of the road, a young woman with strawberry-blonde hair stood holding a leash attached to the collar of a small dog with a fluffy sable coat. The woman, who Ashley guessed couldn't be more than nineteen years old, appeared to be around eight-and-a-half months pregnant. Wearing an unbuttoned blue jacket and a floral dress stretched tight across her stomach, she waddled behind the dog as it sniffed along the edge of the roadway.

Wyatt pounded on the trailer's door. "Lester Warwick," he shouted. "TBI."

But Ashley could tell that he knew that they probably wouldn't receive an answer. Seconds ticked by. The mobile home remained still and quiet.

Wyatt banged on the door again. "Warwick, open up."

High-pitched barking split the air behind her. Pivoting around, Ashley spotted the little dog racing up Warwick's driveway, its leash trailing behind it. The fluff ball had managed to break free from its owner.

The woman tottered after the dog. "Sassy, you come back here," she called.

Sassy bounded up the trailer's porch steps.

Concerned about the woman's advanced state of pregnancy—afraid she might go into labor here and now—Ashley scooped up the dog and carried it back down the driveway.

Placing Sassy on the ground, she handed the looped end of the leash to the woman.

"Here you go," she said.

"Thanks." The woman smiled at Ashley. "Lester ain't home."

The woman was obviously acquainted with Warwick. Did she know where he'd gone?

Ashley was about to ask the question when she heard Wyatt's footsteps coming down the drive. The woman's demeanor shifted from warm to ice cold. Her smile disappeared as she eyed Wyatt with suspicion.

"I gotta get home," she stated. "Thanks again."

Wyatt said, "Wait. We need your help."

The look that crossed the woman's face revealed that she had no intention of volunteering any information to a member of law enforcement. Even if she hadn't heard Wyatt identify himself as a TBI agent, it was clear that she'd pegged him as a cop.

"I don't know nothing," she said. "Ain't seen nothing. Ain't heard nothing."

"It's important that we find Lester Warwick."

The woman shook her head. "Sorry. Can't help ya."

She turned and headed back down the driveway with Sassy at her heels, her pace faster than it had been before. It was apparent that she didn't want her neighbors to see her talking with the police.

Ashley motioned for Wyatt to get inside the SUV. She wanted to speak with the woman alone. He nodded, climbed into the driver's seat, and shut the door.

It appeared as though the woman didn't realize that she was also a cop. And Ashley could use that to her advantage.

She caught up with the woman just as she reached the other side of the road.

"My name is Ashley," she said, hoping the young woman wouldn't tell her to get lost.

The woman glanced back at Wyatt's SUV. "What are you doing with him?" she asked. "He promise you something?"

"He's trying to help me find Lester."

"Oh."

The woman didn't look convinced. She'd probably figured it was the other way around. That Ashley had been helping the police in exchange for something—like a reduced sentence for a crime she'd committed.

"What's your name?" Ashley asked.

"Teresa."

Before she started badgering the woman with questions about Lester Warwick, Ashley wanted to build a rapport. If she could win Teresa over, the woman might divulge some information that would help with the case.

"Are you having a boy or a girl?"

A smile spread across Teresa's face. "It's twins," she said. "Two girls. Twins run in my family. I went and spent a few days with my sister down in Georgia last week. She's got twins too. Only hers are boys."

Now, Ashley knew the reason the woman looked like she was carrying a large beach ball under her dress instead of a child.

"I have some relatives living in Georgia too—in Dalton. When did you get back?"

Ashley hoped the question sounded casual.

"She brought me home Saturday. Her boyfriend was afraid I'd have the babies at their house. But I ain't due for a couple more weeks."

Since Teresa had been in Georgia on Friday, she couldn't have witnessed Cole delivering the subpoena to Warwick.

"Is this your first time being pregnant?"

Nervous apprehension flashed in Teresa's eyes. "Yeah."

As with most first-time moms, Teresa appeared to be wondering whether she had the ability to be a good parent. And the fact that she was expecting twins likely increased her insecurities.

"It feels a little overwhelming—scary—at times, doesn't it?"

Teresa nodded. "You got kids?"

Although she'd been pregnant twice, Ashley had miscarried both times. The losses still haunted her.

"Not yet," she said.

An idea formed in her mind.

"I would really like to find Lester," Ashley said. She placed her hand on her belly and held it there. "There's something I need to talk to him about."

She hadn't stated anything that wasn't true.

A light came on in Teresa's eyes. "Oh, okay."

Ashley could tell that her plan stood a good chance of working. Although she hadn't said the words—hadn't lied—it seemed clear that Teresa assumed that Ashley was also pregnant and that Lester was the father.

Guilt from the deception gnawed at Ashley's heart. But she reminded herself that a man's life was at stake. She had to think about Cole's mother and the pain the woman was suffering. If Cole hadn't yet been murdered, odds ranked high that Lester Warwick knew where he was being held. Warwick could lead them to Cole.

How much time did the sheriff's nephew have left?

"I'm sure you can understand how important this is, right?" Ashley asked.

"Yeah. I guess I can." The woman's gaze fell to the ground.

Ashley wondered whether the father of Teresa's babies was still in the picture.

"Do you know where Lester is?"

Teresa shrugged. "I seen him leave about ten minutes before y'all got here."

"Did you talk to him? Did he tell you where he was going?"

A strained expression crossed Teresa's face as though she felt torn about giving Ashley the information.

The woman hesitated. "I think he went to his girlfriend's house," she finally said. "Her name's Betsy. I guess you didn't know about her, huh?"

"No, I didn't." Ashley hadn't been aware of any of the details of Lester Warwick's personal life. Not until now.

"Do you know where Betsy lives?" she asked.

"She's staying over at her mama's place. When you go out of the trailer park, turn right. You'll pass a red barn with a silo. Betsy's mama lives in that little yellow house across the road, on the left."

Ashley was glad to hear that Warwick's girlfriend lived nearby and not on the other end of the county.

"Thank you, Teresa. I really appreciate your help. And I wish you and your babies the best of everything." She hoped that the young mother had a strong support system, and that her children would grow up happy and healthy.

"You too."

As Ashley started toward the SUV, Teresa decided to reveal another bit of information.

"If you wanna catch Lester, you better hurry," she said.

Ashley stopped, swung around, and met Teresa's gaze. What else did the woman know? "Why?"

"I seen him loading his stuff in the back of his truck this morning," Teresa said. "Him and Betsy are leaving town."

CHAPTER SEVEN

Ashley grabbed the passenger door handle, steadying herself, as Wyatt swung the SUV onto the highway and floored the accelerator. She wondered whether they were too late. Wondered if Warwick had already picked up Betsy and had fled from Fergus County. Ashley doubted they'd be able to get any information from Betsy's mother. Not many people would be willing to point the police in the direction their child had gone—and definitely not a woman with mountain blood flowing through her veins.

Were Betsy and her mother involved in the chop shop network? Did they know what had happened to Cole?

Another question begged answering: Why would Warwick run?

The fact that Warwick had been subpoenaed to give a deposition relating to a minor theft case didn't seem like a strong enough motive. From what Ashley had read in the file, the case might not even make it to trial. The only logical explanation Ashley could think of was that the man was guilty—that he was involved in Cole's disappearance. And now, Warwick likely felt the walls closing in around him. He was probably desperate to flee.

A realization struck Ashley, and her stomach sank. If Warwick believed it was necessary to pack up and leave, that meant that Cole was likely dead. Just as her instincts had screamed.

But Ashley wasn't willing to give up hope just yet. Not until they found a body.

With a deep sigh, she peered through the SUV's windshield and scanned the terrain ahead of them. Teresa hadn't told her how many miles down the highway they would have to go before reaching Betsy's mother's house. Ashley had just assumed that it wouldn't be very far.

She glanced at the speedometer. Wyatt had pushed the SUV to eighty miles an hour in a fifty-five-limit zone. There was one thing she could always count on: her partner's driving skills. He never wasted a second when they were chasing a suspect, and although he'd been forced to dodge obstacles during their vehicle pursuits—including a flying barrel of toxic waste—he'd always gotten them to their destination in one piece.

As the SUV crested a hill, a red barn and silo popped into view on the right. On the other side of the road, through the bare limbs of a grove of hardwoods, she caught sight of a patch of yellow siding.

"There's the house," Ashley said, pointing ahead.

Wyatt reduced his speed. As they neared the small, ranch-style home, she spotted a green Chevy pickup in the driveway with a blue tarp covering the bed. Hope flooded her chest. Warwick was still there.

Coasting into the narrow gravel drive, Wyatt braked the SUV to a stop just before butting the pickup's rear bumper. Ashley cut her eyes at him.

"You don't really think that you can block Warwick's truck in, do you?" she asked. "You know he'll just plow through the yard if he gets the chance."

"I won't give him the chance," Wyatt said with a smirk.

It felt good to know that her partner's confidence level was high. But Ashley feared Warwick wouldn't give up without a fight. The guilty ones hardly ever did.

Ashley motioned toward a wooden shed behind and to the left of the yellow-sided house. A heavy chain and padlock hung from the shed's door.

"Do you think that could be where they're holding Cole?"

Wyatt nodded. "Maybe. It makes more sense than the trailer park."

Hardwood forests flanked both sides of the house, and fenced pastureland lay across the highway. There were no close neighbors to hear Cole scream. It seemed to be the perfect place to hold him captive. But Ashley and Wyatt didn't have a search warrant. Unless they found probable cause, they couldn't bust into the shed.

She hopped out of the SUV and slammed the door. Exchanging glances with Wyatt, she sidled up to Warwick's pickup. The truck was out in the open, in plain view. Anything they could see through the windows or in the back was fair game.

Noticing a wide gap in an unsecured section of the blue tarp, she peeked into the pickup's bed. Wyatt appeared at her side. He leaned over, obviously following her gaze. A television, an iron headboard and bedframe—but no mattress or box springs—and a few cardboard boxes crowded the truck's rear space.

Goosebumps broke out on Ashley's arms. "He didn't pack his mattress," she stated, her voice just above a whisper.

Ashley locked eyes with Wyatt. She could tell he shared her thoughts. Had Cole's blood soaked into Warwick's mattress? Is that the reason it was missing?

As Ashley shifted her attention toward the house, she spotted the blinds in the window on the far right moving. They were being watched. It didn't surprise her. She followed Wyatt up the gravel path to the low, concrete front porch. A festive holiday wreath graced the front door.

Wyatt knocked. "TBI!" he called out.

Ashley heard movement inside the house. Footsteps. But no one came to the door. Again, with no search or arrest warrant, they couldn't force the homeowner to let them in. Betsy and her mother had every right to refuse to answer.

Undeterred, Wyatt pounded his fist against the door, shaking the wreath. "We're with the Tennessee Bureau of Investigation," he shouted. "We need to speak with Lester Warwick. We're not leaving until we do."

Ashley eased closer to the double window over the porch. She heard noises again. Instead of footsteps, it was muffled voices. As Wyatt raised his fist to knock a third time, the door inched open. A woman who appeared to be in her mid-forties, her dark hair rolled in pink curlers, stuck her head out.

"You got a warrant?" she asked.

Her voice carried the low, coarse pitch common among long-time cigarette smokers.

Wyatt held up his credentials for her to inspect. "Ma'am, we only want to ask Lester a few questions."

The woman stared past the badge as though it meant nothing.

"Lester ain't here," she said, her eyes narrowed.

Ashley could tell that Wyatt was trying not to lose his patience. "Ma'am, that's Lester's Chevy parked in your driveway. We know he's here. And right now, I could arrest you for obstruction of justice."

The woman opened her mouth as if to speak, but no words came out. Clearly not knowing how to respond, her fingers flew to her lips.

A male voice echoed from inside the house. "It's all right, Irma."

The woman stepped back from the door.

A ginger-haired man wearing a blue flannel shirt took Irma's place. His face matched Lester Warwick's mugshot.

"I ain't gotta be in court until next week," he spat out.

Except he hadn't actually been ordered to appear in court—not yet. He just needed to provide his deposition.

Wyatt nodded. "Well, the way it looks, you're planning to miss your court date," he stated.

Warwick didn't respond. Although he was playing the tough guy, Ashley thought she saw a hint of fear in his blue eyes.

"Why don't we sit down and talk about it?" Wyatt said. "Or we could haul you to the sheriff's office. Whichever you prefer."

Warwick hesitated for a moment. Then, seeming to give in, he pulled the door open.

Wyatt motioned for Ashley to enter the house first. As she crossed the threshold into the small living room decorated in muted earth tones, she saw Warwick reach his right hand behind his back.

Ashley's breath caught in her throat as her hand snapped to the Glock holstered at her side.

But it was too late.

Warwick grabbed Irma and shoved the muzzle of a pistol underneath her chin.

CHAPTER EIGHT

Ashley froze in her tracks, just a few feet inside Irma's small earth-toned living room, her heart hammering in her chest. She'd crossed the threshold believing that Lester Warwick had given in. That he'd agreed to sit down and answer a few questions regarding the whereabouts of Cole Gowen.

But Warwick had other plans.

He'd reached for the weapon hidden against his back, tucked in the waistband of his jeans. His movement had been unexpected, swift. When Ashley realized what was happening, it was already too late to draw her Glock.

Warwick had Irma firmly in his grasp. "Don't make me kill her!" he shouted.

With his arm crooked around the woman's waist, Warwick pulled her body closer to his, the muzzle of his pistol shoved beneath Irma's chin. He glared at Ashley as though daring her to take one step forward.

Irma closed her eyes. Ashley wondered whether the woman was about to faint. Or maybe she was saying a silent prayer, preparing for the possibility that she might pass into the afterlife.

"Please don't let him kill me," Irma said, her voice sounding much more controlled than Ashley had expected.

Irma seemed to possess the heart of a lion. But then, many mountain women did.

"You don't need to do this," Ashley told Warrick. "It's not worth it."

He ignored her plea. "Take their guns, babe," Warrick said to a petite, young brunette standing next to an artificial Christmas tree dripping with gold and silver ornaments. "And their phones."

With her attention glued to the pistol in Warwick's hand, Ashley hadn't noticed the woman—who couldn't be any older than nineteen or twenty—until now. She guessed that she was his girlfriend, Betsy.

Appearing as though she was accustomed to obeying his commands, Betsy nodded.

Ashley remained still, her hands where Warwick could see them. Betsy patted her down, pulled the phone from her jacket pocket, and then yanked the Glock from Ashley's holster. The woman seemed comfortable handling the pistol. But her familiarity with firearms wasn't too surprising considering the fact that she'd been raised in the mountains.

Wyatt stood behind and to the right of Ashley, in the home's front doorway. She could see him in her peripheral vision. He hadn't had time to draw his weapon either. Not that it would make any difference. She knew that he wouldn't fire at a man whose arms held a hostage.

Wyatt raised his sports jacket and allowed Betsy to take his phone from the inside breast pocket. She ripped the Glock from his shoulder holster. Betsy dropped the weapons and phones on top of the wooden coffee table that skirted the stone-gray sofa.

She motioned toward Ashley. "What are you gonna do with them?"

Warwick kept his pistol pressed tight against Irma's neck. His finger fluttered at the trigger. It was obvious that he still expected Ashley and Wyatt to make a move, even though they were no longer armed. And he realized that they were more concerned with protecting Irma's life than risking their own.

"You got some rope?" he asked Betsy. "Or something to tie them up with?"

The young woman shook her head. "No."

Warwick hesitated as though he was trying to devise a plan. "Let me think about it," he said. "You go get your suitcase."

Without hesitation, Betsy disappeared down a hallway. Warwick obviously had her well-trained. She hadn't uttered a single objection to him threatening her mother's life.

Ashley wondered about the relationship between Betsy and Irma. Since they'd made the decision to live in the same home, it would stand to reason that they cared for each other. That they shared a close bond. But it seemed that Betsy had chosen Warwick over her mother without giving it a second thought.

Wyatt said, "This won't end well, Warwick. Stop and think about it. Drop your weapon."

"Naw. I know what I gotta do."

Determination had replaced the look of fear in the man's eyes. Warwick controlled the room now, and he knew it. But would he really squeeze the trigger?

Would he kill his girlfriend's mother?

"Do you think Betsy will ever forgive you if you shoot Irma?" Ashley asked him.

Warwick didn't answer, but he didn't flinch either. His grip on the pistol held steady.

"Babe," he called out. "You getting your stuff?"

Betsy's voice echoed from the far-right end of the house. "Give me a minute."

Warwick's jaw clenched. "We ain't got all day," he yelled back, ire in his tone. "Get your ass out here!"

Ashley suspected that Warwick was a man who ran low on patience. Did he have a short temper as well? Would he kill Irma in a fit of anger? Ashley needed to try and talk him down, to diffuse some of the tension.

"There's no reason for you to run," she told him, injecting a soothing tone into her voice. "We can work something out."

He looked at Ashley like he thought she was crazy. "If I stay here, I'm as good as dead."

His words made it sound as though Warwick was guilty of Cole's murder and that he feared receiving the ultimate punishment. Was Cole's body locked in the shed?

"We can talk to the DA and let him know that you cooperated. They can take the death penalty off the table."

In Tennessee, capital punishment cases were often negotiated down to life in prison without the possibility of parole. If Warwick handed over his weapon now and surrendered, and if he led them to Cole's body, the odds were high that Warwick would never sit on death row.

Warwick snorted. "Death penalty? You think I'm worried about the law?" he asked, sounding as though Ashley had missed something obvious. "Woman, you don't know shit."

Warwick wasn't concerned about being convicted of murder, and yet, he feared for his life. Had he witnessed someone else killing Cole?

"Is Cole Gowen dead?" she asked him.

He stared at her, confusion clouding his face. "Who?"

Although Warwick's puzzled reaction seemed genuine, it was likely that he was just playing games.

"The process server who delivered a subpoena to you at three o'clock on Friday afternoon."

"How the hell should I know?"

44

"You were the last person to see Cole before he disappeared."

"So what?" Warwick shook his head. "I don't give a rat's ass about some fat server." He glanced toward the hallway. "Betsy!" he shouted. "You gonna make me leave without you?"

Normally when accused of a crime, especially murder, a suspect was quick to declare their innocence. But Warwick acted as though denying involvement in Cole's disappearance wasn't worth his time. As if it was of no consequence to him.

Ashley heard footsteps coming back up the hallway. Betsy rounded the corner carrying mismatched suitcases, one in each hand. A slight smile tugged at the corners of her lips as she eyed Warwick pressing the barrel of his pistol into Irma's chin. It appeared as though it wouldn't faze her a bit if he decided to pull the trigger.

Did Betsy want her mother to die?

Ashley studied Irma's face. The woman's eyes were now open. But instead of fear, Ashley caught a hint of something else in her expression. Smugness?

Ashley's instincts screamed that something was off. Something was wrong with this entire picture.

Warwick asked Betsy, "You got the key to the shed?"

"Yeah. But it might take me a minute to find it."

"Go get it. We'll lock the cops in there."

As Betsy headed back down the hallway, Ashley scanned the living room. She spotted two pistol magazines lying on the small table located at the left end of the sofa. She could see the brass casings of the bullets shining in the sunlight that streamed through the window. One magazine was fully loaded; the second only partially loaded. She eyed the nine-millimeter weapon Warwick held. It was a familiar Smith & Wesson. She had the same model at home: an M&P Shield 2. Warwick's hand covered the end of the firearm's grip, concealing the area where the base of the attached magazine should rest.

In the retail market, the Shield was sold with two magazines— common for nine-millimeter pistols. What were the odds that Warwick had purchased a third magazine? And why would he eject a magazine that still contained bullets?

Ashley's attention shifted back to Irma. This time, the woman met her gaze and held it for a second too long.

The truth struck Ashley like a bolt of lightning.

Irma's eyes revealed the secret Ashley had suspected. The reason Warwick felt comfortable resting his finger directly on the pistol's trigger, instead of safely above; the reason Betsy had smiled at her mother's plight; the reason Irma lacked any display of fear. Everything snapped into sharp focus.

It was all a charade. Planned before Irma opened the front door.

The coffee table stood closer to Ashley than to Warwick. Not wanting him to realize that she'd caught on to their act, Ashley turned her head in the opposite direction, toward the hallway. She waited and listened for the sound of Betsy's boots thumping against the thin carpet.

Just as the woman stepped into the living room, Ashley screamed, "Betsy!"

Warwick's attention flew toward his girlfriend.

Ashley jumped to her left and grabbed the Glock pistols from the coffee table, one in each hand. She aimed both at Warwick.

"Get your hands up!" she shouted.

Warwick's mouth dropped open. "I'm gonna blow Irma's head off," he said, his body tense.

"You couldn't do that even if you wanted to," Ashley told him. "Your pistol isn't loaded. But both of mine are with rounds already chambered. And I can take you out with a single shot."

Ashley had no intention of actually shooting Warwick—he posed no current threat. But she prided herself on being an expert markswoman. If the need arose, she possessed the ability to fire a bullet directly centered between his eyes.

A mixture of hatred and fear flashed across Warwick's face. The unloaded pistol fell to the floor as he let go of Irma.

Wyatt slapped handcuffs on Warwick first, and then repeated the procedure with Irma and Betsy. With the current setup in Wyatt's SUV, they could only safely transport two criminals at a time. Wyatt made the decision that he and Ashley would attend to Warrick, and they'd let the sheriff's deputies haul Irma and Betsy to the station.

Ashley hoped that she could pry some information out of Warwick while they waited for their backup to arrive. They'd separated the three suspects to keep them from talking. Wyatt was already quizzing Betsy in the kitchen.

Warwick sat on his knees in the middle of the living room floor, his hands cuffed behind him. He appeared visibly shaken, nervous. And

Ashley had a feeling it wasn't due to the charges he faced for his ruse of holding Irma hostage.

"What is it that has you so terrified?" she asked him. "Did you witness Cole Gowen's murder?"

Ashley felt as though Warwick knew something, but she doubted that he'd killed Cole himself. Her instincts told her that Warwick didn't have what it took to commit cold-blooded murder.

Warwick didn't answer. He kept his gaze glued to the floor.

"I might be able to help you negotiate for a lesser sentence if you'll tell me what's going on."

At this point, Ashley just wanted to bring Cole—or his body—back home to his mother. If Warwick would agree to provide the information needed to close the case, she'd speak to the DA on his behalf.

"You just don't get it, woman," he said, shaking his head.

"Then explain it to me."

"You go and put me in county jail." Warwick locked eyes with Ashley. "I'll be dead by morning."

CHAPTER NINE

Ashley sank down onto the hard metal chair directly across the table from Lester Warwick in the cramped interview room at the Fergus County Sheriff's Department. Wyatt took the seat opposite Dustin O'Neal. Warwick's attorney—a seemingly eager, dark-haired young man in a pinstriped suit—appeared to be fresh out of law school. Right after Warwick had dropped the bomb on Ashley, stating that he'd be killed in the county jail, he'd invoked his attorney privilege, so the questioning had ceased.

Although he seemed green, O'Neal obviously excelled at negotiations. Either that, or Warwick had strong evidence to back up his claims of being in harm's way as a ward of the county. A deal had been made. After the meeting with Wyatt and Ashley concluded, Warwick would be transported to an undisclosed location, far away from the town of Arbuckle.

O'Neal straightened in his chair, lacing his fingers together on the table.

"My client will only answer questions that pertain to his brief encounter with Cole Gowen," he said.

O'Neal's statement seemed to indicate the threat against Warwick's life was unrelated to Cole. Ashley wondered whether there was more to Warwick's court-ordered deposition for a minor theft case than met the eye.

Wyatt nodded. He looked at Warwick. "Do you know where Cole is?"

"No." Warrick's voice was steady and firm.

"Do you know if Cole is still alive?"

"No."

O'Neal must have instructed his client to stick to one-word responses whenever possible.

"Tell us what happened when Cole arrived at your home on Friday."

Warwick glanced at O'Neal as though he was seeking permission. O'Neal nodded.

"Well, I'd just got out of the shower when he come knocking on my door," Warwick began. "I wasn't gonna answer at first, but he yelled that he had a delivery for me. I told him to leave it on the porch. He said he can't do that. So, I pulled the door open a crack. He asked me if I was Lester Warwick and I told him, 'yeah.' He stuck the envelope through the door and said that I'd been served. And that was it. He left."

"Did you see anyone else with him?"

"No."

Wyatt folded his arms across his chest. "Can anyone back up your story?"

They couldn't just take Warwick at his word. Unless he had a verifiable alibi, he would remain a suspect in Cole's disappearance.

O'Neal spoke up, answering the question for his client. "Mr. Warwick had a three-thirty appointment on Friday with his parole officer here in Arbuckle, which he kept. I'm in the process of obtaining a copy of the sign-in sheet that will show that Mr. Warwick arrived at the office at 3:25 p.m. The parole office is a twenty-minute drive from Mr. Warwick's residence. He remained there until approximately four o'clock. So, if Cole Gowen was a victim of foul play, it definitely wasn't at the hands of my client."

According to Cole's logbook, Warwick's subpoena had been delivered at three o'clock. Ashley knew that Cole's car had been found at 3:38 p.m., fifteen minutes away from Warwick's trailer, in the opposite direction from Arbuckle. If Warwick had been at the parole office during the time stated, there was no way he could have abducted Cole.

The look Wyatt shot Ashley let her know that her partner had come to the same conclusion.

"Thank you for your time," Wyatt said, rising from his chair.

They shook hands with O'Neal. Wyatt pulled open the door of the interview room and motioned for Ashley to enter the hallway first. He closed the door behind them, leaving O'Neal alone with his client.

Side-by-side, Ashley and Wyatt headed down the hallway toward the rear exit of the sheriff's department. Since Warwick obviously had no connection to Cole's disappearance, she wondered what secret the man held.

"Do you think Warwick was being threatened about sitting for his deposition?" she asked, her voice low.

Wyatt stopped walking. He glanced behind them as though making sure he wouldn't be overheard.

"I talked to the sheriff about thirty minutes ago, right after he met with O'Neal," Wyatt stated. "Hyland just found out Warwick has information that will blow apart one of the largest chop shop rings in the southeast. The network runs through Tennessee, Georgia, and Alabama. And Warwick told his attorney that two of Hyland's deputies are involved."

Earlier, Ashley had ducked into the small break room at the department to call and check on her father. Worried for his safety, she'd wanted to make sure that the stalker hadn't visited him again. That must have been when Wyatt spoke to Hyland.

Chop shops were a problem in her hometown as well. And it had long been rumored that law enforcement in Laurel County was paid to look the other way.

"Which two deputies does Sheriff Hyland suspect?"

"I don't know."

Could Cole's friend, Deputy Kelton, be involved? Kelton had found Cole's car. Was that just a coincidence?

Although Warwick held a solid alibi, it was still possible that Cole had stumbled across something he shouldn't have when he'd served the subpoena. His disappearance could be linked to the chop shop ring.

As Ashley pushed through the glass door and stepped into the rear parking lot of the sheriff's department, a strange feeling nagged at her. Something about the encounter between Warwick and Cole just didn't fit. But she wasn't sure what.

"So, where do you think we should go from here?" Ashley asked.

Wyatt shrugged. "Backtrack, I guess. Let's go talk to the farmer Cole visited before Warwick. Maybe he'll remember something."

CHAPTER TEN

As the SUV veered onto the narrow road leading to Jacob Stanley's farm, Ashley logged out of the TBI database and stowed Wyatt's mobile tablet back into its carrying case. During the fifteen-minute drive, she'd studied the photographs of Cole's sedan and had reviewed all the facts pertaining to his disappearance. Still, she couldn't help feeling that she was missing something. A detail she just couldn't pinpoint.

Tucking the tablet into the pocket behind the driver's seat, she stole a glance at Wyatt. Her apprehension regarding their working together had waned a bit. Although he'd been the most talkative she'd ever seen him, venturing into questions relating to her personal life, Wyatt hadn't made any advances toward her since they'd touched hands. And things had gone well when they'd checked into their motel.

After leaving the sheriff's department, they'd stopped by the Arbuckle Motor Inn. Two rooms had been reserved—Ashley's in her own name. And if something were to happen where they'd be forced to move into the same space, she'd been delighted to find that her room had been furnished with two queen-sized beds. She was sure her partner's contained the same. The rooms featured a connecting door between them, but there were locks on both sides, so that fact hadn't concerned her. Maybe Wyatt was only interested in developing a friendship. At least, she hoped that was his only motive.

The SUV rounded a curve, and a red mailbox, shaped like a barn and complete with a black roof, appeared on the left. The navigation system's female voice announced that they had arrived at their destination.

Before serving Warwick with the subpoena for the theft case, Cole had delivered a summons to Jacob Stanley. It seemed that the farmer was being sued over a debt he owed. The sheriff had spoken with Stanley before handing Cole's case over to the TBI, but the notes pertaining to their conversation were brief. Ashley hoped that they'd be able to jog the farmer's memory and learn some new information.

Wyatt piloted the SUV up the long, gravel driveway. Ashley noticed that the woven-wire fencing bordering the pasture was reinforced with an electric fence running along the bottom half. As they neared the large pond located to the left of the drive, she realized the reason the farmer found the electric fencing necessary—a passel of hogs wallowed in the sunshine near the water's edge.

When she was a child, Ashley's uncle had owned a boar and several sows. He'd sell the sows' gilts and barrows to neighbors who would fatten them up and ultimately feed them to their families. As crafty as they were cute, she recalled many times when her uncle's sows and piglets had dug trenches and managed to escape from their pasture. Even an electric fence couldn't be guaranteed to contain them.

A white Appalachian farmhouse, similar to the home in which Ashley had been raised, rested at the end of the driveway. Angling the SUV alongside of a blue pickup, Wyatt shifted into park and cut the engine.

"I hope this doesn't turn out to be another dead end," Ashley said.

Wyatt nodded. "You and me both."

If Cole was still alive, it was doubtful that he had much time left. His family hadn't received a ransom note—not that they could afford a huge payout—and there was sufficient evidence to prove that Cole hadn't taken off for greener pastures on his own. One possible motive was robbery, but that didn't seem very likely since his car and phone were left behind. Another motive could be revenge. With his line of work, it was possible that Cole had made an enemy.

As she slid out of the passenger seat, Ashley heard a male voice echoing from behind the left corner of the house.

"Hello!" the voice called out.

She circled around the front of the SUV and joined Wyatt. A heavy-set man wearing a wide-brimmed hat met them. She assumed the man, who appeared to be in his mid-thirties and had a short, blond beard and rosy cheeks, was Jacob Stanley.

"How are ya?" the man asked, offering his hand to Wyatt.

The farmer's kindness to strangers surprised her. Maybe he thought that they were interested in purchasing some of his pigs. In her past experience, the chance of making a few bucks always seemed to bring out the friendliness in mountain folk.

"My name is Wyatt Clark, and this is Ashley Hope," her partner said, accepting the handshake. "We're special agents with the TBI."

52

"That right? I'm Jacob Stanley," he said, still smiling. "What can I do for ya?"

The fact that Wyatt and Ashley were cops didn't seem to bother the farmer. Maybe he was just an all-around nice guy, working hard to make a living, with no reason to harbor ill feelings toward law enforcement.

"We're trying to locate a man named Cole Gowen. He delivered a summons to you on Friday."

Stanley nodded. "Yeah. I reckon he got here around one. Just after I ate my lunch. I was sorry to hear he'd gone missing."

According to Cole's logbook, he'd served the court summons at 1:05 p.m.

"Can you walk us through what happened when Cole was here?"

"Well, I was outside when he come up the driveway. He was in one of them foreign cars. A dark color. Blue, I think."

Cole owned a dark blue Toyota sedan.

Stanley continued, "Anyhow, he seen me in the pasture, filling up one of the waterers. He come up to the fence and asked me my name. I told him, and he said he had something for me. Then he give me the envelope and said I'd been served. I didn't right know what he meant. So, I said, 'served what?' Cause I knew there weren't no food in that envelope."

Ashley fought to keep her lips from curling into a smile at Stanley's words. She glanced at Wyatt. She could tell that he was doing the same. But guilt was quick to fill her heart. Although the way the farmer had relayed his lack of understanding might have sounded comical, Cole's disappearance was no laughing matter.

Stanley's face remained somber. "Then he told me he was sorry. Said I was being sued. And that he wished he didn't have to tell me. He was right nice about it."

"Did Cole say anything else?"

Ashley saw the farmer's blue eyes light up. She hoped that meant he'd remembered something that would help them find Cole.

"Yep," Stanley motioned toward the pasture. "Said he'd like to have himself a few hogs one day. I took him into the barn and showed him around."

"How long did he stay?"

"Oh, 'bout fifteen—twenty minutes, I guess. I could tell he weren't too happy to leave."

53

Ashley and Wyatt exchanged glances. Was Cole that fond of pigs? Or was he dreading his next delivery—at the trailer of Lester Warwick?

"What do you mean?" Wyatt asked.

"Well, when we went out to his car, he was acting kinda jumpy like."

Had Cole been afraid of Warwick for some reason? Did he know about the chop shop ring?

"Did you tell that to the sheriff?"

"Naw, I'm ashamed to say I didn't. I was real busy when the sheriff come by. One of my boars got loose, and I was on my way to fetch him. Me and the sheriff just talked a minute. I figured the man—Cole—had done showed back up by now."

Sheriff Hyland had obviously assumed that Stanley didn't possess any relevant information, or he would have quizzed the farmer further.

"Did you ask Cole why he was acting nervous?"

"Yeah. He told me he thought some man might be following him."

The news stunned Ashley. Had Cole known he was in danger?

"Did he tell you the man's name?"

"Naw. Just said it was somebody he'd give some papers to. Somebody that didn't take it too good. But I didn't think nothing serious would come of it. Not 'til you told me he was still missing."

So, it seemed that Cole had indeed made an enemy. Ashley wondered whether he'd ever mentioned the mystery man to the sheriff or to his friend, Deputy Kelton. If Sheriff Hyland had known, he would have relayed the information to Wyatt and Ashley.

"Did Cole tell you anything else?"

"Naw. He just said he'd let me get back to my work. I told him I'd be glad to sell him some pigs when he got ready. He thanked me, got in his car, and left."

Wyatt looked at Ashley as though he was checking to make sure that she didn't have any more questions for Stanley. She shook her head.

"Thank you for your time, Mr. Stanley," Wyatt said, shaking the farmer's hand again.

"I hope y'all find him. And if you get a hankering for some good ole country ham, come on back."

Ashley glanced at the little piglets playing down by the pond. Somehow, she doubted her near future would include a craving for pork.

She climbed into the SUV and buckled her seatbelt. "Do you think Cole might have told his boss that someone he'd served was following him?"

Wyatt started the engine. "There's only one way to find out."

The SUV lumbered back down the gravel driveway, headed for Doak Legal Process.

CHAPTER ELEVEN

The narrow red-brick building that housed the office of Doak Legal Process reminded Ashley of an old-timey train caboose. She trotted up the three steps leading to the small porch tacked onto the structure's right end, with Wyatt close behind. If Cole had been harassed by a person he'd served a summons, the company might have kept a record of the incident.

Wyatt had called Sheriff Hyland during the drive back to Arbuckle. As far as the sheriff knew, Cole had never mentioned being followed. Hyland had questioned Cole's mother and his friends at length, and none of them knew of any enemies. The idea of a stalker had never even been broached.

Maybe the first time Cole had seen the person since serving the summons was Friday, sometime before one o'clock. The two could have argued, with the man issuing a threat. Maybe he'd told Cole to watch his back. If an encounter had taken place that morning, it was possible Cole hadn't had the time to notify the sheriff.

A roaring *vrrrr vrrrr* sound met Ashley as she pulled open the company's glass door. Crossing the threshold into the narrow office, she caught sight of a middle-aged woman, with short, auburn curls, piloting a vacuum cleaner. Dressed in a blue western-style shirt, jeans, and cowgirl boots, the woman appeared to be engaged in her own rendition of a country line dance as she moved the machine across the low-pile taupe carpeting, her back toward the front door.

Three metal desks hugged the left wall of the narrow office. There was no reception area, but two closed doors—one marked with a restroom symbol—hid rooms at the rear of the desks.

As the woman swirled around, she finally noticed Ashley and Wyatt. Her face reddened, and she switched off the vacuum cleaner.

"Can I help you?" she asked, a sheepish grin tugging at her lips.

Ashley flashed her TBI credentials. "I'm Special Agent Ashley Hope, and this is my partner, Special Agent Wyatt Clark. We'd like to speak to the manager."

The woman glanced at Ashley's badge. "You're looking at her," she said, offering her hand. "I'm Lynette Doak. Owner, manager, and housekeeper, all rolled into one."

Ashley and Wyatt both shook hands with Lynette.

"We'd like to ask you a few questions about one of your employees, Cole Gowen," Ashley said.

A troubled expression clouded Lynette's face. "He's more than just an employee," she said. "He's been with us so long, both my husband and I think of him as family. And Cole has always been willing to lend a hand whenever we need something. He's helped us move twice. And he takes care of our dogs whenever we go out of town."

Ashley was glad to hear that Cole held a close relationship with Lynette. That meant the woman might know something about his potential stalker.

"Did any of the people who Cole served with a summons ever threaten him?"

Lynette chewed her bottom lip as though she was trying to remember. "Well, I told Sheriff Hyland that I didn't know anyone who could have harmed Cole. But now that you mention it, there was this guy about a year ago. Cole served him with divorce papers. He flew off the handle and threw a punch, but Cole dodged it. The man called here a couple of times. He was trying to get Cole fired. Of course, I brushed him off. But like I said, all that was last year. Nothing has happened lately."

In a messy divorce, it would probably take around twelve to fifteen months to get things finalized. Once the ties to his wife had been completely severed, maybe the man felt it was time to seek revenge against Cole.

"Can you look up the man's name and address?"

Lynette nodded. "Sure. Come on back here."

They followed the woman to the office at the rear of the building. Along with a steel tanker desk, two chocolate-colored, faux-leather armchairs crowded the small space. The dark-paneled walls—which appeared to be a hold-over from the nineteen seventies—added to the claustrophobic atmosphere of the room.

"Grab a seat," Lynette said as she scooted in behind the desk.

The woman's fingers flew across her computer keyboard as Ashley and Wyatt settled into the armchairs. Lynette clicked her mouse in rapid succession as she peered at the screen.

"Okay, I've got his file," she said, a look of triumph spreading across her face. The man's name is Dean Petrie."

Wyatt leaned closer to the desk. "Can you print that out for us? Along with his address?"

Ashley saw something flicker in Lynette's eyes. Almost like she'd seen something on the screen that worried her.

"What is it that you're not telling us?" Ashley asked her.

"Well, it's just that Dean Petrie lives on Birch Bottom Road," Lynette began. "That's in Murdoch Hollow. You don't want to be there after dark. It's not safe—not even for the locals."

Ashley glanced at the clock hanging above Lynette's desk. 3:28 p.m. A little over an hour remained before nightfall.

"How long do you think it will take us to drive there from here?" she asked.

"At least twenty minutes."

Wyatt stood up. "Then we'd better hurry."

The ink-jet printer on the corner of Lynette's desk whirred to life. The machine spit out two pages. Ashley scooped the papers from the tray.

"Thank you for all of your help," she told Lynette.

"I just hope you find Cole. And that he's okay. It's not the same around here without him."

Ashley scanned the details of Dean Petrie's file as she followed Wyatt back out to the SUV. There wasn't all that much to go on. Just a copy of Petrie's DMV photo, his date of birth, address, and place of employment. Only the facts that would be needed to locate the man in order to serve a summons. She noticed an odd coincidence: Petrie worked at the same poultry processing plant as Warwick, the same shift. But she guessed that it wasn't that unusual since the plant was the largest employer in the county.

A chill hit her as she read Petrie's height. It might have been the brisk December breeze that made Ashley shiver. But the icy sensation that spread throughout her body was most likely spurred by the fact that Petrie fit the only known physical attribute of their suspect's profile.

He stood five feet, eight inches tall.

Ashley climbed into the passenger seat of Wyatt's SUV and grabbed his mobile tablet. As the engine roared to life, she logged onto the TBI database. Since Petrie had already displayed a penchant for violence, it was possible that he had a criminal history. For all they knew, the forty-year-old man could have already done time for manslaughter or even murder.

And Ashley wanted to know exactly what they were facing before they reached Murdoch Hollow.

CHAPTER TWELVE

Trepidation surged in Ashley's chest as she read through the list of prior offenses marring Dean Petrie's criminal record. His most recent arrest was for a DUI, but he held two prior convictions for assault and had been charged with domestic abuse. If Cole had crossed paths with Petrie while the man was drinking, Petrie could have snapped. Hell-bent on revenge, he could have followed Cole to Warwick's trailer.

Maybe Petrie had blocked the narrow country road near the mobile home park. Cole could have gotten out of his car to confront the man. And then …

Ashley struggled to keep her mind from painting the picture she feared.

Wyatt must have noticed a worried expression cross her face.

"I take it Petrie has a bad record," he stated.

She nodded. "And his priors fit the profile close enough to make him our number-one suspect."

Ashley hoped that they were on the right track this time. That they would find Cole safe—a hostage on Petrie's property. Her thoughts turned again to Cole's mother. If for some reason they weren't able to save Cole—if they arrived at Petrie's too late—she knew Rosalie's wounded face would haunt her every time she closed her eyes.

The narrow highway snaked to the left as the SUV began the descent into Murdoch Hollow. Ashley pulled out her cell phone and checked the signal bar. No service. She wasn't surprised. Mountains had a habit of blocking cell signals from entering the surrounding, low-lying valleys. The hollows near Ashley's own hometown suffered from the same type of outages.

Another realization struck her. It was possible the steep terrain that edged the hollow would also interfere with the broadcast waves from Wyatt's police radio. She just prayed that they wouldn't need to call for help.

She leaned over and turned up the radio's volume. Chatter from the Fergus County deputies reverberated through the SUV's cab. Their ability to communicate with the dispatcher remained clear for now, but they hadn't yet reached the lowest elevation of the hollow.

Wyatt glanced at her. "I was just about to check that," he said.

Concern that they might need backup obviously plagued her partner's mind as well. He picked up the mic.

"This is TBI Special Agent Wyatt Clark. Dispatch, do you copy?"

"Loud and clear, Agent Clark."

The female dispatcher's voice brought a slight sense of relief to Ashley, but the respite was destined to be short-lived.

She saw Wyatt eyeing the SUV's navigation screen.

"My partner and I are headed to 157 Birch Bottom Road," he stated. "Please be advised that we might need assistance."

After a three-second pause, the dispatcher answered. "There's radio blackout in that area, Agent Clark."

Ashley's anxiety level ratcheted up a notch. She could tell by Wyatt's strained expression that he felt the same.

"If I don't contact you again in one hour," he said into the mic, "please send out reinforcements."

"Will do, Agent Clark."

Ashley was thankful that Wyatt had the forethought to notify dispatch. But she wondered whether an hour was too much time. A lot could happen in sixty minutes. And how long would it take the deputies to get to the hollow? Twenty minutes or longer?

The road corkscrewed to the right. Rushing water glinted in the waning sunlight as the SUV approached a narrow, concrete bridge. She noticed the sign posted next to the road that read, *Murdoch Creek*, had been defaced.

Her breath caught in her throat as Ashley recognized the symbol painted onto the sign.

The capital letters *S* and *A* intertwined together stood for Soldiers of Armageddon. The clandestine, backwoods mountain cult had been born in the Appalachians in the early eighteen hundreds. Rumors abounded that the group offered human sacrifices to the spirits they worshiped.

Her gaze shifted to Wyatt. His normal poker face had returned. Either he hadn't seen the cult's symbol, or he didn't know what the letters represented. She decided that this wasn't the best time to explain it to him. They both had plenty of worries already.

After the SUV crossed the creek, the road leveled out. They were no longer traveling down an incline. She guessed that they'd reached the base of the hollow.

The warning, "*Satellite Transmission Failure,*" popped up on the navigation system's screen, and Ashley felt her stomach drop. She checked the police radio. Static echoed through the speakers. It was official: they were now completely cut off from civilization.

She heard Wyatt sigh. "At least we're almost there," he said. "And we won't stick around. We'll take Petrie back to the sheriff's department."

Ashley realized that hauling Petrie to the station for questioning might not be as easy as Wyatt hoped. "What makes you think that he'll agree to come with us?"

"Keep your eyes open. Look for drugs. Anything that will give us grounds to arrest him."

Maybe Wyatt would get his wish. Finding a legitimate reason to arrest Petrie might not be that difficult. The man had been convicted of aggravated assault which was a class C felony. It was against the law for convicted felons to possess a firearm. Considering the location where Petrie lived—and the reputation of the cult who had marked the territory—Ashley could almost guarantee that he kept a loaded weapon in his home. He wouldn't rely on law enforcement for protection.

As the SUV rounded a curve, the sign for Birch Bottom Road appeared ahead on the left. Wyatt eased off the accelerator and rolled into the turn. The SUV bounced as the tires left asphalt and hit gravel.

Dense forest flanked both sides of the slender road. Ashley had studied the map of the area on Wyatt's tablet while they were still in Arbuckle. She knew that Petrie's property was located approximately a mile down, on the left. She glanced at the clock on the dashboard. Lynette had guessed the drive would take at least twenty minutes. Wyatt had made it in fifteen.

A dented aluminum mailbox stood at the end of Petrie's dirt driveway. Ashley spotted a patch of dingy white through the branches of the dormant hardwoods. As the SUV wound its way up the rutted drive, the patch morphed into an aging mobile home stained with green algae. An older model tan pickup, sporting a cracked windshield, rested to the trailer's right. According to the DMV, the truck was the only vehicle registered in Petrie's name.

An eerie feeling washed over her as she slid out of the SUV. It was almost too quiet. No birds called or sang. Not even the crows or the ever-present grackles. The only sound was the wind whispering through the limbs of the naked trees.

Ashley scanned the property, the grass hidden beneath a sea of brown leaves. She noticed Petrie had dug a fire pit in the front yard. Logs smoldered in the center of the pit ringed with river rocks. A dirty cast iron skillet lay on a slab of limestone peeking out of the ground. Petrie had obviously cooked a meal outside. Did the trailer lack a stove?

She followed Wyatt up to the sagging wooden front porch. To her surprise, the front door of the mobile home stood ajar.

Wyatt knocked on the door's frame. "Dean Petrie," he shouted. "TBI!"

After receiving no answer, Wyatt pushed the door the rest of the way open with his foot. They could look, but they couldn't go inside without just cause. The living room lay empty. No furniture. No television. Dead leaves littered the dirty brown carpeting. Petrie must have practiced the habit of leaving his door open.

Wyatt called again, "Petrie! Come on out!"

Still, no response.

The man was either not home, or he was hiding in one of the other rooms. At the moment, Wyatt and Ashley didn't have an excuse to demand that he come to the door.

"I want to check out the cab of his truck," Wyatt stated, his voice hushed.

Ashley nodded. She trotted down off the porch. Drawing her Glock as a precaution, she circled around the left side of the trailer into the back yard. An unusual structure on the far side of the yard caught her attention. It reminded her of the fort she and her brothers had built when they were children.

Logs had been cut, stacked, and nailed together to form four walls that stood around four-and-a-half feet tall. She guessed the small gap at the corner between two of the walls was used as a door. There was no roof, but an old car hood had been hoisted a few feet above the walls. Suspended from a thick tree limb with rope, the hood seemed to serve as a canopy. While not covering the entire area, the steel hood likely kept some of the rain out of the fort. Petrie probably had kids, and this was their clubhouse.

She peeked inside. The fort was empty.

Gazing into the forest behind the trailer, Ashley saw another building. A shed with a metal stove pipe sticking out of the tin roof. Located a fair distance from the mobile home, she wondered what was inside. A moonshine still? Or was the space crammed with a wood stove and old furniture? There was one way to find out.

She glanced back toward Petrie's pickup. She didn't see Wyatt. She guessed that he was still nosing around the front of the trailer. Maybe he'd found something interesting.

Ashley headed into the woods. The path leading to the shed appeared well-worn. Petrie had obviously made trips to and from the building on a regular basis. It seemed clear that the structure's purpose included more than just storage of old discarded items.

The further she hiked from the trailer, the more ominous the property felt. She looked straight up through the canopy of bare hardwood branches at the slate blue sky. It would be dark soon. She still hadn't seen or heard any birds in the trees. Were they afraid to fly here for some reason? The notion seemed silly. And yet …

Ashley wondered whether Petrie belonged to the Soldiers of Armageddon.

As she drew closer to the shed, she noticed a padlock hanging from a hasp on the door. The panes of the window to the right of the door had been covered on the inside by what appeared to be aluminum foil. Was the foil used to reflect the sun's rays in an attempt to keep the shed cooler? Or was it to block the view?

What could Petrie be hiding?

Had Cole been bound, gagged, and locked in the shed?

She rounded the corner of the building, checking for gaps between the rough wooden boards, hoping that she'd be able to peer inside. Although the planks were old, they all appeared flush.

"Cole," she said, her cheek pressed to a joint in the coarse side wall, "are you in there?"

Silence met her. But that didn't mean that Cole wasn't inside. He could be drugged. Or worse. She continued along the wall.

Just as she reached the rear of the shed, Ashley heard a shout in the distance.

"Stop! TBI!" Wyatt yelled.

Ashley's heart skipped a beat. She ran back toward the yard.

Rifle fire exploded near the trailer.

CHAPTER THIRTEEN

Fear sliced through Ashley's heart as the crack of a rifle split the air. Her fingers gripped tight around her Glock, she zoomed down the path that led through the forest to the back yard of Dean Petrie's mobile home. She'd heard Wyatt shout for someone—likely Petrie—to stop. But instead, the man had decided to fight.

Had Wyatt been hit?

The fact that her partner hadn't returned fire worried her. Images of Wyatt lying on the ground next to the trailer, helpless and bleeding, flooded her mind. What would Kaylee do if she lost her father? Ashley couldn't let that happen.

Would she have to take Petrie out in order to reach Wyatt?

As she raced toward the edge of the tree line, the rifle blasted again. She stopped short, taking cover behind an oak, trying to determine from which direction the shot had originated. It seemed to have come from her left. But she didn't see anyone.

Where was Petrie hiding? Maybe behind a tree in the woods that bordered that side of the yard. Could she circle around behind the man and take him by surprise?

Ashley scurried from tree trunk to tree trunk, heading toward the left side of the property. She struggled to keep quiet as the thick carpet of brittle leaves crunched beneath the soles of her hiking boots. She scanned the yard and forest as she went, but still, there was no sign of Petrie. Or of Wyatt.

A thought struck her: Petrie might not be alone. He could have help. Maybe the gunfire had come from two different rifles. She turned and looked behind her. It was possible that someone was planning to ambush her as well. She didn't see anyone or any signs of movement, but the creepy sensation she'd felt when she'd first arrived at the trailer still plagued her.

She crept toward a broad hickory, her pulse racing. Ashley's breath caught in her throat as another shot exploded from the rifle. Only this time, she heard Wyatt return fire.

A splinter flew from one of the logs at the top of the fort-like structure, hit by her partner's bullet. Relief that Wyatt was still alive—able to shoot—filled her heart. And now she knew the reason he'd held off firing for so long. He couldn't get a clear shot.

Petrie had taken cover inside the fort.

They couldn't see him. And there was no guarantee they could hit him, even if their bullets penetrated the thick, hickory-log walls. They'd likely just be wasting ammo if they fired blind. They needed to make sure that every round would count.

She wondered whether Petrie had been inside the trailer when they'd arrived. Had he watched them through a window? It was possible he'd been outside, somewhere in the forest. Maybe he'd been hunting. Had he seen Ashley? Did he know that she was on the property? Or did he believe Wyatt was here alone?

As she moved in behind a maple, Ashley studied the fort. A plan began to form in her mind.

From the direction of the pistol fire, it seemed Wyatt was hiding behind the old, tan pickup. She hoped Petrie would keep his attention focused on the driveway. She wanted to get closer to the fort.

Angling toward the left corner of the yard, Ashley dashed toward the edge of the tree line. Just as she took cover behind an oak, rifle fire thundered through the forest. A shower of bark exploded from the hickory tree on her right.

Petrie had spotted Ashley. Now, she was in his crosshairs.

He was likely watching her from a thin crack between two of the fort's logs. And since she hadn't seen his head rise above the wall, his rifle was probably aimed through a small gap as well. Again, she wondered whether Petrie was alone in the fort, or if he had someone else covering his back.

In order for her plan to work, Ashley needed to move closer to the structure. She would have to obtain a clear line of sight through the woods. Her best vantage point would be from the tree line running down the left side of the yard. But could she make it there without being shot?

Taking a deep breath, she sprinted toward a nearby maple. Petrie fired again. The bullet whizzed past Ashley's ear as she dove for cover. Her heart pounded in her chest like a jackhammer. The shot had come close to hitting her skull. Too close.

66

As she struggled to calm down, to restore her breathing to normal, a realization struck her. From where she stood, her back pressed against the tree, she couldn't see the narrow door of the fort. If Wyatt was stationed behind the pickup as she suspected, his view would be even more limited than hers. It would be easy for Petrie—or a cohort of his—to sneak out of the structure and circle around behind Ashley.

Petrie knew exactly where she was hiding.

If she ran out from behind the tree, he would fire at her again. But if she remained still, she risked being ambushed from the forest. And she knew that Petrie would continue to shoot at Wyatt. Her partner had no doubt realized that Ashley had become a target. Would he try to come to her rescue by attempting to circle around the front of the trailer? If Wyatt broke from the cover of the pickup, Petrie could kill him.

If that happened, Ashley would never forgive herself.

Her heart screamed that she had only one choice. Instead of continuing to her left, she'd run deeper into the forest. Maybe Petrie would think she'd given up—that she was running away. After gaining ample cover in the woods, she'd veer back around and skulk toward the tree line on the left side of the yard. Then she'd be at the proper place to follow through with her plan. Hopefully, Petrie would never see her coming.

Ashley counted to ten, steeling herself for the rifle blast she knew would come. She bolted from the maple tree.

Shots rang out.

One blast ... two ... three ...

Tree trunks splintered to her left and right as she zigzagged through the woods, heading away from Petrie's yard. After a few seconds, the rifle fell silent. But Ashley kept running. She feared Petrie could still have her in his sights. She had to put as much distance, and as many obstacles, behind her as she could before changing her direction.

Once she felt she had advanced far enough to lay a padding of forest between herself and the scope of Petrie's rifle, Ashley stopped. She leaned against a sycamore to catch her breath. As she glanced at the maple across from her, Ashley's heart skipped a beat.

Red paint marred the maple's bark. Capital letters *S* and *A* intertwined together. The land where she stood had been claimed by the Soldiers of Armageddon. And the sky overhead was growing dim. But Ashley couldn't allow herself to worry about the cult and the rumors of their ritual sacrifices. She had to get back to Petrie's trailer.

Cutting toward the left side of Petrie's property, she sped through the woods. Would he be watching for her return? Her eyes scanned the forest as she tried to judge how much farther she had to go. She realized that it was possible Petrie had sent someone to search for her. She might meet them head-on.

The crack of rifle fire ricocheted through the trees. Petrie was obviously shooting at Wyatt again. Ashley prayed that her partner was safe—that he hadn't made a risky move in an effort to reach her. He had no idea what she was planning. He might think she'd been injured and needed help.

She had to hurry. A stitch burned in Ashley's side as she pushed her muscles to their limit.

Finally, she caught sight of a break in the tree cover ahead to her right. Petrie's back yard. Slowing her pace, she angled toward the area where she knew the fort rested. When she saw the log structure peeking through the trees, she switched into stealth mode.

An eerie stillness—a strange silence like she'd never experienced during all of her years growing up in the backwoods—blanketed the forest. Did evil spirits lurk here? Were they influencing Petrie? Ashley had never believed otherworldly entities to be real, but now, she was beginning to wonder. Either way, if she made one wrong move, Petrie would hear her approaching.

Creeping from tree to tree, she sneaked closer to the fort. As she inched between two hickories, her boot smashed a small branch hidden beneath the layer of dead leaves.

Snap!

The abrupt sound echoed through the forest. Ducking behind a tree, Ashley held her breath. She now had a clear view of the fort, which meant that Petrie would be able to see her as well. He had to have heard the branch break. She'd no doubt drawn his attention.

Ashley stood still and counted off the seconds, hoping Petrie would turn his focus back toward the driveway or the rear of his property. But she knew she couldn't wait long. In order to be in the correct position for her plan to work, she needed to move a yard or so to her left.

As she slipped out from behind the hickory, the crack of rifle fire exploded in her ears.

Pain ripped through her body.

Ashley had been shot.

CHAPTER FOURTEEN

A scream stuck in Ashley's throat as the bullet from Petrie's rifle tore through the left arm of her navy cargo jacket, searing her flesh. White hot pain ripped through her shoulder, but she couldn't cry out. She didn't want Wyatt to hear her. She feared that he'd leave the safe haven behind the pickup truck and run into the forest in an attempt to rescue her. If he darted out into the open, Petrie would likely kill him.

She couldn't live with Wyatt's death plaguing her conscious.

Knocked off balance by the blast, time seemed to shift into slow motion as Ashley careened toward an ancient sycamore.

The crack of rifle fire split the air again.

Dodging the bullet, Ashley hit the ground and rolled. Another shot echoed through the forest in rapid succession. The toe of her boot slammed against bark. Ashley snapped into a ball, curling her body behind the wide trunk of the sycamore tree. Her heart hammered in her chest. She forced herself to take deep even breaths. For this brief second, she was safe.

Slipping her arm out of her jacket, she examined her shoulder. Blood soaked the sleeve of her honey-colored shirt. The wound hurt like hell, but it didn't appear deep. Relief flooded her mind when she realized that the bullet had only grazed her. She might need a couple of stitches, but she'd be okay.

Ashley felt herself sigh. Now that Petrie knew her location, how would she stop him? She needed to take aim at the fort. But if she peeked out from behind the tree, he'd shoot her again. And the next time, the damage might prove fatal.

Leaning her head back against the tree trunk, she closed her eyes for just a second. She had to gather her thoughts and figure out a way to put her plan into action. She knew that the Soldiers of Armageddon stalked these woods. With their symbol marking the maple so close to Petrie's property, it was likely that he was a member of the cult. Hearing the barrage of gunfire, would the group rush to his aid?

How much time did Ashley have before the soldiers surrounded her?

She opened her eyes and gazed up at the tree branches. Spiky, brown, sycamore seed balls dangled above her. Her back still pressed against the trunk, she pushed herself to her feet. Raising her right hand above her head, she realized that she could reach the lowest limb. Could she climb up this side of the tree without Petrie seeing her?

He probably expected Ashley to run again. His vision would likely be focused on the ground, not above. Swiveling around to face the trunk, she studied the sycamore's structure. The branches were large enough and spaced in such a way that they should provide her with ample cover.

It just might work.

With her left shoulder still throbbing, Ashley gripped the limb with both hands. She hooked her right leg over the thick branch and then pulled herself up. It had never dawned on her that all those years of practice climbing trees during her childhood could end up saving her life.

Stretching her arms over her head, she continued to climb. She wanted to make sure that she was above Petrie's general line of sight, but she couldn't go too high. She needed to be at just the right angle to fire her pistol. Checking her balance, preparing to jerk back out of harm's way, she chanced a look around the sycamore's trunk.

The car-hood canopy blocked the view inside the fort. But if Petrie suspected she'd ventured up into the tree, the barrel of his rifle would likely be visible just above the log wall. It wasn't. He probably had his weapon trained on the base of the sycamore.

A blast from Petrie's rifle startled her.

The sole of Ashley's hiking boot slipped on the bark of the tree branch. A bolt of fright struck her as she felt herself falling. Her pulse racing, she grabbed a nearby limb. She struggled to calm her nerves as she steadied herself in a crook of the tree.

Wyatt returned Petrie's fire. He had to be shooting blind. But why? Why would he waste precious ammo? Fear wormed its way into Ashley's heart as she guessed what was happening. Wyatt must have decided to storm the fort. He probably thought that Ashley was in trouble—that he had no choice.

Petrie fired two more rounds.

Ashley had to get into position before it was too late. Before one of Petrie's bullets struck Wyatt. Getting a firm grip on an adjacent branch, she scooted around to the left side of the tree trunk. She braced her body between two sturdy limbs and then focused her attention on the oak tree that towered over the fort.

The old steel car hood that shielded the interior of the log structure hung from a rope wrapped around a thick branch of the oak, at a level just slightly lower than where she perched.

Rifle fire thundered beneath her. Again, Wyatt shot back.

Ashley couldn't see her partner from her current vantage point, but it sounded as though he was moving closer to the fort. She had to hurry. She couldn't allow Wyatt to make a fatal mistake.

As she raised her pistol, Petrie blasted off another round.

Blocking out the sounds of the gunfire, Ashley aimed her Glock. She breathed in deep. Exhaling, she squeezed the trigger.

Her bullet hit its mark, severing the braided nylon rope.

The steel car hood crashed into the fort below.

Her eye caught movement on the ground to her left. It was Wyatt. He ran toward the fort. Rather than climb back down the tree, Ashley readied her Glock, just in case Petrie crawled out from beneath the car hood.

Ashley watched as Wyatt circled around to the fort's narrow door. She saw him lift the car hood and prop it against one of the log walls. Petrie lay face down on the ground, his weapon at his side. She hoped that he wasn't dead. Wyatt knelt down, grabbed the rifle, and then checked the man's pulse.

After a few seconds, Wyatt stood and scanned the tree line, obviously looking for Ashley.

"Up here," she called.

A look of surprise crossed his face as his eyes met hers. His lips curved into a smile. "Petrie's out cold," he said.

She was grateful that their suspect was still alive. They needed answers. They needed to find Cole.

"Okay, I'll be right down."

As dusk pushed into the hollow, Ashley holstered her Glock and descended from the boughs of the sycamore tree. She dropped to the ground and headed toward the fort. Wyatt knelt on one knee next to a handcuffed Petrie. Blood streaked a cut beneath the suspect's blond facial stubble, but she didn't see any gashes on his skull. She hoped that was a good sign.

Wyatt gave the man a shake. "Wake up, Petrie."

A grunt escaped the suspect's lips. His eyelids fluttered.

"Petrie." Wyatt shook him again.

The man's eyes opened. He struggled against the handcuffs.

"Get off my land," he yelled, his words sounding slurred.

Ashley didn't think he was drunk. The blow to his head had likely garbled his speech.

Wyatt pulled the suspect to his feet. He checked the man's vision and vitals, making sure that Petrie hadn't sustained a concussion.

After determining their suspect was in good shape physically, Wyatt stated, "Dean Petrie, you're under arrest for attempted murder."

"I ain't killed nobody."

"You just fired several rounds at two TBI agents," Wyatt pointed out, anger in his tone. "Why? Why did you shoot?"

"I didn't know you was the law."

Wyatt shook his head. "That's hard to believe. I identified myself as soon as I saw you."

"That don't matter," Petrie said. "They always lie. They pretend to be somebody else."

"Who are you talking about? Who lies?"

A look of fright crossed Petrie's face. "The soldiers. I thought you was them. That you'd come to kill me."

"Petrie, you're not making any sense. And you're in big trouble, so don't even think of copping an insanity plea."

Ashley stepped toward Wyatt and Petrie. "The people he's afraid of are members of a vicious mountain cult: the Soldiers of Armageddon. I saw the symbol marking their territory out in the woods behind his trailer."

Wyatt stared at Ashley as though she was speaking a foreign language. He'd clearly had no idea that such groups existed. After a second's hesitation, he turned his attention back to Petrie.

"What did you do with Cole Gowen?" Wyatt barked, the ire from being shot at still obvious. "Is he locked in your shed?"

Petrie looked at Wyatt like he was the crazy one. "Who the hell are *you* talking about?"

"The man who served you with divorce papers last year."

Petrie huffed. "That asshole? I ain't seen him since."

72

Ashley said, "There are witnesses who say you took a swing at Cole. Then you called his place of employment and tried to get him fired."

"Who cares?"

She locked eyes with Petrie. "You should," Ashley stated. "Cole disappeared on Friday—we think he may be dead—and you're our number one suspect. It's quite possible that you could be sentenced to the electric chair."

"No way," Petrie said, shaking his head. "I told you, I ain't been nowhere near that guy. If I had, you'd found his body full of lead. And I'd be bragging."

Hatred radiated from the man's pores, probably both for Cole and law enforcement, but Ashley couldn't tell whether Petrie was telling the truth or not.

"Then you'd better hope that you can prove you didn't abduct Cole."

Petrie stared at her. "When did he go missing?"

Was their suspect weaving together an alibi?

"Sometime between three and four in the afternoon."

"See, it can't be me," Petrie said, a smirk on his face. "Check with the Bonner County Sheriff. I was all the way over there, picking up trash on the highway. Court ordered for a DUI."

Ashley glanced at Wyatt. If his story checked out, Petrie would have an airtight alibi. But she wasn't ready to believe the man yet. They didn't wear shackles on litter clean-up duty. Maybe he'd slipped away from his group.

Wyatt touched Ashley's arm. He'd noticed the bullet tear in her jacket.

"Did you get hit?" he asked, concern spreading across his face.

She shrugged. "After we get Petrie settled in at the sheriff's department, I might need to take a quick trip to the ER."

Even if her wound didn't require stitches, she would likely need a tetanus shot and maybe some antibiotics.

Stars broke out across the darkened sky as they marched Petrie to the SUV. Wyatt chained the prisoner to a metal ring built into the rear floorboard and then bucked the seatbelt around him.

As Wyatt slammed the door, he looked at Ashley. "Take your jacket off before you get inside."

"What?"

"We need to clean your bullet wound," he said, worry in his eyes.

She should have guessed that was his plan.

"It's just a graze—nothing serious. I'll be fine."

"Just do it."

Ashley didn't see any point in arguing. She nodded. She stripped off her jacket and climbed into the passenger seat.

Wyatt flipped on the interior cab lights and popped open his first aid kit. Ashley was glad that she'd decided to wear short sleeves that morning. She winced as she pulled the fabric of her shirt sleeve up over her shoulder, exposing the gunshot.

When the alcohol swab touched her skin, pain stung her like a nest of hornets. She gritted her teeth and allowed Wyatt to clean off the blood.

"Petrie can wait," he told her, his jaw set in a firm line. "We're going to the ER first."

Anxiety sprouted in Ashley's chest. Maybe the wound was more serious than she'd thought.

After Wyatt taped a temporary bandage onto her arm, she leaned her head back against the seat and closed her eyes. Along with her aching shoulder, her head had begun to throb. And she still hadn't shaken the eerie feeling that had permeated her soul since they'd arrived at Petrie's property.

Ashley just hoped that they didn't run into the Soldiers of Armageddon on their way out of the hollow.

CHAPTER FIFTEEN

Jerry Osborne's eyes popped open. He pushed himself up on the sofa and looked at the television. Something had jolted him out of a deep sleep. A noise. Or maybe a vibration. He wasn't sure what had roused him, but he realized that it wasn't the sitcom on the screen. The TV volume was turned too low.

Was Marilyn home?

He glanced at the clock hanging on the living room wall. 9:40 p.m. Maybe his wife had fought with her hot-headed mother again. Marilyn must have decided to leave Sparks County, driving home early. In all honestly, he was glad. Not because his wife and mother-in-law didn't get along. He wished their on-again, off-again relationship wasn't so rocky. But he didn't look forward to milking the cows by himself in the morning.

"Marilyn?" he called out.

The house stood silent. Maybe she'd taken her luggage upstairs. Although Marilyn was slim and fit, her weight landing on the squeaky third step was probably the sound that woke him. The creaking was a trigger noise for Jerry, one he couldn't block out. It grated on his nerves each time he heard it. But adding caulk and screwing down the warped, one-hundred-year-old oak treads hadn't fixed the problem, so he was forced to live with the irritation.

He swung his legs off the sofa. As his toes hit the hardwood floor, the sensation of pins and needles shot up his right leg. His foot had fallen asleep. Cursing under his breath, he stumbled into the foyer and gazed up toward the second floor.

"Marilyn?" he shouted again.

Still, no answer.

Maybe she'd gone back out to fetch something from the car. The last time she visited her mother, she'd brought home jars of pickles, green beans, and peaches her aunt had canned. He should find out if Marilyn needed help.

With his foot still numb, he left the foyer and crossed back through the living room. When he reached the doorway to the kitchen, a frosty draft struck him. His attention jerked toward the right as he stepped over the threshold.

The door leading outside gaped open.

A chill shot down the back of Jerry's neck.

Marilyn would never intentionally leave the door standing open. It was the one quirk she'd inherited from the female side of her family. If Jerry dared to leave an outside door ajar, just a crack, she'd ask, *"Were you raised in a barn?"* in the same condescending tone her mother often used.

Could the wind have blown the door open?

Holding his breath, he crept across the kitchen. Bitter cold seeped through his socks as he inched out onto the wooden back porch. Except for his pickup, the driveway lay empty. Marilyn was still at her mother's house.

He padded back into the kitchen, pressed the door closed, and locked it. He stood still, listening. The December breeze buffeted the glass panes in the door behind him, but inside, all sat quiet. He told himself that there was nothing to worry about—that he was in the house alone—but he decided to go upstairs and get the loaded pistol from his nightstand, just in case.

He walked toward the living room.

Thump!

Jerry froze, his pulse racing.

The noise had come from the direction of the utility room. Being as quiet as possible, he pivoted on his heels and moved toward the short hallway off the kitchen. As he neared the door to the utility room, another noise broke the silence. A faint squeaking, like metal hinges turning.

His heart pounded as he recognized the sound. It was the door of the breaker box opening.

Someone had broken into his home.

The premonition that he would soon meet his death flashed through Jerry's mind.

Fear split his chest as darkness engulfed the farmhouse.

CHAPTER SIXTEEN

Ashley scratched her arm, her fingernails skirting the bandage covering her gunshot wound. Along with the pain that throbbed throughout her shoulder, the area itched like crazy. But according to the doctor at the Fergus County Hospital emergency room, the wound should heal with no problems. Except for a small scar, there would be no permanent damage. The doctor had sewn three stitches into her shoulder and had sent her on her way.

With a sigh, she sank down onto the side of her motel room bed. After booking Dean Petrie into jail for their attempted murders, Wyatt had contacted the sheriff's department over in Bonner County. Petrie's alibi had checked out. The suspect had been present for roll calls on the highway litter detail at one o'clock, three o'clock, and five o'clock on Friday afternoon. There was no way he could have kidnapped Cole.

The investigation had rocketed back to square one.

Where was Cole? And why had he been abducted? Something deep in the recesses of Ashley's mind still nagged at her concerning Lester Warwick. But she couldn't pinpoint exactly what it was that bothered her. She didn't think the man was personally guilty of Cole's disappearance, but her instincts told her that something was off.

As Ashley made her way toward the vanity area to brush her teeth, her cell phone rang. She felt a smile spread across her face when she glanced at the caller ID on the screen.

She was quick to answer. "Hi, Daniel."

"Hi, sweetheart. How's everything going in Fergus County?"

The sound of his voice seemed to melt away all the tension that had built up inside her during the chaotic day.

She hesitated for a second, wondering what she should tell him first. An update on work won out. "Well, the investigation is at a standstill right now," she said.

"Yeah? What else is wrong?"

It amazed Ashley how well Daniel could read her. She wasn't sure how he did it, but whenever something was bothering her, he always picked up on it.

She'd been contemplating how to tell him that she'd been shot. In the past when he'd thought that she was in danger, he'd tended to overreact. When she'd received the first note from her stalker, he'd called in the TBI forensic team to investigate and had even personally gone door-to-door to question her neighbors. But even though the news might upset him, she'd vowed to herself to tell Daniel about everything important. She was finished with keeping secrets.

"I'm okay—so don't freak out."

"What happened?" he asked, his tone tinged with anxiety.

Ashley took a deep breath, hoping that she could phrase her words in a way that would help ease Daniel's mind. "It's nothing serious," she stressed again. "My shoulder was grazed by a bullet earlier today. But the doctor at the emergency room told me that the wound will completely heal in a few weeks, so there's no reason to worry."

Daniel remained silent for a moment as though he was processing the information. "Are you in much pain?" he finally asked.

"It's not too bad," she said, downplaying the situation. "And the doctor gave me some medication that should help. I'll take it right before I go to bed."

She glanced at the time on her phone. 10:02 p.m.

"Where are you staying?"

Ashley guessed what he really wanted to know was whether or not she and Wyatt were bunking in the same room again.

"It's the only place in town—the Arbuckle Motor Inn. I have my very own room, number 128, on the first floor, right next to the ice machine."

Although dimly lit, with worn brown carpeting, gold bedspreads, and battered oak furniture, the room looked a lot cleaner than the one she and Wyatt had been forced to share. But she had noticed a faint, odd smell lingering in the air.

"Sounds good."

She could hear his relief. She was about to ask how his day had gone when a muffled male voice echoed over the line. She couldn't understand the man's words, but his tone had sounded urgent.

78

"Hey Ashley, I'm going to have to go," Daniel said. "I'm on a stakeout, and our suspect's on the move. I'll call you back in the morning. Around six."

One upside to dating another TBI agent was that they both understood the demands of the job and the strange working hours.

"Okay," she said, wishing they could talk longer. "Good luck—and please be careful."

As she ended the call, a low battery alert popped up on her phone. She only had a few minutes left before it went dead. She was about to dig her charger out of her suitcase when she heard a knock on the door that separated Wyatt's adjoining room from hers.

Ashley unlocked the door and pulled it open. Wyatt had changed into a TBI T-shirt and a pair of gym shorts.

"You ready to tape up your shoulder?"

She had asked him earlier to help cover her wound, using a small plastic trash bag, so she could take a shower.

"Yeah, come on in."

She led him to the vanity area. She pulled up her shirt sleeve and watched in the mirror as he sealed the plastic over her bandage. It felt a little awkward with him standing so close, touching her skin, but she couldn't waterproof her shoulder alone, one-handed. And so far, he hadn't made any advances toward her.

"All right, that's got it," he said, placing the roll of medical tape on the vanity counter.

"I really appreciate your help," she told him. "Not only now, but also in the SUV with the first aid kit."

If Wyatt hadn't insisted that they go to the ER before taking Petrie to jail, it was possible that her wound would have had time to become infected.

"No problem. I'll see you in the morning."

Ashley followed him back to the door that connected their two rooms and reengaged the lock. Then she headed for the bathroom.

As she stood underneath the hot spray of the shower, she reviewed the details of Cole's case in her mind. The only thing they knew for certain was that the kidnapper stood no taller than five feet, nine inches. But then a realization struck her. That assumption had been made based on the fact that the driver's seat of Cole's car had been moved forward. Cole's friend, Deputy Kelton had discovered the car on Rattler Ridge.

What if Kelton was involved in the chop shop ring? He would have had ample opportunity to adjust the seat in order to falsify evidence.

Kelton definitely stood taller than five-nine. Moving the seat would be one way to cast suspicion in another direction.

First thing in the morning, Ashley would share her thoughts with Wyatt. They could find out Kelton's patrol location and ask him a few more questions.

After toweling off, Ashley slipped into her nightgown. The events of the day had caught up with her. She struggled to keep her eyes open as she brushed her teeth. She switched off the lights and collapsed onto the bed.

As she slid beneath the covers, both of her feet hit something ice cold. She gasped in shock. She flipped on the light that rested on the bedside table and yanked back the sheet.

Ashley screamed.

Dead frogs—dozens of them—crowded the bottom half of the bed.

CHAPTER SEVENTEEN

Sprawled across his motel room bed, Wyatt sighed as he gazed at the sleeping form of his daughter, Kaylee, broadcast from the nanny cam at her mother's home to the app on his cell phone. He wished things were different. That he could be there to tuck her beneath the covers every night. But he realized that even if his job allowed him to work a nine-to-five shift, Lauren would never agree to him visiting her place that often. She valued her independence. Her freedom. She didn't want Wyatt interrupting her routine.

"Sweet dreams, baby," he said aloud, though he knew that Kaylee couldn't hear him. "I love you."

He logged out of the app, slid his phone onto the battered nightstand, and flipped off the light. Just as his head hit the pillow, a woman's scream cut through the paper-thin wall that butted the bed.

It was Ashley.

Alarmed, he jumped up and ran to the door that connected the two motel rooms.

"Ashley!" he called out. "Are you okay?"

He remembered the shout that had escaped his own lips the night he'd found a roach crawling across his chest. Maybe Ashley had experienced the same. At least, he hoped that was the case. As he raised his hand to knock on the door, it opened.

Ashley stood before him, wrapped in a blue silk robe, her face drained of color. Something was definitely wrong.

"What's going on?" he asked her.

Instead of speaking, she stepped back and motioned for him to enter her room. The first thing he noticed was a strange smell, almost like formaldehyde. And then he saw the bed.

A sea of dead frogs covered the foot of the mattress.

The sight seemed so bizarre that he almost couldn't believe his eyes.

"What in the hell ..."

"I guess my stalker decided to leave me a present while we were out," Ashley said.

He pulled open the drawer of the nightstand and fished out the cheap, plastic, ballpoint pen the motel provided. He poked at one of the frogs, flipped the corpse over with the pen. He could tell the animals had been preserved. That was the reason the room reeked of formaldehyde.

"They were probably stolen from a school," he said. "These frogs were meant to be dissected."

"Well, that makes sense because bullfrogs hibernate underwater in the wintertime. It wouldn't be easy to find this many in the wild right now."

Wyatt knew the person following Ashley most likely lived in Laurel County. The mountain people were known for their strange ways but filling a bed with frogs in order to seek revenge seemed odd even for them.

"It might be a good idea to keep one. For when you press charges. Have you got an evidence bag handy?"

Ashley grabbed her cargo jacket from the desk chair and pulled a plastic bag from one of the pockets. She handed it to Wyatt. Still using the pen, he knelt down and scraped one of the frogs off the mattress and into the mouth of the bag.

He looked at the second bed in the room. Had it been booby-trapped as well? He dropped the bagged frog on top of the desk. The spread covering the bed that rested next to the window seemed taut and flat. But that didn't mean there wasn't a surprise lurking beneath it. He stripped back the covers. No frogs. And the sheets appeared clean.

"They knew which bed you'd pick."

Each bed stood a fifty-fifty chance at being used, and yet, the stalker had guessed right. Did that mean he knew how Ashley's mind worked? Were they well-acquainted?

"That's probably because I took the spread off of the bed I planned to sleep in when we first arrived."

That made sense. The stalker must have watched Wyatt and Ashley check in. And after they'd headed out on their way to the Stanley farm, he'd broken into the room. The bed was already turned down, waiting for him.

Wyatt hadn't seen any cameras mounted outside the door. A habit gleaned from his years of detective work, he always checked for

82

surveillance without even thinking about it. Unless they could find a witness, it would be difficult to determine who had broken into the room.

"I'll be right back," he told Ashley.

He wanted to take a few pictures to document the scene before he cleaned up the mess. He headed into his room and scooped his phone off of the nightstand. Ashley had to be upset. Frightened. But there were no other motels in Arbuckle. They had nowhere else to go.

And even though a strong need to protect Ashley tugged at his soul, Wyatt knew better than to invite her to stay with him in his room. She'd made it clear that she still didn't trust him enough. He guessed that she'd heard the gossip floating around the bureau. Rumors about him that proved less than half true.

Regardless of his not-so-deserved reputation, Ashley was safe with Wyatt. Although he couldn't forget the jolt of electricity that had surged through his body when their fingers had touched (it had haunted his mind all day), he would never make a move unless she gave him an indication that it was something she wanted. And right now, she was dating Daniel Lansing. A man with a sterling character. So, Wyatt likely didn't stand a chance.

With phone in hand, he slipped on his shoes and trotted back to Ashley's room. He snapped photos of the dead frogs from several different angles. Whenever they uncovered the identity of her stalker, she had enough evidence to hang the man. Not just for the stalking charge, but also for breaking and entering.

Satisfied that he'd taken enough photographs, Wyatt pocketed his phone. He folded the bottom and top sheet together, encasing the frogs like an envelope, and stripped them from the bed. The mattress would likely retain the formaldehyde odor, but at the moment, there was nothing he could do about that.

"I'll take them out to the trash," he said.

A look of relief flashed across Ashley's face. "Thank you."

As he crossed the motel room's threshold, he scanned the parking lot. Was the stalker watching him now? Only a few streetlights dotted the pavement. The man could be hiding in the shadows, peering at him through the window of a car or pickup. If the stalker was here, he might decide to sneak into Ashley's room while she was sleeping.

Wyatt needed to figure out a way to ensure Ashley's safety.

After tossing the frogs into the dumpster, his gaze swept the parking lot once more. He still didn't see anyone. He headed back into the motel room. He caught Ashley pacing in the vanity area, her arms folded across her chest. He could see the wheels of her mind turning. It was obvious that she was trying to come up with a plan.

But an idea had already struck Wyatt.

"Let's switch rooms," he said. "Just for sleeping. Leave all your stuff here, so that if they break in while we're gone, they won't notice it. But if they come in at night, they'll have to deal with me."

He knew how easy it would be for someone to open the swing-bar safety latch on the motel door using only a piece of string. An instructor had demonstrated the technique at a TBI conference several years earlier.

Ashley stared at him for a moment as though she was considering the proposition.

"I don't want to be responsible for putting you in danger," she said.

"You won't be. I'll rig up something at the door that will make noise. I'll have my Glock drawn before they step into the room."

He hoped that she would listen to him. He wouldn't forgive himself if he allowed someone to hurt her.

Ashley chewed her bottom lip. "Okay," she finally said, nodding. "As long as you're sure it's what you want to do."

"I'm sure."

He'd go even further to protect Ashley if she'd let him.

Wyatt wandered toward the window, giving her a bit of privacy as she gathered up a few essential items—toiletries and a change of clothing.

"I guess I'll see you in the morning then," she said.

Ashley disappeared through the connecting doorway. He noticed that although she'd chosen to shut the door, he hadn't heard the lock click into place. She was obviously rattled, and he couldn't blame her.

Moving into the vanity area, he found Ashley's bottle of liquid laundry detergent on the counter. The bottom was concaved by just the right amount. He balanced the bottle on top of the motel room's doorknob and tested it to make sure it would stay put. If someone tried to get inside, the bottle was heavy enough that he'd hear it when it hit the floor.

Wyatt switched off the lights and crawled into the clean bed by the window. Despite the night's excitement, he drifted off to sleep within just a few minutes. Images of Kaylee, laughing in the sunshine, playing on a swing set, filled his dreams. And then Ashley appeared. Her blue eyes sparked as she reached for his hand. As their fingers intertwined, her beauty took his breath away. She leaned toward him, her lips seeking his—

An urgent ringing sound jerked Wyatt awake. He glanced at the clock on the nightstand. 6:04 a.m. Groggy, his hand searched the top of the small table for his cell phone. Then he realized the ringing had come from the landline.

He picked up the receiver of the motel phone.

"Clark," he said, his voice laden with sleep.

No one spoke.

"Hello?"

He heard a familiar sound on the other end of the line. Faint chatter and the keying of a mic. A police radio. Was it the sheriff calling?

He sat up in bed. "This is Wyatt Clark," he stated.

A dial tone answered him. Whoever it was, they'd decided to hang up. It had most likely been a wrong number. Someone with a police scanner.

And then a realization hit him. Had Ashley's stalker called?

Maybe it would be best not to mention it to her. Knowing about the call wouldn't change anything, and she had enough to worry about already. Sighing, he slung his legs over the edge of the bed. His alarm was set for six-thirty, so he might as well get up now. He could make a coffee run.

As he stepped into his chinos, his cell phone rang. He checked the caller ID. This time, it really was Sheriff Hyland.

"Clark," he answered, his voice firm.

"Hate to call so early, Agent Clark," Hyland stated, his voice on edge. "But we've got a new development. And I think it's connected to Cole."

CHAPTER EIGHTEEN

Ashley slid out of the bed in Wyatt's motel room and pulled on her robe. Her shoulder ached, and her eyes felt grainy. Sleep had evaded her for most of the night. Visions of decapitated opossums and zombie-like frogs had haunted her dreams. Knowing that someone possessed the ability to sneak into her apartment and her motel room at will, and that they'd likely pawed her most intimate belongings, chilled her to the core.

Who had followed her to Fergus County? And why had they chosen frogs to put into her bed?

The members of her ex-husband's family had proven ruthless in the past. They'd once burned down an enemy's barn with his livestock trapped inside. But if they wanted to terrorize Ashley with dead animals, why not pick something they could catch in the wild?

Although winter had descended upon the mountains, the forest still teemed with wildlife. Rabbits, quail, turkeys, beavers, and of course, deer, all roamed the land. And the Barrett clan was known for their expert hunting skills. Why would they go to the trouble of breaking into a school to steal bullfrogs? It made no sense.

Unless they were trying to send a specific message.

What did the frogs and the opossum symbolize? They had to be connected to her past with Ethan in some way. But Ashley couldn't figure out how.

She shuffled into the vanity area and washed her face. Had she made the wrong decision by switching rooms with Wyatt? The fact that she may have put him in harm's way pricked at her soul. She'd agreed to his plan based on one assumption. If the stalker came in and found Wyatt, she guessed that the intruder would flee rather than confront the TBI agent. And she'd also taken Wyatt at his word that he would engineer an alarm system, so that he would hear someone coming before they breached the door.

Wyatt had assured her that he would be waiting for the stalker, Glock poised for action.

Pulling on her jeans, Ashley glanced at the clock on the nightstand. It was already a couple of minutes past six. Daniel would be calling soon. Ashley sighed as she realized that she'd left her cell phone back in her original motel room.

Was Wyatt awake yet? She didn't want to disturb his sleep, but she also didn't feel comfortable sneaking into the room. What if he'd chosen to sleep in the nude? She might see something that she would prefer remained a mystery. She'd just have to call Daniel back later. He'd understand. And she knew that he'd be grateful that Wyatt had offered to switch rooms.

Ashley scooped the remote from the top of the chest of drawers and switched on the television. As she flipped through the channels, searching for the weather station, she thought she heard a faint ringing coming from her old room. She hit the mute button.

She perched on the side of the bed, listening. It wasn't her cell phone or Wyatt's cell that she'd heard; she knew that. But she thought maybe it was a ring tone he'd set as a wake-up alarm. If he was up now, she could get her phone. Maybe she wouldn't miss Daniel's call after all.

Deciding to give Wyatt a minute or two to get dressed, she turned up the volume of the television. It appeared as though today would be a carbon copy of yesterday as far as the weather was concerned.

Another faint ringing seeped into the room. This time, she recognized the jingle. It was Wyatt's cell phone. A call at this hour was likely bad news.

Had they found Cole's body?

Concern filled her chest as she switched off the TV. She rose from the bed and inched toward the door that connected the two rooms. But then she stopped short. She didn't want to eavesdrop in case the call turned out to be personal.

With her nervous energy building, she strode to the window, parted the curtain, and peeked out at the parking lot. Was the stalker here? Waiting for Ashley to leave so he could slip into her room again? What other surprises did he have planned?

A knock echoed from the connecting door.

"Ashley?" Wyatt called out.

The tone of his voice let her know that she'd been right. The call had contained bad news.

She raced toward the door and pulled it open. Before she could ask what had happened, Wyatt spoke.

"The sheriff just called," he said. "There's another missing person. And Hyland thinks this case might be connected to Cole. I told him we'd be right over."

Although it unnerved her to hear that someone else had gone missing, she was relieved that the sheriff hadn't called to inform them that Cole had been found murdered.

"I'm ready to head out whenever you are," she told Wyatt.

He nodded. "In case someone's watching, we should leave from our assigned rooms," he said. "Make sure to take your hairbrush and … other stuff back with you so they don't get suspicious. And lock the connecting door."

Ashley gathered up her things and returned to her original room. She grabbed her cell phone from the nightstand next to the frog bed. Irritation shot through her as she checked the screen. She'd forgotten to plug her phone into the charger. During the night, the battery had died.

Daniel's call this morning would have been sent straight to voice mail.

Luckily, she'd packed her vehicle charger. How long would it take to juice the battery enough to power the phone back on? She needed to send Daniel a text letting him know what had happened. She didn't want him to think she'd ignored his call.

She stuffed her charger into her jacket pocket and glanced around the room. Everything looked right. Felt right. If the stalker broke in again while she was gone, he'd think she was still sleeping here.

Eager to learn the details surrounding the new disappearance, Ashley raced out the motel room door.

CHAPTER NINETEEN

Ashley plucked her cell phone from the center console of the SUV and pressed the power button. She glanced at the clock on the dashboard. Only fifteen minutes had passed since she'd plugged the phone into the charging port, and she feared it might not work yet. But she hoped to be able to send Daniel a text before she and Wyatt reached their destination.

Investigating the scene of the second disappearance might take a couple of hours. And she didn't want Daniel to have to wait that long, wondering why he hadn't been able to reach her this morning. With everything that had transpired lately—the threats from her stalker and the fact that she'd been shot—she didn't want him to worry that something bad had happened to her.

Relief rushed through her heart as the manufacturer's logo popped up on the screen. After entering her passcode, she checked for a voicemail notification. There was nothing new.

Opening the text app, she tapped out a message.

Sorry we didn't get to talk this morning.
My cell battery died.
Can't wait to hear your voice again.
Call me when you can. I miss you.

As Ashley tapped Send, the computerized female voice from the SUV's navigation system announced that 1252 Homestead, the missing man's residence, was just up ahead. Woven wire fencing lined the right side of the road. At the top of the slope, a herd of light-brown Jersey cows huddled near a gray metal barn. The man and his wife obviously ran a dairy farm.

Wyatt piloted the SUV up the long gravel drive to the left of a white two-story farmhouse. Two Fergus County Sheriff's Department cruisers crowded the parking area, resting behind a green pickup and a blue sedan. As Ashley hopped out of the passenger's seat, Sheriff Hyland emerged from the front door of the house. He trotted down the porch steps and headed toward the driveway.

"Thanks for getting here so fast," Hyland said, nodding at both Wyatt and Ashley. "The wife is pretty upset. Her name's Marilyn Osborne. She's chomping at the bit to talk to you two."

If the mountain local was eager to talk to state law enforcement, she likely feared her husband was in real danger, not just taking a break from the routine of his life on the farm.

"Lead the way," Wyatt told Hyland.

The sheriff motioned for Ashley to go first. She strode up the pea gravel path and mounted the front porch. A dark-haired deputy met her at the door, pulling it open. After slipping protective covers over the soles of her hiking boots, she crossed the threshold into the foyer.

Glass shards littered the hardwood floor. The remnants of what had once been a vase, filled with silk flowers in shades ranging from light pink to cranberry, rested beside a small, overturned, accent table to the left of the staircase.

The deputy pointed to the doorway at the end of the foyer. "Mrs. Osborne's in the living room," he said, his voice hushed.

"Thank you."

Ashley felt Wyatt's presence behind her. She glanced at him over her shoulder and then veered around the glass, hugging the foyer wall, as she made her way toward the living room. As she entered, a slender woman with shoulder-length brown hair, who appeared to be in her early thirties, rose up from the plaid sofa.

"I'm TBI Special Agent Ashley Hope," she said.

"Marilyn Osborne."

Instead of shaking Ashley's offered hand, the woman pressed a photograph onto her palm. "We had this picture took just a couple months ago," Marilyn said. "That's Jerry."

Ashley studied the photo. It appeared to have been shot at some type of harvest festival. An attractive man with sandy hair stood next to Marilyn, a wide smile striping his face.

Wyatt walked to the woman's side. "I'm Special Agent Wyatt Clark."

Marilyn nodded. The woman's face appeared ashen, her eyes red and puffy. "Y'all have a seat," she said.

Ashley sank onto the sofa next to Marilyn. Wyatt chose the adjacent armchair.

"When did you first discover that your husband was missing?" Ashley asked.

"It was early," Marilyn began, her voice strained. "I spent last night at my mama's house. I got home around four this morning to help Jerry with the chores. We milk twice a day. At five in the morning and five in the evening. Anyway, when I come home, I seen the back door was standing open. I knew something was wrong."

"Did you see anyone—or any strange vehicles—near the house?"

"No. Just Jerry's pickup in the driveway."

Marilyn cleared her throat. She continued, "When I got inside the kitchen, the lights wouldn't come on. I had to get my flashlight out of the car. Then I seen one of the chairs was knocked over. The kitchen table was moved too. Like somebody bumped into it. I hollered for Jerry, but he didn't answer me. I found out the breaker box was switched off. After I got the lights on, I searched the whole house and the barn." Her voice faltered. "Jerry was gone," she squeaked, tears welling in her eyes.

Ashley's heart went out to the woman.

"Did you notice any items or money missing from the house?"

It was possible that Jerry had interrupted a robbery. If the Osbornes sold milk or butter to their neighbors, they might keep cash on hand.

"Naw, there wasn't nothing stolen."

Her husband must have been targeted for some reason. Likely by someone who was aware that Marilyn had gone away for a visit.

"Can you think of anyone who might have a grudge against Jerry?" she asked.

Marilyn stared at the wad of tissues clasped in her hands as though she was thinking the matter through. "No. I don't reckon he has any enemies."

"Has anything odd happened during the last few days? Did Jerry mention that he thought he was being followed, or that he'd noticed something unusual?"

Marilyn shook her head. "Everything was good."

Ashley decided to switch gears. "Do you know a man named Cole Gowen?"

The woman answered without hesitation. "I don't. But Jerry might. Is that man a criminal?"

"No, he's not," Ashley answered, not wanting to divulge any further information. "What about a man named Lester Warwick?"

Ashley felt Wyatt's gaze shift from Marilyn to her. She hadn't yet told him that she couldn't shake the feeling that something wasn't right about Warwick.

Marilyn's eyes widened. "Lester worked for us a while back. Do you think he done it?"

Maybe the abductions were tied in with the chop shop ring after all. Sheriff Hyland must know that Warwick had once worked for the Osbornes. Maybe that's the reason he'd linked Jerry's disappearance with Cole's.

"When was the last time that you saw Lester Warwick?"

Marilyn clenched her bottom lip between her teeth. "About two years ago. Right after we bought our cow, Mable. That's when Lester got the job at the poultry plant."

The timeframe didn't fit the way Ashley had expected. Maybe Jerry had seen Warwick recently.

"How was the relationship between Lester and Jerry? Did they socialize together or have any friends in common?"

"Naw, nothing like that. They ain't friends, but they don't have no ill will between them either."

Ashley wanted to find out whether the Osbornes knew Deputy Kelton, but she feared her words would be overheard. She leaned toward Marilyn. "Does Jerry have any friends who work at the sheriff's department?" she asked in a hushed voice.

A shocked expression crossed Marilyn's face. "I don't mean no disrespect, so don't take this wrong. But we don't hang out with cops."

The woman's disdain for the police came as no surprise. But Ashley suspected that Deputy Kelton might be working on the wrong side of the law. And it was possible that Jerry had acquaintances and associates that Marilyn didn't know about.

Was there a reason that Jerry might need to leave town? Had he run for his life? Did he possess the same information as Warwick?

The next question Ashley needed to ask would be the most difficult. "Can you think of any reason that Jerry might want to stage his own disappearance?"

Marilyn pressed her lips into a thin line. "And that's the reason we don't like cops. Y'all always think the worst of everybody." She bolted up from the sofa. "Y'all need to be out looking for Jerry. Not asking me a bunch of stupid questions."

"I didn't mean to offend you, Mrs. Osborne," Ashley stated, rising from her seat. "But we have to explore all of the possibilities in order to find your husband."

Although the woman seemed distraught—possessed an air of innocence—Marilyn obviously realized that she was a suspect in Jerry's disappearance as well. At least for the time being.

A look of fury replaced the tears in Marilyn's eyes. "I'm gonna go upstairs now," she said. "Y'all know the way out."

Ashley watched as the woman stomped toward the foyer. Was her anger really due to a belief that her husband would never fake his own death? Or was Marilyn hiding something? Had she realized that there was a possibility that Jerry had run out on her?

Right after Marilyn marched out of the living room, Sheriff Hyland appeared at the doorway.

"Something go wrong?" he asked.

Wyatt and Ashley exchanged glances.

"Just the usual," Wyatt said. "Mrs. Osborne didn't like one of our questions."

Hyland nodded, an expression of understanding crossing his face. "Did you get in touch with forensics?"

"Our team's driving over from Briarwood," Wyatt stated. "They'll be here in a few hours."

When the TBI forensic techs arrived, they would dust for prints and scour the place for evidence. But Ashley wanted to conduct a search of her own.

"Have you been all the way through the house?" she asked the sheriff.

"Yeah. The upstairs seems clean. And I didn't find anything in the barn."

From where she stood, Ashley had a narrow view into the kitchen. She wondered whether the intruder had busted open the back door or if he'd picked the lock. Maybe Jerry had let the man inside.

Was Jerry's abductor someone he knew?

Ashley headed through the doorway that led into the kitchen. Just as Marilyn had said, the round, wooden table had been shoved up next to a bank of cabinets, and one of the chairs had been overturned. But she noticed something else the woman hadn't mentioned. A knife was missing from the block on the counter. Was the knife in the dishwasher? Or had it been used to threaten Jerry?

She moved to the back door and checked the frame and the lock. There were no obvious signs of a forced entry. Once Marilyn calmed down a bit, Ashley would ask whether an extra key was hidden somewhere on the property. Since Warwick had worked on the farm, he might know how to get inside the house. And he could have divulged the information to a member of the chop shop gang.

Wyatt wandered past Ashley toward an adjacent hallway. She followed. Just as she crossed the threshold, Wyatt stopped short in front of her. Their bodies almost collided.

"At least we've got the answer to one question," he stated, motioning toward the floor to his left.

The blade of a butcher knife glinted beneath the overhead light. The black handle matched the set in the wooden block. Wyatt snapped several photos with his cell phone. Then he pulled on a pair of latex gloves and picked up the knife with his fingertips.

"I don't see any blood," he said.

Since the weapon had been left on the floor in plain sight, it was doubtful that it had been wiped down. Maybe Jerry had grabbed the knife for protection, and the intruder had knocked it out of his hand. Rather than bagging the weapon, Wyatt placed it back on the floor for the forensic techs to examine.

Ashley trailed Wyatt into the utility room. The breaker box hung on the wall next to the hot water heater. If the abductor had switched off the power, how did he see to attack Jerry? Did he have night vision goggles? They'd become quite popular with hunters in the mountains.

Across from the utility room was a small dining room. Ashley circled around the long oak table and emerged back into the foyer. She'd completed the tour of the downstairs. From what she'd seen, she guessed Jerry had been subdued after a fight near the staircase. He'd probably been knocked unconscious.

She edged around the shards of glass from the destroyed vase. Kneeling down, she took one last look at the flowers strewn across the floor. Ashley's breath caught in her throat as she realized what the silk blooms had masked. The tiny pink and yellow dots on the hardwood hadn't come from the floral arrangement. They were pieces of Mylar confetti.

Anti-felon identification tags fired from a police Taser.

CHAPTER TWENTY

Kneeling in the foyer of the Osbornes' farmhouse, Ashley fished a pair of latex gloves from one of the pockets in her cargo jacket and snapped them on. Shards from a broken crystal vase glimmered around her on the hardwood floor next to an overturned wooden accent table. Hidden among the silk flowers that had once filled the vase, she found a smattering of tiny pink and yellow confetti.

The Mylar anti-felon ID tags had been shot from a police Taser.

Did Deputy Kelton abduct Jerry Osborne?

The tags contained the serial number of the cartridge that had fired them. Would the unique number trace back to the Fergus County Sheriff's Department?

One thing bothered Ashley. Kelton knew the tags bore a tracking ID. Would he have left them behind? Although difficult to pick up by hand, the twenty to thirty tags the cartridges emitted could be collected with a vacuum cleaner. Maybe Kelton had run out of time.

Had the abductor been in the house, planning to conduct a cleanup, when Marilyn returned?

Ashley placed her index finger on one of the pink tags. The Mylar dot stuck to her glove.

Sensing movement behind her, she turned and looked up. Wyatt had walked into the foyer.

"You're not going to believe what I just found," she stated, holding up her hand.

Wyatt squinted at her finger. "Is that—"

"Yes, and it could belong to one of the deputies involved in the chop shop ring. I think we need to have a talk with Sheriff Hyland."

She peered out through the glass panes in the front door. The sheriff stood in the yard, smoking a cigarette, and talking with the deputy that had met them when they'd first arrived at the farmhouse.

Pulling the door open, Wyatt called out. "Sheriff? Could you come inside for a minute?"

Hyland stubbed out his cigarette with the toe of his boot and headed up the porch steps. She knew his office would have the serial numbers on file for all of the Taser cartridges they'd purchased.

"You find something?" he asked.

Ashley glanced toward the top of the stairs. "Maybe we should move into the living room where we can have a little more privacy."

She hoped the deputy would remain outside.

The sheriff nodded and followed Ashley and Wyatt into the next room.

She held out her hand so that Hyland had a clear view of the AFID tag. "Does this look familiar?" she asked him.

"Well, I know what it is, if that's what you're asking. Where'd it come from?"

She knew he was referring to the location where she'd found the tag. But the most important question was: who had fired the Taser?

"We were hoping that you could give us that information. And that you would tell us everything you know about Deputy Kelton."

"Kelton?" A puzzled look crossed Hyland's face.

"He was the person who found Cole's car," Ashley reminded the sheriff. "He could have moved the seat up toward the steering wheel to throw us off track. And we know that one or more of your deputies are accomplices in the car theft ring."

"Now wait," Hyland said, his voice firm. "You're barking up the wrong tree. First of all, my department doesn't have Tasers. Our budget's too tight. And second, Kelton's not involved—I'd stake my job on that. I've known him his all his life. Him and his folks. They're good people."

Although the sheriff held Kelton in high regard, Ashley knew from experience that some people—even those we believed to be the closest to us—were often not as trustworthy as they appeared.

She exchanged a glance with Wyatt.

"Then which of your deputies do you suspect of being mixed up with the chop shop?"

Hyland sighed. "I wish I knew. Warwick hasn't given up any names. His lawyer's trying to work out some kind of deal with the DA. We won't get any info until that's done."

It disappointed Ashley to learn that the sheriff had no idea which of the members of his force had switched to the dark side, and to find out that his department didn't own Tasers. But the TBI would still be able

96

to trace the serial number of the cartridge. The process would just take a little longer.

Placing the ID tag inside an evidence bag, she shoved it into her pocket.

Sheriff Hyland had overlooked the Mylar confetti in the foyer. She wondered whether he'd missed other important clues on the property. Since Marilyn was still upstairs, Ashley decided she'd check out the Osbornes' barn.

Leaving Wyatt and Hyland conversing in the living room, she padded into the kitchen and slipped out the back door. Her breath clouded in the frosty morning air as she crossed the back yard. It was possible Jerry had continued his business relationship with Warwick long after the man had left his employ. The Osbornes could have used the dairy farm to launder proceeds from the chop shop.

The odor of manure drifted toward her as Ashley pulled open the steel gate that led into the pasture. Careful to look where she stepped, she picked her way up the slope to the gray metal barn. One of the fawn-colored Jersey cows ambled to her side.

"Hi, girl," Ashley said, patting the cow's neck.

She slid open the barn door. A large stainless steel milk collection tank rested in the room to her right. The room on the left contained feed bins and shelves stocked with iodine, which she knew was used to prep the cows' teats before milking, as well as antiseptics and worming medications. There was no desk or filing cabinet in sight. Nothing that would hold financial documents.

Exiting the supply room, she wandered down the concrete aisle that striped the center of the barn. Straw covered the floor of the milking areas that flanked the aisle. Ashley didn't see anything out of the ordinary.

Sighing, she headed back toward the barn's entrance. She wanted to poke around on the second floor of the Osbornes' home, but since Marilyn had already stated that she wanted Ashley and Wyatt to leave the premises, it was doubtful the woman would allow it. Maybe the forensic techs would fare better with Marilyn. Hopefully, they'd find something that would help further the investigation.

Ashley eased the barn door open. Her attention shifted toward the farmhouse, and she stopped in her tracks. She almost couldn't believe what she was witnessing. Ducking down behind the friendly cow so she wouldn't be spotted, she watched the house in astonishment.

A window on the second floor gaped open. Marilyn, bundled in a red coat, climbed out through the window onto the roof of the back porch. Seeming as though she was well-practiced in using the escape route, the woman inched toward a maple growing next to the house. Grabbing hold of one of the branches, she swung into the tree and then shimmied to the ground.

Obviously unaware that she had an audience, Marilyn ran toward the forest bordering the west side of the farm.

Ashley followed.

CHAPTER TWENTY ONE

Curiosity piqued Ashley's mind as she raced across the cow pasture at the Osbornes' farm, keeping Marilyn in her sights. Why had the woman sneaked out of the second-floor window of her own home? Where was Marilyn going? And why did she want her absence kept secret?

Ashley just hoped the woman wouldn't look back over her shoulder and realize she was being pursued. If that happened, relevant facts surrounding the case might never come out.

Had Ashley hit on the truth when she'd suggested Jerry had staged his own disappearance? Was Marilyn on her way to meet her husband? The man could be lying low in a hunting cabin nestled in the woods. Only one thing didn't fit. If Jerry's abduction had been faked, he wouldn't have needed to fire a Taser.

After seeing the overturned table in the Osbornes' foyer, Ashley felt certain that someone had been subdued by the Taser's barbs. Maybe Jerry had been the one who'd fired the weapon. Like Warwick, he could have information that would blow apart the chop shop ring, securing a long prison sentence for the members. Maybe the ringleader had sent a henchman to shut Jerry up permanently. But instead, Jerry had won the fight. And now, fearing for his life, he'd gone into hiding.

Darting through the pasture's gate, Ashley swerved toward the western edge of the property. Up ahead, Marilyn disappeared into the dense hardwood forest. Ashley feared that the woman might get away. Increasing her speed, she flew across the Osbornes' back yard. As she neared the tree line, she spotted a path snaking through the underbrush. Marilyn and Jerry had obviously hiked the trail on a regular basis. Where did it lead?

Trying to catch up, Ashley pushed her muscles harder. As she rounded an oak tree, a wave of frustration struck her. She stopped cold. The path forked at her feet. Had Marilyn continued straight ahead? Or had the woman veered to the left? Each branch of the trail appeared equally well-traveled.

Ashley had to make a decision. Fast. Every second she faltered added distance between herself and Marilyn. But what if Ashley made the wrong choice? If the path led her to a dead end, by the time she backtracked, Marilyn and Jerry could be gone. They might flee the state, taking their knowledge of what had happened to Cole with them.

Letting her instincts act as her guide, Ashley plowed straight ahead.

As the soles of her hiking boots pounded against the uneven ground, Ashley's left shoulder throbbed. Focusing on the forest ahead, she struggled to block out the pain. The medication the emergency room doctor had given her lay tucked in one of the pockets of her cargo jacket, but she fought the urge to swallow the pills. Her thoughts needed to remain sharp and clear. Allowing her mind to become sluggish wasn't an option.

The path corkscrewed between the trunks of a stand of hickories. Ashley caught sight of a patch of cream through the bare branches. Another farmhouse rested up ahead. She slowed her pace as she neared the clearing.

Ducking behind the wide trunk of a sycamore, she scanned the home's rear yard. A chicken coop stood halfway between the forest and the cream-sided house. A spot of color drew Ashley's attention: Marilyn's red coat. The woman had just trotted up the wooden steps of the farmhouse's back porch.

A series of loud thumps echoed through the trees as Marilyn banged on the home's door.

Wanting to get a closer view, Ashley bolted from the woods and zoomed toward the safety of the chicken coop. The hens pecked at the ground inside their sprawling wire cage, ignoring her arrival. She was glad the chickens had stayed quiet. As Ashley peeked around the wooden building's corner, angry voices drifted toward her.

A dark-haired man, seeming to be in his late thirties, had joined Marilyn on the porch. The two appeared to be about the same height which meant the man was shorter than five-nine.

A realization struck Ashley. It was possible that a woman had driven Cole's car to Rattler Ridge. She didn't know why she hadn't thought of that prospect before now. Instead of one man being responsible for the disappearance, it could be a team. A husband and wife. Or a man and his lover.

Was Marilyn romantically involved with the man on the porch?

Ashley strained her ears, trying to make sense of the couple's heated conversation.

"… delivery to Alabama!" Marilyn shouted.

Although she'd been unable to decipher the first half of the woman's sentence, Ashley wondered whether Marilyn was upset about stolen car parts shipped out of state. Warwick had told his attorney that the chop shop ring included members in Alabama and Georgia.

The next words out of the woman's mouth rang clear. "Prove you ain't killed Jerry!" Marilyn cried out.

The woman had obviously lied when she'd stated that her husband had no known enemies. Maybe Jerry and the man on the porch were partners in crime. It was possible that they'd only recently butted heads over an Alabama parts delivery. Speculation aside, Marilyn had reason to believe that the man had harmed her husband.

Ashley took full cover behind the chicken coop. She needed to text Wyatt and let him know where she'd gone and what she had discovered. Her hand flew to the pocket where she kept her phone. It was empty. She'd left her cell charging in the SUV. She'd be forced to confront the arguing pair alone.

The slamming of the farmhouse's rear door split the air.

Peering back around the edge of the coop, Ashley saw a third person now on the porch. A blonde, thirty-something, woman. Was she the man's wife?

"Go home!" the blonde woman screamed at Marilyn.

The man stepped between the two women. Ashley couldn't hear what they were saying, but all three parties still seemed enraged. It was time to make her presence known. Before the situation escalated. As she took a deep breath, steeling herself for the confrontation, she glanced back toward the forest.

Wyatt stood at the tree line, partially hidden by the same sycamore Ashley had sheltered behind. He must have seen her running across the Osbornes' back yard and decided to follow. She was thankful that he'd chosen the right direction when he'd encountered the fork in the trail.

Drawing her Glock, Ashley motioned for Wyatt to move in.

Her partner probably hadn't overheard Marilyn accuse the dark-haired man of killing Jerry. Although they had no grounds to arrest the trio—not yet—she and Wyatt could haul the group back to the sheriff's department and hold them for twenty-four hours based on the suspicion of murder.

Jerry might still be alive somewhere, but Ashley knew deep in her gut that the neighbors were involved in an illegal enterprise. Most likely, they were guilty of stealing cars and possibly laundering money for the chop shop through the dairy farm. Ashley wanted to convince them to squeal on each other. And to compel them to confess what they knew about Cole.

As Wyatt sprang from the forest, she leapt out from behind the chicken coop and rushed the porch.

"TBI!" Ashley shouted. "Everyone freeze—hands above your heads!"

The trio appeared stunned. Both of the women obeyed her command, flinging their hands into the air. But the dark-haired man just stared at her. Taking a step backward, he lunged through the rear door of the house, slamming it behind him.

Shit!

The man had obviously known that since he'd posed no immediate threat, Ashley wouldn't fire at him.

Wyatt ran past Ashley, his Glock drawn. "I'll cover the front door," he called out.

A defiant look flashed in the blonde woman's eyes. Was she planning to flee as well?

"Don't even think about it," Ashley barked, leveling her Glock at the woman's chest. "Both of you, come down off of the porch right now, single file. And move slowly."

With Marilyn taking the lead, the women trudged down the porch steps.

"Get down on your knees."

Ashley slapped handcuffs on the blonde woman first and then repeated the process with Marilyn. The man worried her. He'd likely grabbed a weapon and could have called in armed reinforcements to surround the farmhouse.

"You ain't got no right coming onto our property!" the blonde woman screamed. "You can't prove nothing."

A panicked expression crossed Marilyn's face. "Shut up, Vera," she said.

"Don't you tell me to shut up. I can say whatever I damn well please."

Ashley had no intention of interrupting the argument. She wanted Vera to talk. Maybe the woman would spill something that would incriminate the three neighbors. But Vera seemed to realize this. She fell silent.

Pulling the women up onto their feet, Ashley marched them back toward the porch. She didn't have time to play babysitter. She cuffed Marilyn to the porch railing. Wanting to keep the two women separated so they wouldn't concoct a story, she walked Vera to the chicken coop and cuffed her to a metal pole on the rear side. If the women wanted to speak with each other, they'd be forced to yell.

Gunfire erupted from the west side of the farmhouse. The dark-haired man must have slipped out a window or a side door. He was shooting at Wyatt.

As Ashley sped along the rear of the house, she saw the man dart behind an oak tree. She hadn't spotted Wyatt yet. Using a hickory as cover, she watched. Her pulse racing, she waited for the man to make his next move. Her partner was likely doing the same.

Her aching shoulder reminded her how deadly the situation had become.

Did Wyatt call the sheriff for backup?

Taking his chances, the dark-haired man popped out from behind the oak. He fired another round from his pistol as he ran toward the safe harbor of a sycamore. Wyatt's Glock remained silent. Had her partner been unable to get a clear shot? Or had he been hit?

Pushing the concerning thoughts aside, Ashley edged out from the hickory and dashed toward a conjoined pair of beeches. She studied the trees to her right. She finally caught sight of Wyatt hiding behind an oak. He seemed to be okay.

"Give it up!" Wyatt shouted at the man. "It's not worth it. In about two minutes, this whole place will be surrounded. You won't get away."

Ashley hoped Wyatt's words were true. That the sheriff and his deputies were in route to the farm.

But the dark-haired man wasn't ready to surrender. He had other plans. He swung out from the sycamore. The man fired three shots from his pistol in rapid succession.

This time, Wyatt returned fire.

Ashley gasped, her heart leaping to her throat.

The dark-haired man crashed to the ground next to the sycamore

Was he dead? Or just injured? Aiming her Glock, Ashley moved out from behind the twin beech trees. She glanced at Wyatt. He was heading toward the dark-haired man as well.

As they approached, it became apparent that the man was still conscious.

He lifted his pistol.

"Drop it!" Wyatt yelled, his Glock trained on the man's center mass.

The man's hand trembled. Ashley held her breath. A full four seconds ticked by and then the man's fingers parted. The pistol fell to the ground.

Inching closer to the man, Ashley's gaze settled on the right side of his chest. Blood stained his light blue shirt. Anxiety fluttered in her stomach as she realized the wound was serious. Would the man die before an ambulance arrived?

Wyatt picked up the pistol and knelt beside the man, checking his vitals.

A worried look crossed her partner's face. Ashley guessed that the man's pulse had proved weak.

Police sirens wailed from the direction of the road. The sheriff would be here in a matter of moments.

Pulling out his cell phone, Wyatt called for medical help.

"Stay with me," he told the dark-haired man.

If the man succumbed to his injury, it was possible that the truth about what had happened to Cole and Jerry would die with him.

Ashley just hoped that Marilyn and Vera would agree to cooperate. Marilyn obviously didn't know where her husband was located, but Vera might. Were Jerry and Cole being held alive somewhere?

Or had their bodies been buried here on the farm?

CHAPTER TWENTY TWO

Brett Holbrook wheeled his Lexus into the crowded parking lot of the Walmart Supercenter in Briarwood. He spotted Zeke's black pickup parked in the designated location in the far corner, a good distance away from the security cameras, next to a Bradford pear tree. But Brett didn't stop. Not yet. Although fairly certain none of his family or friends shopped at the big-box store, he wanted to ensure that no one he knew would witness the meeting. He scanned the sea of cars as he circled the lot.

Satisfied that he wouldn't later be connected to the Laurel County native, Brett veered his sedan into the parking spot next to the pickup.

Zeke hopped out of his truck and slid into the passenger seat of the Lexus.

"I done just like you said," the muscular, ginger-bearded man stated.

He handed over his phone.

Brett smiled as he swiped through the photos on the screen. Pictures taken inside of Ashley's motel room in Fergus County. He zoomed in on a shot of the dead frogs filling the lower half of the bed. He would have been willing to pay a million dollars to see his ex-fiancé's reaction when her feet touched the corpses.

Although Brett would have loved to hear Ashley scream, setting up cameras and microphones in her apartment had proven child's play compared to installing surveillance in a motel room. At the motel, there were housekeepers, travelers, and maintenance people to deal with. Brett was just glad that Zeke had been able to deliver the surprise without being detected.

Had Ashley realized the significance of his gift?

Did she remember?

He hoped that the message would evade her mind for a while. But it stood as no real consequence to Brett whether Ashley connected the frogs with their past together or not. There was no evidence linking him to the crime. He'd used cash and a front man to purchase the preserved animals from an underpaid Nashville science teacher. Likely passed off as a teenage prank, the teacher's theft of the thirty-five frogs hadn't even made the news.

After giving the man back his phone, Brett popped open the sedan's center console. He pulled out a Kraft envelope.

"As promised, two-thousand dollars, all in twenties," he said.

Brett would have paid more than double the amount. In fact, enacting revenge on Ashley would be worth his entire fortune. He was alone now. With Cherie gone, he had no one else to spend the money on. No lover to lavish with gifts or to take on luxurious vacations. Because of Ashley, his dreams for the future had been shattered.

He placed the envelope on Zeke's outstretched palm.

"Mighty obliged." Flecks of smokeless tobacco marred the man's toothy grin. "Just let me know when you're ready for the next job."

The plan required finesse. Brett would terrorize Ashley, taunting and toying with her like a cat playing with a helpless mouse. Each step needed to be timed perfectly. All leading up to an explosive climax.

"I'll be in touch," he told Zeke.

The man nodded. "Happy to do the work." He pushed open the passenger door of the Lexus. "One thing I been wondering. What did Ashley Hope do to you?"

Rage flowed through Brett's veins as he thought about his answer.

"A woman I loved more than my own life was murdered," he finally stated. "It's Ashley's fault she's gone."

But Brett planned to even the score.

He refused to quit until Ashley was dead.

CHAPTER TWENTY THREE

Ashley peered through the one-way mirror into the interview room at the Fergus County Sheriff's Department. The blonde woman, who had been identified as Vera Mansfield, sat handcuffed to the metal table. Her husband, Tim, had been transported to the nearest trauma center, located in Peck County, and was now undergoing surgery to repair the damage from Wyatt's bullet.

According to Sheriff Hyland, the members of the Mansfield and Osborne families were well thought of in the county. And Tim, Vera, Jerry, and Marilyn all lacked a criminal record. But it was clear that they were involved in something illegal. Otherwise, Marilyn wouldn't have voiced the accusation regarding Jerry's murder, and Tim wouldn't have fled the scene, firing his pistol.

What were the neighbors hiding? And how had they managed to fly beneath the radar?

The minute Ashley and Wyatt had hauled Marilyn into the station, she'd invoked her right to an attorney. So, they wouldn't be allowed to question the woman yet. Thankfully, Marilyn and Vera had been kept apart, riding to the sheriff's department in different vehicles. If Vera found out Marilyn had lawyered up, she'd likely do the same.

Wyatt poked his head through the doorway of the viewing room.

"You ready?" he asked.

Ashley couldn't wait to grill Vera. "I'm right behind you."

She followed Wyatt into the interview room and eased down onto the metal chair opposite the suspect. Per their discussion in the SUV on the way to the department, Ashley would take the lead interrogating Vera. Wyatt believed the woman would be reluctant to answer questions posed by the agent who had shot her husband, and Ashley had agreed. He planned to remain a silent sentinel of support.

"Would you like something to drink?" she asked Vera. "We can get you a soda, bottled water, or some coffee."

One thing Ashley had learned was that in order for an interview to be successful, it was necessary to show empathy. To make the suspect feel as though you cared about their wellbeing, and that you were there to offer help. Otherwise, they'd likely shut down and refuse to talk.

Vera kept her gaze fixed on the tabletop. "I just want my husband to pull through," she stated, her voice shaky.

Although the woman was likely a criminal, Ashley hated seeing her suffer. She knew firsthand how it felt to have a loved one in the hands of a surgeon, not knowing whether they would live or die. She'd struggled through the same ordeal twice. First with her father when he'd had his heart surgery and then with her younger brother when he'd been attacked by Ethan Barrett.

"I wish things had gone differently at your farmhouse this morning," Ashley said. "What made Tim think that he needed to run away?"

Vera sat silent for a moment. Then she tore her attention from the table and glared at Wyatt. "I ain't saying nothing with him in here."

The declaration didn't seem to faze Wyatt. With a quick nod, he rose from his chair and headed back out the door. Ashley knew that he'd retreat to the viewing room. Sitting on the other side of the one-way mirror, he'd be able to watch and listen to the entire interrogation broadcast through a pair of speakers.

After giving Wyatt a moment to get settled in the next room, Ashley leaned toward Vera.

"I know that talking to me has to be hard for you right now," she began. "But the sooner we can get a few things cleared up, the sooner you'll be able to visit your husband."

"You think I'm stupid? Y'all ain't gonna let me see Tim."

Vera didn't yet realize that they lacked the proper evidence to arrest her. As it stood, they could only hold her for a maximum of twenty-four hours. Maybe it was the handcuffs that led her to believe that she was in jail to stay. Was that the sheriff's motive for leaving them on her?

"If you'll cooperate with me—answer a few questions—then I'll arrange a visit."

Even if they did end up arresting Vera, a deal could be worked out. It would be beyond cruel to deny the woman a chance to see her dying husband.

"I don't know nothing to tell you."

"Well, you can start by explaining what you, Tim, and Marilyn were arguing about on your back porch."

"Just neighbor stuff. Nothing you'd be interested in."

"Why don't you let me decide that?"

Vera stared off into space as though she was thinking. Was she weaving together a lie?

"It's the cows. Jerry don't keep his fences mended. They got out the other day and come into our yard."

The woman would have to do better than that. Ashley wasn't stupid either.

"So, you expect me to believe that Marilyn would accuse Tim of murder just because a few dairy cows broke loose?"

Seeming to only now realize how ludicrous her explanation had sounded, Vera shrugged.

"Tell me about the delivery to Alabama," Ashley said.

Vera's eyes grew wide. "I don't know what you're talking about."

She obviously wasn't going to give anything up. Not yet. Ashley decided to shift gears. "How long have you known Cole Gowen?"

Ashley wasn't one hundred percent sure that Vera and Jerry were acquainted with Cole. But just in case they were, she wanted it to seem as though the relationship was common knowledge.

"Can't say that I really know him. He just hangs out at Treva's Tavern sometimes. Why you asking about him?"

"Because we have reason to believe that Cole was abducted on Friday afternoon, and now Jerry is missing as well. Did Tim have something to do with their disappearances? Is that why he ran this morning?"

Vera shook her head. "Tim didn't do nothing to Jerry," she stated her voice firm. "He done told Marilyn that."

The look in her eyes made it seem as though Vera was actually telling the truth for once.

"Did Tim get into an argument with Cole? Maybe over something related to the Alabama delivery?"

Vera bit her bottom lip.

If she was trying to come up with another lie, she'd better hope that it was more plausible that the last story.

After a slight hesitation, Vera asked, "Where'd Cole go missing from? Here, in Fergus County?"

"His car was found abandoned up on Rattler Ridge."

"I don't know nothing about no delivery. But it's true me and Tim was in Alabama Friday. So, you can't pin Cole missing on us. And we've got proof we was there. A cop pulled us over in Montgomery for speeding. Gave Tim a ticket."

The alibi would be easy to confirm. The drive from Montgomery to Fergus County spanned at least four hours. If Tim and Vera had been in Alabama in the afternoon, they couldn't have kidnapped Cole. But that didn't mean that they weren't involved in some way.

Ashley decided to switch to the hardline approach. She'd throw her theory at Vera and see if it struck a nerve. "We know that you, Tim, Jerry, and Marilyn have a side business that you're running. An illegal business. Did Cole find out?"

The color drained from Vera's face. But the woman didn't deny the accusation. "I want me a lawyer," she said.

They were the words every cop dreaded hearing. Vera's request for legal counsel brought the interview to a screeching halt. Ashley wouldn't be able to pry loose any further information.

Stifling a sigh, she stood up from her chair. "I'll let the sheriff know you need an attorney."

Ashley met Wyatt in the hallway as he exited the adjacent viewing room. "Brenda just called," he told her. "The judge approved the search warrant for both farms."

The TBI deputy director never wasted time, and she'd proved to be an expert when it came to dealing with rural county judges. Since they lacked physical evidence tying Cole and Jerry to the Mansfields' property, Ashley had worried the warrant for the second farm wouldn't go through.

"Then maybe it won't matter that Vera and Marilyn have attorneys," she stated. "We might be able to find out everything we need to know without their help."

Side-by-side, Ashley and Wyatt strode down the hallway toward Hyland's office. They needed to break the news that Vera had decided to hire a lawyer. And Ashley wanted to find out whether the sheriff had an update on Tim's condition. She hoped that the man would live. If Cole and Jerry were dead, and Tim shared responsibility for the crime, she wanted him to stand trial. Obtaining justice through the legal system would likely be the only way Cole's mother could gain full closure.

As they rounded the corner, a seed of optimism sprouted in Ashley's heart. She felt certain the key to uncovering the neighbors' illegal activity lay somewhere on the Mansfields' property. Were Cole

110

and Jerry being held prisoner in one of the outbuildings? She just prayed that the search wouldn't end with the discovery of a pair of freshly dug graves.

CHAPTER TWENTY FOUR

An uneasy feeling blanketed Ashley as the SUV sped along the highway that led to the Mansfields' farm. She shifted her position in the passenger's seat and tapped the icon for her phone's message app. Daniel hadn't yet responded to the text she'd sent that morning. And he hadn't called.

It was totally out of character for him to go that long without sending a reply. She hoped that his silence only meant that he was busy working his TBI case. But the fear that he might be lying unconscious in a hospital bed somewhere nagged at her. It was the nature of their job.

Each workday held life-threatening dangers.

Her aching shoulder acted as a testament to the fact. Sighing, she tapped out another message.

Hope you're okay.
I miss you.

At least Ashley knew that her father was safe. Worried that the stalker might return to Laurel County, she'd called to check on Spencer when she was still at the sheriff's department. So far, he hadn't received any more threats.

The more Ashley thought about the note slipped into her grocery cart, the more she believed that it was a ploy to get her out of her apartment. Knowing that she would rush right to her father's house, the stalker had a guarantee of four-and-a-half hours before she returned. Had he used the time to search through all of her belongings? What could he have been looking for?

Forcing herself to push the thoughts of her stalker from her mind, Ashley directed her attention out through the SUV's windshield. The rear brake lights on Sheriff Hyland's cruiser flared as they slowed to make the turn onto Homestead Road. Hyland had decided to participate in the search of the Mansfields' property.

The TBI forensics techs had already descended on the Osbornes' home. And an additional team was in route from Briarwood to scour the Mansfields' farm. Ashley hoped that she and Wyatt would find evidence that would lead them to Cole and Jerry before the techs arrived. She knew that they were running out of time.

The cream-colored farmhouse popped into view. The SUV rocked as the tires left the asphalt road and crawled onto the Mansfields' pothole-laden gravel driveway. When the sheriff had informed Vera of the search warrant, the woman had volunteered the location of a spare house key hidden inside the chicken coop. Ashley guessed that Vera feared they would break down her front door. And they would have.

Slowing to a halt behind Hyland's cruiser, Wyatt threw the SUV's transmission into park. Ashley hopped out of the passenger seat. Joining the sheriff, they walked past the two pickup trucks belonging to Vera and Tim. She wondered whether the techs would find blood inside one of the vehicles.

Hyland said, "I'll get the key. Vera told me it opens the back door."

Ashley mounted the steps of the rear porch with Wyatt at her heels. Out of sheer curiosity, she tested the doorknob. To her surprise, it turned.

Glancing back over her shoulder, Ashley called out to Hyland, "Sheriff, the door is already unlocked."

Tim must have left it open when he'd dashed inside to get his pistol.

Hyland nodded. "I'm gonna check the barn," he called back.

After donning a pair of shoe covers, Ashley pushed the door open and crossed the threshold into a narrow utility room. When the TBI team arrived, they'd go through everything with a fine-toothed comb. But for now, Ashley and Wyatt were looking for the obvious clues. She lifted the lid of the washing machine, checking for blood-stained clothing. It was empty, as was the dryer. On the surface, she didn't see anything that seemed out of place.

Continuing on, she entered the kitchen. The scent of bacon grease from the Mansfields' breakfast still lingered in the air. A stack of dishes crowded one side of the stainless-steel sink, and a dirty skillet rested on top of the stove. Wyatt followed as Ashley moved through the living room and then into the foyer.

The treads creaked as they trudged up the staircase leading to the second floor. Four doors opened into the hallway at the top, each standing slightly ajar.

"I'll take the rooms on the right," Ashley told Wyatt.

The hinges moaned as she pushed the first door the rest of the way open. An old desk, which appeared to have been handcrafted from cedar, stood next to the window. An open laptop computer rested in the center of the desk. The financial records for the Mansfields' illegal business were most likely located on the computer's hard drive.

The search warrant the TBI had secured included all of the electronic devices on the property. Ashley eased down into the wooden straight-backed chair and studied the laptop's screen. She realized right away that the operating system was an older version of Windows. All of the normal icons—browser shortcuts, trash bin, etc.—dotted the desktop. The Mansfields used Microsoft Outlook for their email. Ashley snapped on a pair of latex gloves and clicked the Outlook shortcut. A password prompt popped up. Although she couldn't snoop through the emails now, a TBI computer tech would be able to crack the code.

Next, she opened the Documents folder. The list seemed to include mostly recipes and saves from computer games. Scrolling down, she browsed through the file names. Nothing caught her interest. She scanned the pictures folder as well, but only found holiday and vacation photos.

Ashley didn't see a shortcut for any financial software on the desktop. But she did notice a file folder labeled "*Boswell.*" The name didn't ring any bells. For most people, the files earning desktop status were the ones most often used. So, whoever—or whatever—Boswell happened to be, they were obviously important to Tim and Vera.

Ashley clicked open the folder.

The files inside were named for the months of the current year. By the extension, she could tell that they were Microsoft Excel spreadsheets. Could that mean they held some type of financial data? December's spreadsheet had been modified the prior day. She clicked on the file.

Again, Ashley was hit with a password prompt.

Her gut screamed that the spreadsheets were connected with the illegal enterprise run by Tim, Vera, Jerry, and Marilyn. Maybe Boswell was the name of the person who actually hotwired and stole the

114

automobiles. It was possible that the vehicles were chopped in the large barn on the Mansfields' property, and the parts were delivered to Alabama and Georgia. The proceeds could be laundered through the dairy farm.

Hearing footsteps, Ashley tore her attention away from the computer. She looked up to see Wyatt walking through the door.

"The bedrooms are clean," he stated. "I didn't find anything."

Ashley must have spent more time examining the laptop than she'd realized.

"I may have found some files that are linked to the chop shop," she told Wyatt. "But I can't open them because they're all password protected."

She didn't know enough information about Tim and Vera to hazard a guess at the word or phrase that would unlock the files.

Wyatt peered over her shoulder at the computer screen.

"Boswell? Without a first name, it might be hard to pin down a criminal record. But we can try."

"And it's also possible that Boswell *is* the man's first name instead of his last."

"True."

With the upstairs proving empty of any apparent evidence relating to Cole or Jerry, it seemed that their sweep of the inside of the house was finished. Ashley pushed herself up from the chair.

"I wonder if Sheriff Hyland found anything interesting in the barn," she said.

"Let's go see."

They trotted back down the stairs and circled around to the rear door. As she walked out onto the porch, Ashley scanned the Mansfields' back yard and dormant corn field. The barn door gaped open, but she didn't see the sheriff. He must still be inside. She wondered whether he'd discovered a stolen car. Or maybe something worse.

Hurrying down the steps, Ashley and Wyatt crossed the yard. The chickens clucked inside their wire pen as Ashley skirted past the coop.

Stepping into the barn, she stopped to give her eyes a second to adjust to the lack of direct sunlight. But then she saw the beam of a flashlight cut through the gloom at the rear of the building. Following the glow, she found Sheriff Hyland crouched beside a dark pool on the dusty concrete floor.

Fear gripped her heart. Was it blood?

As she inched closer, Hyland looked up. He must have read the thoughts going through her mind.

"Fresh motor oil," he stated.

Relieved, Ashley wandered toward the heavy farm machinery to the left.

"Do you think it came from the tractor?" she asked him.

"Could have. Or it could be from a car or truck." He sighed. "I didn't find anything else. No sign of Cole."

But the motor oil might be evidence of the chop shop operation.

Wyatt said, "I noticed a padlock on the door of the other outbuilding."

"That's not a problem," Hyland replied.

The sheriff picked up a crowbar that had been lying hidden at his feet. Ashley and Wyatt followed him to the shed that loomed to the right of the barn. It only took Hyland a couple of minutes to pry the padlock's hasp from the aged wooden door.

A rush of musty air struck Ashley as the door squeaked open. Rusting farm equipment packed the building. There wasn't even any room left for them to squeeze inside. The thick layer of dust topping the ancient machinery proved the equipment had lain untouched for quite some time. Likely several years.

Disappointment settled over Ashley. It was another dead end.

She knew of only one place left to explore on the farm. The second path in the forest. As well-worn as the trail leading from the Osbornes' property to the Mansfields' back yard, the path had obviously been used by the families on a regular basis.

"We might need your crowbar again," Ashley told Hyland. "I think there could be another building of some sort located out in the woods."

The sheriff raised his eyebrows. "Lead the way."

The trio headed toward the tree line at the east side of the property. A crow cawed from the branches of an oak as they entered the forest. With Ashley in front, they plodded along the hard-packed dirt path that snaked through the underbrush.

Apprehension fluttered in her chest as they reached the path's fork. Although eager to find out what lay at the end of the trail, Ashley worried that Cole and Jerry might already be dead. They could be buried here in the woods.

Moving ahead, she scanned the edges of the underbrush, looking for freshly turned earth. The path veered to the right. As she rounded the curve, Ashley caught sight of a large building with brown metal siding nestled among the trees.

Her pulse quickened.

The building featured a rolling garage door. This could be the chop shop. A dirt drive wound from the garage bay through the forest, in the opposite direction from which they'd come. Ashley could tell the driveway didn't intersect with Homestead Road. It probably led to a much smaller side lane, or maybe an old logging road.

Sheriff Hyland strode past the garage bay to the building's main door. "I don't think we can pry this baby open," he said.

The steel door featured a metal guard that covered the portion of the frame where the deadbolt connected, protecting the lock. There was no way to force it open with the crowbar.

A single window stood to the right of the door, draped inside by a heavy black curtain. They'd have to break the glass panes. As Ashley moved toward the window, a humming sound split the air.

"Did you hear that?"

But it was obvious that both Wyatt and Hyland had.

They circled around the corner of the building. The noise had come from a central heat and air unit that had switched on. The presence of the CHA unit convinced Ashley that they'd found the nerve center of the Mansfields' and Osbornes' illegal operation.

"Break the window," she told Hyland. "I'll climb inside and unlock the door."

They returned to the front of the building. Ashley and Wyatt stood back as the sheriff swung the crowbar. Glass spit onto the ground as he smashed the windowpanes.

After Hyland knocked out all the remaining shards, Ashley slipped off her cargo jacket. Folding the jacket, she placed it across the windowsill. She crawled through the opening and dropped to the other side.

Stunned by the sight before her, Ashley felt her eyes grow wide

CHAPTER TWENTY FIVE

As her feet landed on the concrete floor, Ashley brushed the heavy, black window curtain aside and scanned the interior of the huge metal building in amazement. Nestled in the forest on the Mansfields' farm, she'd expected to find a warehouse full of automobile parts and the skeletons of cars and SUVs that were in the process of being dismantled.

But the true nature of the business the Mansfields and Osbornes ran was now crystal clear.

The shipment they'd delivered to Alabama didn't contain stolen vehicle parts.

Rows of potted marijuana plants filled the cavernous space. Grow lights hung from the ceiling, blazing so bright that the heat warmed Ashley's cheeks. Fans from a ventilation system whirred overhead, but still, a pungent odor—like a mixture of rotting lemons and sulfur—hung in the air. She'd never seen anything like it before.

Although several states had legalized marijuana for medicinal or recreational purposes, cultivating the plants still stood as a criminal offense in Tennessee. There had to be at least three to four hundred plants growing in the warehouse. Classified as a class B felony, Tim, Vera, Jerry, and Marilyn were each facing a sentence of up to thirty years in prison.

Ashley heard Wyatt's voice calling through the broken window. "Everything okay, Ashley?"

Transfixed by the elaborate cultivation system, complete with irrigation pipes, she'd almost forgotten about Wyatt and Hyland waiting outside.

"Yeah, it's fine," she shouted back.

The glass shards from the shattered windowpanes crunched beneath the soles of Ashley's hiking boots as she headed toward the steel door. A series of questions niggled at her mind. They knew that Warwick had gotten mixed up with the chop shop ring and that the man had once worked for the Osbornes. Had he been involved in the drug business as well? And how was the pot operation related to Cole? Were they even connected at all?

Maybe the sheriff had been wrong. Maybe Jerry's disappearance had nothing to do with Cole's abduction.

She flipped the deadbolt lock and pulled the door open.

The sheriff entered the warehouse first. "Well, I'll be damned," Hyland said, appearing almost as shocked as Ashley had been.

Wyatt pulled out his cell phone. "I'll call Brenda and tell her to send out a DID team."

The bureau's drug investigation division was a separate unit with their own specialized agents. The DID would take over the part of the investigation that included collecting evidence for the prosecution of the marijuana cultivation charges.

"I better get a couple of my deputies out here," Hyland stated. "For backup."

As the men placed their calls, Ashley wandered along the rows of plants, each rooted in their own pot of soil. The warehouse seemed to be divided into sections according to the various stages of the marijuana's development. Some of the plants were small and just starting to sprout, while others were full and taller than Ashley, with thick buds waiting to be harvested. As she drifted past the marijuana plants with flowers budding, her nose wrinkled. The buds smelled like they'd been sprayed by a skunk. She hoped the funky odor wouldn't cling to her clothing.

Moving toward the rear of the building, Ashley peered through the leaves of the thick stand of greenery. She spotted a hallway up ahead. Curious, she circled around the last few rows of plants. As she approached, she saw four doors dotting the dim hallway. Two flanked her left side, one stood to her right, and the last—a match to the steel front door—stood at the end of the hall.

Ashley eased open the first door. It was a bathroom with two stalls. She continued on. Just as she reached the room on the right, a man wearing a black hoodie burst through the doorway.

"TBI!" Ashley shouted, reaching for her Glock.

But as soon as the words escaped her lips—before her fingers could wrap around the grip of her weapon—something hard and heavy smashed into the side of her jaw.

The momentum of the blow hurled Ashley to the side. She crashed to the concrete floor.

"Ashley!" she heard Wyatt yell.

Then she heard the rear exterior door of the building slam shut.

Dazed, she tried to push herself up from the floor. A bout of wooziness struck her. Pressing her eyes closed in an attempt to stop the room from spinning, she sank back down. She felt Wyatt and Hyland rush into the hallway.

Wyatt knelt down beside her. "Are you all right?"

Now, she had a throbbing pain in her jaw to match the one in her shoulder.

Ashley forced her eyes open. "Don't worry about me," she said. "Go after the man. Don't let him get away."

Wyatt stood and looked at the sheriff. "Stay here with Ashley. The man might bring a buddy back with him."

The sheriff nodded, and Wyatt raced out the rear door.

Hyland crouched next to her. "You think you can stand up?"

Although she still felt shaky, the dizziness had passed. "Yeah."

The sheriff helped her to her feet. "Did you recognize the guy?" he asked her.

Ashley shook her head. "I wasn't able to get a look at his face." She motioned toward the room on the right. "He ran out of that door and surprised me."

Flexing her jaw, she wondered what the man had used to hit her. She knew it wasn't his fist. She inched toward the dark room where he'd been hiding. Was someone else still in there? Out of caution, she drew her Glock. Stepping on the threshold, she reached her left hand inside and flipped on the light switch.

Dim overhead bulbs sparked to life. Where the cultivating section of the warehouse was lit as bright as a July day, here, there was barely enough light to see.

The sheriff followed her inside. Marijuana buds hung from rows of stainless-steel racks. Fans circulated the pungent air. It all felt surreal to Ashley.

"It's the drying room," Hyland told her.

Ashley wasn't familiar with the steps involved in cultivating and processing the marijuana for sale, but the sheriff had likely busted his share of grow operations in the past. He knew what they were looking at.

Hearing a noise, Ashley flew back into the hallway. Wyatt pushed through the rear door. A discouraged expression masked his face.

120

"The man disappeared," Wyatt said. "I never even got a glimpse of him."

Ashley wasn't that surprised. Mountain locals were skilled at hiding in the forest. And the man was on his home turf.

She asked the sheriff, "Do you know anyone by the name of Boswell?"

Hyland appeared to be thinking. He shook his head. "Not that I can recall. Why?"

"I came across a folder with that name on the Mansfields' computer. I just wonder if Boswell is the man who hit me."

If Boswell was a local criminal, the sheriff should be familiar with him. Maybe the Mansfields were using code names. It was also possible that Boswell didn't live in Fergus County.

The ringing of Wyatt's cell phone echoed in the hallway.

He glanced at the screen. "It's Brenda," he told Ashley.

Wyatt snapped the phone to his ear. "Clark."

Ashley could hear the muffled tones of the TBI's deputy director on the other end of the line, but she couldn't decipher the woman's words.

She watched as a look of astonishment spread across Wyatt's face.

"Right. Got it," he said before ending the call.

Wyatt shoved his phone back into his pocket. He locked eyes with Ashley.

"You're not going to believe what Brenda just told me," he said.

CHAPTER TWENTY SIX

The man crouched behind the wide trunk of the sycamore at the edge of the forest and scanned the yard of the small, gray-sided, ranch-style house. A feeling of accomplishment swelled in his chest. The blue Ford sedan rested in the home's driveway.

After weeks of searching, he'd finally found Scarlett.

She had to be stupid to think she could hide from him forever.

But Scarlett wasn't the only one there. Her second cousin's white sedan also sat in the driveway. Despite what Toby had said, it would be difficult to subdue both women at the same time. Scarlett had to remain unblemished for the most part. And the man didn't need to take the cousin.

He needed to think of a way to get Scarlett alone.

The man fished a joint from his pocket and flicked the flame of his lighter over the end. He took a long drag, savoring the taste of the weed as it hit his lungs. As he exhaled, he called up a vision of Scarlett in his mind. Her long, black hair, her crystal blue eyes, her voluptuous curves. He imagined the shocked expression that would spring to her face when she saw him again. She thought that by lying low, hiding out in the neighboring county, she'd gotten away with it. But she was wrong. She'd be forced to pay the consequences. The smoke drifted from the man's mouth in a thin stream as he considered his next move.

An idea began to form in his mind.

During his search, he'd found out the cousin's husband, Ben, worked at the poultry processing plant. And he also knew that the company's employees weren't allowed to carry their cell phones into the building. The cousin wouldn't be able to call Ben to check out the story. And she'd probably be too upset to question it anyway.

Feeling confident that his ruse would work, the man stubbed out the joint on the sole of his boot. He pulled out the crumpled paper where he'd written down the cousin's information. He just hoped that she'd answer the ring of an unknown caller. He couldn't afford to leave a message with his callback number on her voicemail. And he couldn't risk having his voice recorded.

The man tapped *star 67* on his phone to block his number from appearing on the caller ID and then he dialed the cousin.

A seed of doubt sprouted in his chest as four rings echoed through his phone. It appeared as though the woman had decided to ignore the call.

The man was about to hang up when Daisy answered.

"Hello?" she said, her voice hesitant.

"This is Al Reeves," the man lied. According to the information he'd gleaned, Reeves was the name of the day-shift supervisor at the poultry plant. "I'm trying to reach Ben Nolan's wife."

"I'm his wife." A hint of fear infused Daisy's tone.

The man realized he'd already hooked the cousin.

"We've had us a little accident down here at the plant. Now, Ben's okay, he's just a little banged up. Has a bump on his head. He says he don't wanna go to the hospital. But we can't let him drive home. We need you to come get him."

"Yeah, okay," Daisy replied in a shaky voice. "I'll be right there."

A smile tugged at the man's lips as he ended the call.

He knew Scarlett would stay behind. She wouldn't risk being seen back in Fergus County. It would take Daisy at least forty minutes to drive to the poultry plant and probably another ten to figure out that she'd been duped.

By that time, it would be too late.

The man peeked back around the trunk of the sycamore. Daisy rushed through the rear door of the house and trotted down the steps of the wooden deck. She hopped in her sedan. Gunning the engine, she hooked a U-turn and sped off down the driveway.

The man's pulse quickened as he inched out from behind the tree.

Now, he could kidnap Scarlett.

CHAPTER TWENTY SEVEN

The expression that lit Wyatt's face as he ended the phone call with the TBI's deputy director sent a jolt of energy racing through Ashley's body. Had Wyatt received word of a break in the investigation? Had Brenda given him a new lead on how to locate Cole?

"Please tell me that you have some good news for a change," Ashley said.

Wyatt glanced at Sheriff Hyland. The sheriff stood next to Ashley in the hallway at the rear of the Mansfields' cavernous marijuana cultivation building. It dawned on her that the information Wyatt had to share might not be facts that Hyland wanted to hear.

"The techs found something in Cole's car," Wyatt stated, his voice now edged with apprehension.

Ashley's hope that the new information would lead to finding Cole alive vanished. Had they found blood in the car's trunk? Or some other type of forensic evidence pointing to Cole's murder? She braced herself for the worst.

Hyland's lips pressed into a thin line. He obviously now expected bad news as well.

"Give it to me straight," the sheriff said.

Wyatt nodded. "They found a hidden compartment in the car. It was filled with twelve pounds of marijuana."

The news stunned Ashley.

Possessing that amount of weed could only mean one thing. It appeared as though Cole had been dealing. His involvement in illegal activity also explained the reason there were so few calls listed in his cell phone records. Drug dealers relied on burner phones. Whoever had taken Cole would have made sure to take the burner cell also. They'd want the information contained on the phone destroyed.

Although learning his nephew was a weed dealer had to be difficult for Hyland, at least there was a slim chance that Cole was still alive somewhere.

124

The sheriff sighed. "That's a rough one to swallow." His gaze dropped toward the concrete floor, and he shook his head. "Was Cole really selling under my nose? I know my nephew's not perfect— nobody is. But he's always been a good kid. Never gave Rosalie a lick of trouble. He always followed her rules. I never pegged him for a dealer."

It pained Ashley to see the anguish and disappointment in Hyland's eyes. And she didn't even want to think about how the news would affect Cole's mother. But at least now there was a solid connection between Cole and the Mansfields.

The motive for the abduction of Cole and Jerry was likely tied to the marijuana operation. But who had committed the actual kidnapping? The Mansfields' alibis had checked out. Tim and Vera had been four hours away from Fergus County on Friday afternoon. They couldn't be the culprits.

A thought struck Ashley.

Was there a rival marijuana farm in the county?

Maybe Cole and Jerry had been abducted as a threat. Maybe the competition wanted the Mansfields' weed farm shut down.

Ashley asked Hyland, "Where is Deputy Kelton right now?"

Kelton was Cole's close friend. He had to know about Cole's second job.

The sheriff checked his watch. "Kelton should already be here. He's probably down at the Mansfields' farmhouse."

Ashley still didn't trust the deputy. Maybe Kelton was dealing weed too. Or being paid to look the other way. Maybe when he'd found out that the cultivation building had been discovered, he'd decided to skip town.

"I think I'll head on back down the trail and see if I can find him," she stated.

"Yeah, that's a good idea." Wyatt said. "I'll come too."

The look in her partner's eyes revealed that he suspected Kelton as well.

Hyland nodded in response. Likely chiding himself for not discovering Cole's double life sooner, he seemed to want to be alone with his thoughts.

Wyatt motioned for Ashley to go first. She made her way down a narrow aisle between the rows of marijuana plants with her partner close behind. As they neared the door leading outside, a realization hit

125

her. Although the families of Cole and Jerry had not received a demand for money, it was still possible that the men were being held for ransom.

A ransom of a different kind.

Maybe the rival organization was trying to take control of the Mansfields' operation. And maybe Tim and Vera had balked at the idea of working for someone else. The rivals could be holding Cole and Jerry hostage, waiting for the Mansfields to give in.

Anxiety knotted in Ashley's stomach as she realized something else.

Once the word got out that the Mansfields' grow house had been confiscated by the TBI, and that the business was shut down, the rivalry and fight for control over the drug territory would end. There would be no more competition.

And no further reason to keep Cole and Jerry alive.

Ashley struggled to prevent the image of Rosalie's grieving face from haunting her mind as she crossed over the building's threshold. Even if the TBI put a lid on the marijuana bust and swore the sheriff's department to secrecy, the information would leak out to the locals. It always did.

The man who'd hit Ashley and fled the building had likely already spilled the news.

Ashley and Wyatt retraced their steps down the winding path through the forest. As they approached a sharp turn, she heard a noise. Holding up her hand to alert Wyatt, Ashley stopped short. She stood still, listening.

Footsteps thumped on the trail ahead, moving toward them.

Deputy Kelton stepped out from behind the branches of a pine tree at the curve. An older, red-haired deputy lumbered not far behind him.

"Agent Hope, Agent Clark," Kelton said in way of a greeting. He motioned toward the man bringing up his rear. "This is Deputy Gilroy."

Ashley introduced herself and Wyatt, shaking Gilroy's hand.

"We were hoping to speak to you in private for a few minutes, Deputy Kelton," she said.

A strange look crossed Kelton's face. One Ashley couldn't quite gage.

"You go on ahead," Kelton told Gilroy.

Ashley gave Deputy Gilroy ample time to move out of earshot.

"We know about Cole's side job selling weed," she stated.

Kelton's eyes widened. "Wait—hold on a second. What are you talking about?"

She held the deputy's gaze, trying to decide whether or not his shocked reaction was genuine.

"Do you expect us to believe that you weren't aware that Cole was dealing?"

Kelton didn't attempt to look away. "Sure, he smokes a little now and then. A lot of people do, but Cole doesn't sell the stuff."

"By 'a little,' do you mean twelve pounds?" Ashley asked. "Because that's the weight of the marijuana found hidden in the secret compartment in Cole's car."

The words seemed to hit the deputy like a sledgehammer. He appeared even more dumbfounded. He hesitated for a moment, as though the wheels of his mind were turning. "He's always got cash," Kelton finally said. "But I just figured it was from his father's life insurance policy."

Although Ashley still had qualms regarding Kelton, his body language led her to believe him. He spent a lot of time with Cole. If the deputy had been in the dark regarding Cole's side job, maybe he possessed pertinent information and just didn't realize it.

"Can you tell us anything about a person named Boswell?"

He shook his head. "I don't know anybody by that name."

And then a look of understanding flashed across Kelton's face. It was as though a long-forgotten detail had clicked in his memory.

The deputy pulled a small notepad and a pen from his pocket. He scribbled something down and then ripped the page from the notebook.

He handed the paper to Ashley.

"This   is   where   you   need   to   go," he   told   her.

CHAPTER TWENTY EIGHT

Scarlett tightened the drawstring on the laundry bag and jerked it free from the hamper in Daisy's master bathroom. She and her second cousin had never been friends before. In fact, Daisy's jealousy had led them to hate each other while they were growing up. But the twelve years that had passed since their high school graduation had changed her cousin for the better.

Maybe it was her secure marriage to Ben that had done the trick. Having confidence in the solidity of her current relationship, she no longer feared that Scarlett would steal her man away.

Upon meeting again three months earlier, with both women having gained maturity, the bond of their shared blood had finally overcome the rivalry of their youth. And when Scarlett bottomed to her lowest point, with nowhere to go, Daisy had taken her in.

Now, after only a few weeks, the two had grown as close as sisters.

As she lugged the bag through the bedroom and down the hallway to the cramped laundry room, Scarlett whispered a prayer for Ben. She hoped that his injury wasn't serious. And she wished that she could have ridden along to the poultry plant to provide support for Daisy. But the risk of returning to Fergus County proved too great. For now, anyway.

The hinges on the ancient top-loading washing machine squealed as Scarlett lifted the lid. She planned to go back to work once it was safe. Although she'd taken on most of the chores since moving in, she still didn't feel as though she earned her keep. She wanted to be able to bring some money into the household.

With the mortgage to pay and food prices skyrocketing, she knew the budget was already stretched thin. What if Ben was forced to stay out of work for a while? Would they be able to hold on? Scarlett might need to look for a job sooner than she'd expected. Maybe she could find an administrative position. Something that would keep her out of the eye of the public.

As she poured detergent into the washer, a creaking sound drew Scarlett's attention. Was it the back door opening? In her rush to get to the poultry plant, maybe Daisy had forgotten something.

Scarlett capped the detergent bottle and eased toward the door to the hallway. She strained her ears, listening.

"Daisy?" she called out.

There was no response.

A cold chill rushed through her.

Knowing everything that had transpired in Scarlett's life, Daisy wouldn't play games. If she was in the house, she would answer. But the noise hadn't been a product of Scarlett's imagination. It had been real. She was certain of it.

Stowing the detergent back on the shelf, she crept down the hallway. She paused in the living room, listening once again. All was quiet. She checked the front door. To her relief, it was locked. She moved to the right, into the kitchen.

The door to the deck was closed. The knob was locked as well. As a precaution, Scarlett engaged the thumb-turn deadbolt. What could have made the noise she'd heard? She peered through the door's glass panes. Except for a flock of grackles pecking at the ground, she didn't see anything.

Puzzled, she headed back to the laundry room.

An uneasy feeling nagged at her as she loosened the drawstring and dumped the contents of the laundry bag onto the floor. Could the sound have been caused by the house settling? Sifting through the clothing, she fished out the items constructed from dark-colored fabrics. With a load in her arms, she stood and stepped toward the washer.

A noise echoed behind her. Footsteps.

Fear cut through Scarlett's soul.

Dropping the clothing, she whirled around.

She screamed as her eyes locked with his.

He'd found her. And he held a Taser in his hand.

Pop!

Barbs pierced Scarlett's right arm and left leg. A pain more excruciating than any she'd ever felt ripped through her body as every one of her muscles contracted.

As she fell to the floor, her head struck the corner of the cast iron laundry sink.

Scarlett's vision blurred just before the darkness engulfed her.

CHAPTER TWENTY NINE

As Ashley settled into the passenger seat of the SUV, the impulse to swallow one of the pain pills she'd received in the emergency room tugged at her once again. This time, the urge proved even stronger than before. Her jaw had swollen from the blow she'd taken in the Mansfields' weed growing building. Every time she opened her mouth, a searing sting shot up through her cheek bone. And the relentless ache in her shoulder from the bullet wound still plagued her.

But Ashley knew from past injuries how her body reacted to Oxycodone. The drug made her sleepy. And sometimes dizzy. She couldn't risk either side effect right now.

Sighing, she resigned herself to suffering through the pain. It wouldn't be the first time, and in her line of work, she was certain that it wouldn't be the last.

She thought about Tim Mansfield and the pain he must be going through. She prayed the surgeon would be able to repair the damage from his bullet wound. And she knew that Wyatt felt the same way. He'd called several times requesting an update on Tim's condition. For now, it was touch and go.

The SUV hit a pothole, radiating another shockwave through Ashley's body, as Wyatt pulled out onto the highway leading back toward Arbuckle. She remembered seeing the pink brick building that housed Teague's Florist the first time they'd driven through town.

According to Deputy Kelton, the shop was owned by the parents of Cole's ex-girlfriend. Cole and Jessica had remained friends after the breakup. Kelton said that he'd often wondered why the two—who seemed so perfect together—had decided to part ways. But now that the truth had come to light regarding Cole's side job of selling weed, many puzzling things the deputy had overheard between the couple now made sense to him.

Kelton believed Jessica knew all about Cole's double life.

Was the woman's disapproval of the drug dealing the reason the pair had split?

Ashley wondered how much information Jessica could provide them. She'd read through the notes Sheriff Hyland had taken when he'd originally spoken with Cole's ex. Nothing stood out. But at the time of the interview, Hyland hadn't known the right questions to ask.

Pondering the situation between Cole and Jessica, Ashley's thoughts veered toward Daniel and her own romantic relationship.

She pulled her cell phone from her pocket and opened the text app. All of the messages—four in total—that she'd sent Daniel throughout the day showed as being delivered. But he hadn't texted back. Ashley told herself that Daniel's failure to respond was due to the fact that he was busy chasing bad guys. Or that he was working undercover using a burner phone and had left his own cell at home.

Ashley refused to allow her mind to consider the alternative. She pushed away the thought that Daniel might have been seriously injured in the line of duty.

Shaking off her growing doubts, she directed her attention through the windshield at the storefronts lining Arbuckle's Main Street. She spotted the pink brick building from a block away.

"That's it, Teague's Florist, just ahead on the right," she told Wyatt.

He angled the SUV into an empty parking space near the door of the shop. The green awning that graced the front of the store complimented the color of the brick. Ashley unbuckled her seatbelt and slid out of the passenger seat.

A bell tinkled as Wyatt pulled open the shop's door and motioned for Ashley to enter first. The strong scent of carnations wafting in the air reminded her of a funeral parlor. She edged between the displays of colorful flower arrangements, peace lilies, and dieffenbachias. As she approached the rear of the store, a sandy-haired, middle-aged woman, wearing a green apron, emerged from a doorway behind the counter.

"How can I help you?" the woman asked.

Wyatt made the introductions. "We'd like to speak with Jessica Teague."

The woman's face clouded. "Jessica is my daughter," she said. "Can I ask why you want to talk to her?"

Ashley stepped closer to the counter. "Your daughter is not in any kind of trouble," she assured the woman. "We're investigating the disappearance of Cole Gowen and believe that Jessica might be able to help us find him."

Mrs. Teague hesitated, her distrust of law enforcement evident in her eyes.

Ashley softened her voice. "You probably know that Cole's father died just two years ago," she stated. "And now his mother is sick with worry that she might lose her son too. It's possible that Jessica could have information that would bring Cole home."

The plea seemed to work. Mrs. Teague nodded. She stuck her head back through the doorway leading to the employee's section of the building.

"Jessica?" she called. "Can you come out here please?"

A few moments later, a slender woman, seeming to be in her early twenties, with honey-colored hair and bright blue eyes, appeared behind the counter.

This time, Ashley introduced herself and Wyatt and explained the reason for their visit.

The bell jingled behind her as a customer entered the flower shop.

"We'll be discussing details that we don't want to slip out," she told Jessica. "Is there someplace we can go to speak in private?"

Jessica glanced at her mother. "Yeah," she said. "Follow me."

Ashley was actually glad that the customer had picked that moment to visit the florist. It gave them an excuse to separate Jessica from her mother. If Mrs. Teague had sat in on the discussion, her daughter might not feel comfortable giving up information regarding Cole's involvement in the marijuana trade.

Jessica led them around the counter, through the door, and down a hallway.

"We can use my mom's office," she said, ushering them into a small room furnished with a desk and office chair, two hard-backed chairs, and a metal filing cabinet.

Ashley pushed the door closed. As Jessica slid into the chair behind the desk, she sank down onto one of the hard-backed chairs next to Wyatt. She took a second to gather her thoughts, trying to come up with a way to broach the subject of Cole's drug dealing without triggering Jessica's defense instinct.

"It's important for you to realize that our only motive is to find Cole," Ashley began. "We're not trying to trap you or get you to admit to any illegal activity. We're just fitting the pieces together so that we can determine who abducted him. Do you understand?"

Jessica nodded, concern clear in her eyes. "Yeah. I want him found too."

With that settled, Ashley dove in. "We're aware that you knew Cole was selling marijuana," she stated, matter of fact, as if it was no big deal.

A panicked look crossed Jessica's face.

Apparently, the woman had failed to believe Ashley's earlier statement. Given law enforcement's reputation in the area, who could blame her?

Ashley leaned toward the desk. "It's okay," she said. "You're not in trouble."

"Did you tell my mom?"

"No. And we don't plan to discuss any of this with her, so you don't have to worry. You can speak freely. Again, our focus is on finding out exactly what happened to Cole."

The words were true. At this point, saving the lives of Cole and Jerry was the only thing that mattered to Ashley. She believed Wyatt felt the same.

Jessica seemed to relax a bit. "Okay, I'll tell you what I know."

"Good. We think it's possible that Cole may have been kidnapped by a rival drug supplier. Do you know whether the Mansfields had any competition?"

A look of confusion flashed in the young woman's eyes. "Who are the Mansfields?"

Ashley exchanged glances with Wyatt. "Cole never mentioned the farm where the marijuana was grown?"

Maybe Ashley had it backwards. Maybe Cole worked for the competition. The Mansfields could have kidnapped him, which led to Jerry's abduction in retaliation.

"No." Jessica sighed. "And there's something important for y'all to understand. I know selling weed is illegal, but Cole is a good-hearted man. He never wanted to hurt anybody. If his daddy hadn't died and left his mama in debt, he never would have started it."

Ashley could tell when she'd met Rosalie that the woman had relied heavily on Cole. She just hadn't realized the mother-son relationship included financial dependence. She wondered whether the sheriff was aware of that fact, or if Rosalie was too proud to admit it.

"Did Deputy Kelton know that Cole was selling marijuana? Was he being paid to look the other way?"

Surprise lit Jessica's eyes as though she couldn't believe Ashley would ask that question. "Never in a million years. Cole was scared half to death that Mike Kelton would find out. Mike's a straight arrow. He loves Cole like a brother, but he would have turned him in. Cole knew that Mike would've told Sheriff Hyland."

Listening to Jessica's firm reply, Ashley began to believe that Sheriff Hyland had been right. That Deputy Kelton had nothing to do with Cole's disappearance.

Jessica continued. "There's something else I want y'all to know. Cole is not like other weed dealers. He cares about people, especially kids. Cole's customers are at the college in Peck County. Nowhere else. He won't sell to anybody younger than eighteen. And he worried that if he got caught, it would make his uncle look bad. So, he never sells in Fergus County."

The young woman's fervent need to defend Cole made it clear that she still harbored deep feelings for him.

"Did Cole ever tell you the name of his marijuana supplier?"

Jessica nodded. "He gets the weed from Leif."

Ashley wondered whether the man was using a nickname—a play on the word *leaf* as in marijuana leaves.

"Have you ever met this man before?"

"Yeah. A couple of times. He lives in Peck County. About ten minutes from the college. I used to go with Cole to pick up the weed."

So, the rival marijuana farm might be located somewhere in the neighboring county. That could be where they'd taken Jerry. But there was still no information pointing to the location where Cole was being held.

"What kind of relationship do Cole and Leif have? Do you ever remember them arguing or anything?"

Jessica hesitated a moment, as though she was thinking. "Cole doesn't like Leif. Doesn't trust him. He always calls him a thug— behind his back though. But as far as I know, they don't fight or anything like that."

The possibility existed that Leif and Cole had a falling out that had led to Cole's death. But that didn't explain Jerry's disappearance. For now, Ashley nixed the idea in her mind. The theory of a war waged between rival farms seemed much more plausible.

Jessica knew where Leif lived. If they could haul in Cole's supplier, who was likely a middleman, they had a good chance of finding out who owned the rival farm.

"Did Cole ever tell you Leif's last name?"

Jessica nodded again. "It's Boswell," she said.

CHAPTER THIRTY

Dressed as a cable television line repairman, Daniel sat in the driver's seat of the white utility truck and struggled to focus his attention on the apartment across the alleyway. Perez, the man Daniel and his partner had under surveillance, was suspected of one of the vilest crimes being committed in Nashville: human trafficking.

According to the intelligence they'd gathered, Perez had a meeting scheduled with his boss sometime this afternoon. But they had no idea of the identity of the man at the top of the chain. They were waiting for Perez to make his move, so that they could follow.

But instead of concentrating on Perez's silhouette, visible through the front window of the apartment, Daniel's mind was fixed on Ashley. He couldn't shake the sick feeling in the pit of his stomach that had been plaguing him since early that morning when he'd called Ashley's motel room.

When a still half-asleep Wyatt had answered her phone.

Daniel had believed Ashley when she'd told him that she had her own room at the motel in Fergus County. But obviously, something had changed during the night. And he feared that he knew exactly what that something had been.

Wyatt had seduced Ashley.

She'd promised that nothing physical would ever happen between her and her TBI partner. That she was only interested in Daniel. But in the end, Ashley hadn't been able to stop herself. Like many women before her, according to the rumors, she couldn't resist Wyatt.

It had felt as though a knife had been plunged into Daniel's heart when he'd heard Wyatt's voice on the other end of the phone line. Taken by surprise, he'd frozen in place, his words failing him. So, instead of shouting profanities at Wyatt or demanding to speak with Ashley, he'd cut the connection.

But the next time he saw Wyatt, he knew exactly what he would do. He planned to punch the agent square in the face. And if Brenda suspended Daniel from duty for his actions, so be it.

136

"Hey, you hungry?" Rick's voice interrupted his thoughts.

Earlier, Daniel had noticed his ginger-haired partner eyeing the burger joint situated across from the apartment complex. Like Rick, he was usually always hungry. But right now, the idea of food made him nauseous.

"No, I'm good."

Rick shook his head. "You might not be hungry, but there's no way you're good. Something's been eating at you all day. Is it Ashley?"

He avoided Rick's gaze. Although his partner, who had been married for almost ten years, might be able to provide some helpful advice, Daniel didn't feel like divulging the events of his morning. He wasn't ready to admit out loud that Ashley had cheated on him. He decided to keep his answer vague. "She's away on assignment."

"Still partnered with Wyatt Clark?"

Rick was well aware of Wyatt's womanizing reputation.

"Yeah."

"Man, I don't know how you do it. It would drive me crazy to know my wife was spending hours alone with a guy like Clark."

Daniel didn't know how to respond. He had trusted Ashley. He'd believed that being unfaithful wasn't a part of her nature. But his instincts had let him down. How long had she been harboring feelings for her partner?

"Yeah, I get it," he said, nodding.

Lately, Ashley had been quick to jump to Wyatt's defense. The two of them seemed to be growing closer. Forming a bond. Which would have been fine as long as they'd kept the relationship on a platonic level.

But the fact that Ashley and Wyatt had shared a bed last night couldn't be denied.

"Well, you've got a hell of a lot more self-confidence than me," Rick said. "I'm going to walk over and grab a burger. You sure you don't want anything?"

"I'm sure. But make it quick. We don't know when Perez will decide to take off."

Rick slid out of the passenger seat and slammed the door of the utility truck.

Daniel pulled his phone from his pocket and tapped open the text app. He reread through the messages Ashley had sent. It was obvious that she was worried about him. Wondering why he hadn't responded.

137

But he couldn't think of the right words to say. Still, it was unfair to leave her hanging. He typed out a reply.

I'm fine. Can't talk now.

And that was all he wrote. Daniel was angry. More pissed than he'd been with anyone in a long time. But he refused to tell her what was wrong in a text.

He wanted Ashley to come clean. To volunteer the information that she and Wyatt had slept together. He didn't want to be forced to confront her about it. After all the time they'd spent together, after all the things they'd shared, she owed him the courtesy of being honest. But he knew that when she finally uttered the words, it would sting like no pain he'd ever felt.

The truth was that he'd fallen completely and hopelessly in love with Ashley.

When he'd looked into her eyes, he'd imagined marriage, and babies, and grandchildren, and growing old together.

He'd planned on sharing his feelings with her that past Sunday, right after dinner. But then Wyatt had called. And Ashley had brought up Daniel's failed marriage to Melody.

He'd been caught off guard. He hadn't realized Ashley had been comparing herself to his ex-wife. The two women were nothing alike. Not even close.

Or so he'd thought.

Who had Ashley been trying to convince when she'd stated, "*I'm not Melody?*" Daniel, or herself? Maybe she'd had an inkling of what would end up happening during her trip to Fergus County. Knew that she might hurt Daniel in the same way his ex-wife had done.

Melody was selfish and manipulative. Character flaws Daniel had overlooked, partly because of his youth, and partly because he'd thought that she'd outgrow them. That she'd change once they were married. Now, he knew how foolish he'd been back then.

And he realized that he'd been just as foolish with Ashley.

He'd believed her to be caring, supportive, gracious, and loving. Not to mention the fact that she was beautiful. He'd never felt so close to anyone before. So connected. His heart had convinced him that Ashley was everything he'd ever wanted.

But obviously, his heart had been wrong.

Daniel had repeated the same mistake he'd made in college. He'd allowed himself to overlook the one thing about Ashley that had concerned him in the beginning—her habit of keeping secrets. She'd been hiding the fact that she'd felt drawn to Wyatt. Maybe she'd even been hiding the truth from herself. And now, Daniel was paying the price.

Just like Melody, Ashley had been unfaithful.

Daniel shoved his phone back into his pocket.

Although the thought of living without Ashley ripped his heart apart, he decided that he would break the news later tonight. Daniel would tell her that their relationship was over.

CHAPTER THIRTY ONE

As she and Wyatt sat in the parking space in front of Teague's Florist, Ashley grabbed the mobile tablet from the pocket behind the driver's seat of the SUV, freed it from its case, and switched it on. She'd only been a little bit surprised to learn that the person supplying Cole with weed to sell was named Boswell. Just like the file folder she'd found on the Mansfields' computer.

Cole had actually been working for the Mansfields all along, but the odds ranked high that he didn't know it. Tim and Vera were likely insulating themselves by using the middleman.

"Boswell probably manages a whole network of salespeople scattered throughout all the neighboring counties," she said to Wyatt.

And it stood to reason that all of the dealers were kept in the dark regarding the origin of the merchandise.

"That's a safe bet."

But the drug trade was a treacherous business. And Ashley realized for the first time that the lives of the people at the bottom of the food chain didn't matter. If one of the salespeople was eliminated—maybe by a rival grower—they could likely be replaced in short order.

"Jerry's abduction seems fairly easy to explain," she stated, pondering the situation out loud. "He sits at the top of the organization. The competition would know that the Mansfields need him to launder the proceeds from the marijuana sales."

If a rival grower wanted the Mansfields out of business, one of the best ways to accomplish the task would be to interrupt the flow of money. With Jerry gone, Marilyn could be threatened and coerced into parting ways with the Mansfields.

"Right. It does no good to make money if you can't spend it."

"But what made them think that they needed to get rid of Cole?"

Wyatt shrugged. "We're obviously missing part of the picture."

As one of many dealers, Cole was just a peon. It didn't make sense.

Unless he'd stumbled onto a piece of information that someone wanted to keep hidden.

Ashley tried to connect the dots in her mind. "What if a rival grower decided to lure Boswell away from the Mansfields? They could have promised him a large amount of money. Maybe even offered him a cut of the business in exchange for helping them take down the Mansfields' operation from the inside."

"Yeah. That sounds plausible. It would be the easiest way to eliminate the competition."

Maybe Cole had overheard Boswell discussing the matter when he'd picked up the packages of weed. Boswell might not have realized it until later.

"Cole could have found out about the Mansfields' farm," Ashley stated. "And about Boswell's plans to destroy, or take over, their operation."

A realization struck her. "I'll bet that Boswell is the person who was following Cole," Ashley said.

Cole had told the pig farmer that he was being stalked by someone he'd served a summons. But what was he supposed to say? That he was being pursued by a drug dealer?

She met Wyatt's gaze. "If Boswell was the person Cole was afraid of, it makes perfect sense why he didn't tell the sheriff or Deputy Kelton about it," she said. "If he had, they would have found out that Cole was leading a double life and that he was involved in something that could land him in jail."

Ashley logged onto the TBI database. She searched the criminal records for Leif Boswell. In just a few seconds, a hit popped up. "He's only got a few priors," she told Wyatt. "There's one assault charge—it looks like he got into a bar fight. And I see a couple of charges for simple possession. That's it."

She'd been expecting more in regard to the sale of marijuana. But then, he had an army to do that for him. Like the Mansfields, he could keep his hands clean.

Ashley pulled up Boswell's mug shot. "Okay, our suspect is thirty-four years old with brown hair, brown eyes, and a full beard. He weighs one-hundred-and-seventy-five pounds. And guess what else?"

"He's five-nine or shorter."

She nodded. "He's listed as being five feet, eight inches tall."

Maybe this time, they'd found the right man. Maybe Boswell would lead them to Cole and Jerry. She just prayed that the two missing men were still alive.

141

Ashley punched Boswell's address into the SUV's navigation system. The female computerized voice directed them back onto Main Street to begin the trip to Peck County.

As she clicked her seatbelt into place, Ashley's cell phone chimed. It was her text message alert. Hoping that Daniel had finally responded to the many messages she'd sent, she rushed to pull her phone from the pocket of her cargo jacket.

Her lips curved into a smile when she saw Daniel's name on her phone's screen.

But then, a wave of disappointment hit her as she read his text. Five short words. He was fine, but he couldn't talk. The message felt cold and detached. Not like Daniel at all.

In the past, even when he'd been knee-deep in the midst of a murder investigation, he'd always told her that he missed her and that he was thinking about her. But this text seemed as though it had been written by a completely different person.

Did someone else have Daniel's phone?

Maybe that was it. Maybe Daniel had been forced to leave his phone somewhere, and he'd asked his partner to send Ashley the message. But that didn't make sense. If Rick had sent the text, he would have identified himself and let her know what was going on.

Something was wrong. Ashley felt it deep in her gut. But she had no idea what.

She stared at the screen, waiting to see the three little dots indicating that Daniel was typing again. Wishing that he would take two seconds to at least say he missed her.

The dots never appeared. Finally, she decided to tap back a reply.

I'm so glad you're okay.

I can't wait to hear your voice again.

I miss you so much.

Ashley settled back in the passenger seat and peered out the side window. Wyatt apparently noticed the shift in her mood.

"Everything okay?" he asked.

She nodded in response, but Wyatt must not have been looking at her.

"Ashley?"

"I'm fine, Wyatt," she said, realizing that her tone had sounded harsher than she'd intended. "Thanks for asking about me," she added to soften the blow.

142

"Is everything all right with your father? And your brothers?"

Although she appreciated her partner's concern, she almost wished that they could go back to the way things were before their last assignment. To the time when Wyatt didn't seem to care about her personal life. After seeing the look on his face when they'd touched hands, it was hard for her to accept his friendship without questioning his true motive.

She still worried that Wyatt wanted something more. Something she could never give him.

Forcing a cheery note into her voice, hoping that Wyatt would stop grilling her, she said, "I talked to my father earlier today, and he and my brothers are all doing well."

Concerned the stalker would make a return visit to Laurel County, Ashley had touched base with her father every few hours. Every time she'd had the chance to make a phone call. Although Spencer had hinted that she should focus her mind on her work and trust him to take care of himself, until the stalker was caught, she'd continue to check on her father. Even if it irritated him.

"That's good to hear."

Swinging his gaze from the road, Wyatt stared at her as though he was expecting her to say more. To explain the reason why, upon receiving the text, her mood had changed from being excited about solving the case to sullen. She didn't.

Ashley had no intention of talking to him about Daniel.

"You know," Wyatt began, his voice soft. "I'm here if you need me."

They weren't the words she'd anticipated. She realized Wyatt was speaking from his heart. Although she was wary, his words touched her. But she still wasn't ready to allow them to grow closer just yet. Not until she was certain that he only wanted to be friends.

Unsure of what to say, she decided to keep it simple. "Thank you."

Ashley's cell phone rang, saving her from further awkward conversation.

Checking the screen, she saw that the caller ID had been blocked. Was it Daniel?

"Hello," she said, anxious to speak with her boyfriend.

The line crackled.

And then she heard the clipped computerized voice.

Did. You. Like. My. Gift?

"Who is this?" she demanded, more angry now than scared.
Laughter echoed in the background. Human laughter. A man.
And then the computer spoke again.
You. Will. Die. Soon.
Ashley's blood ran cold as the call disconnected.

CHAPTER THIRTY TWO

"Was that him?" Wyatt asked her. "Was it the stalker?"

Shaken by the phone call, Ashley nodded. Anxiety cramped her stomach. The man who was harassing her had proven he could launch an attack any time he chose. He'd been inside her apartment. He'd been inside her motel room. No place was truly safe.

And Ashley believed the man planned to make good on his threat.

He wanted her dead.

But the question remained: who was threatening her? Although she was fairly certain that the man would prove to be a relative of her ex-husband, Ethan, she had no idea which one. As soon as this case wrapped up, she'd go back to Laurel County. She'd dig deep into the Barrett clan. And she wouldn't stop until she identified the culprit.

She hated feeling vulnerable. Hated feeling as though she had to constantly look over her shoulder, but she didn't know from which direction the stalker would strike. He could be following their SUV down the highway at that very moment. He could be hiding in her motel room shower when she returned. He could surprise her when she least expected it.

But Ashley refused to allow fear to control her.

"I'm not going to let him win," she voiced the resolution aloud.

"I know," Wyatt said. "You're too strong for that."

As the SUV crested a hill, the vehicle's navigation system alerted them to the turn they needed to take up ahead. They'd almost reached Boswell's house.

Ashley forced the thoughts of her stalker aside. She had a job to do. The lives of Cole and Jerry were at stake. She had to focus all of her energy on finding them.

Would she and Wyatt be able to get Boswell to talk?

Boswell likely had a stash of marijuana at his home, ready to distribute to his dealers. But without a search warrant, unless Ashley and Wyatt saw the weed in plain view, or smelled it, they had no grounds to arrest him.

"You know that Boswell will probably make a run for it," Ashley said.

The guilty ones usually did. And with Boswell's line of work, the man probably remained on high alert. All of the time.

"Yeah, he will. Why don't you go up to the front door? I'll stay out of sight. Sneak around the back."

It sounded like a decent plan.

Wyatt wheeled the SUV onto the road where Boswell lived. Hardwood trees flanked both sides of the narrow strip of asphalt. He craned his neck to the right as they reached Boswell's driveway, but Wyatt didn't slow down. He kept going. Once they were out of the direct line of sight from the house, he eased the SUV onto the road's shoulder.

"I'll cut through the woods and meet you there," he said.

A gust of wind whipped through the bare branches of the trees as Ashley hopped out of the passenger seat. Zipping up her cargo jacket to ward off the chill, she trudged along the side of the road heading toward Boswell's driveway. The late afternoon sun hung low in the sky, threatening to dip beneath the horizon. Standing tall in the waning rays, the trees cast long shadows at her feet.

As she neared the single-story home, clad with beige vinyl siding, she noticed a light burning in the front room. The left end of the house featured a two-car attached garage. According to the DMV records, a black Ford sedan was registered in Boswell's name. But with the garage door closed, there was no way for her to know whether or not the car was parked inside.

Hiking up the gravel driveway, she approached the house with caution, wondering whether she was already being watched from one of the windows. It wouldn't surprise her to learn that Boswell had cameras hidden outside. In fact, she almost expected to be under surveillance.

She mounted the concrete porch steps and then paused before the door. She hoped Wyatt was already in place in the back yard. The muffled sounds of a television show seeped through the front wall of the house. She thought that it might be an old rerun of Gilligan's Island.

Ashley rang the bell.

Light footsteps echoed inside.

The door swung open. A young boy, no older than ten, stood before her. Wearing a pair of faded jeans and a red T-shirt, he had a mop of brown hair that was tousled and in need of a cut.

Apprehension gnawed at Ashley. The child was a complication they didn't need.

"Yeah?" the boy said in place of a greeting.

"I'm here to see Leif Boswell," she told him. "Is he home?"

"Who wants to know?"

Boswell had obviously trained the kid well.

"My name is Ashley. What's your name?"

The boy studied her a moment as though he was contemplating whether or not she posed a stranger danger. He was probably used to weed dealers coming in and out of his house. She wondered if any of them were female.

"Logan," he said after a few seconds. He stood at the threshold, still eyeing her.

She decided to ask again. "Are your mom and dad home?"

"Mama don't live here. It's just me and daddy. He's in the bathroom."

Maybe she was finally getting somewhere. "Would it be okay for me to come inside and talk to him?"

"I guess."

Logan stepped aside and Ashley crossed into the living room. A leather sectional sofa crowded the space and a large television hung on the wall. A gaming console rested on the floor beneath the TV. All most likely purchased with funds from the Mansfields' illegal operation.

"Daddy!" Logan yelled out. "There's a pretty lady here wanting to see you."

He plopped down onto the sofa, tucking his socked feet under him. He focused his attention on the TV screen.

The faint odor of pot drifted toward Ashley. Boswell not only supplied the dealers with weed, but he also obviously smoked it as well.

It was a lucky break. Ashley had been invited into the home, and now she had probable cause to arrest Boswell and conduct a search of the premises. But again, Logan concerned her. She worried how it would affect the child to see his father led away in handcuffs.

She pulled out her phone and tapped a text to Wyatt.

I'm inside.

There's a child here.

Weed odor.

Maybe Ashley could distract Logan while Wyatt cuffed Boswell.

Shoving her phone into her pocket, she leaned across the back of the sofa toward Logan.

"My friend, Wyatt, drove me here. Would it be okay for him to come inside and talk to your dad too?"

Logan shrugged. "I guess," he said, keeping his eyes glued to the television.

Wyatt was already trotting up the porch steps when Ashley pulled the front door open.

"Boswell is supposedly in the bathroom," she told him, her voice hushed. "I've just been waiting."

A surprised expression on his face, Wyatt eased through the door and pushed it closed behind him.

"Logan," Ashley said. "This is my good friend, Wyatt."

The boy didn't move a muscle. Didn't even glance behind him. "Okay," he said.

A grin tugged at Wyatt's lips. He circled around the end of the sofa and sank down onto the cushion next to Logan.

On the TV screen, Ginger sang, *"Boop-boop-a-doop"* to the stranded castaways.

Wyatt looked at Logan. "Ginger's pretty, huh?"

"I like Mary Ann."

"Yeah, me too."

Maybe Ashley had it backwards. Wyatt should be the one to keep Logan occupied while she arrested Boswell.

Footsteps drew her attention. Boswell emerged from the hallway. He wore jeans, but no shirt. Water plastered his dark brown hair to his head, and a blue bath towel draped his shoulders.

His eyes widened when he saw Ashley. "Who the hell are you?" he barked.

Clearly fresh from the shower, Boswell obviously hadn't heard the doorbell ring or Logan call out to him. He'd had no idea guests were inside his house.

Logan said, "That's Ashley."

Wyatt stood up from the sofa.

Ashley extended her hand, not that she really expected Boswell to shake it.

"I'm Special Agent Ashley Hope and this is my partner, Special Agent Wyatt Clark," she stated. "We're with the TBI."

He stared at her, hatred spreading across his face. "Logan, go to your room," he said, his voice firm.

"But Daddy, my show's almost over."

"I said, go!"

Logan peeled himself from the sofa and then disappeared into the adjacent hallway. It relieved Ashley that the child was out of the room. She didn't have to worry about him witnessing his father's arrest.

She waited a moment, giving Logan time to get out of earshot.

"Mr. Boswell, the odor in your home is clear evidence that you're in possession of an illegal substance," Ashley said. "We're going to have to place you under arrest."

Since they'd caught him by surprise, unless Boswell had a knife in his pocket, she didn't think he was armed.

Wyatt said, "On your knees."

Boswell complied. Wyatt pulled the man's hands behind his back and snapped the cuffs on his wrists. He checked Boswell's pockets. They were empty.

Ashley and Wyatt would haul the suspect to the sheriff's department in Fergus County and question him there. That way, Logan wouldn't overhear the fact that his father might be guilty of kidnapping and possibly murder.

But it might take child protective services a while to arrive at the house. Someone would have to wait here with Logan. Maybe the Peck County sheriff had a deputy nearby on patrol.

"I'll grab a shirt and a coat for you if you'll tell me where to look," Ashley said to Boswell.

But before the man could answer, Logan's voice thundered into the living room. "Get away from my daddy!" he screamed.

Ashley's gaze swung to her right. Her breath caught in her throat.

Logan stood at the mouth of the hallway, a pistol clamped tight in his hands.

149

CHAPTER THIRTY THREE

Ashley's heart hammered in her chest as she watched Logan inch into the living room, pointing a pistol toward Wyatt. Although she'd thought the child was tucked in his room, out of earshot, Logan had obviously been eavesdropping. He knew his father had been arrested.

But it seemed that Wyatt had sensed the child coming. Maybe he'd seen Logan sneaking down the hallway because he'd already drawn his Glock.

Wyatt's weapon was trained on Boswell, who was still crouched on his knees next to the sofa.

She knew Wyatt would never aim at a child. Not even one who wanted to kill him.

"Let my daddy go!" Logan shouted.

"I can't do that," Wyatt said, his voice calm. "Put the gun down."

Logan's face flushed red. "I'll shoot you."

Boswell piped up, "Do it, Logan. Right in the heart."

Ashley couldn't believe her ears. Boswell was ordering his young son to murder a TBI agent. Did he actually think he could get away with it? Did he not care what would happen to Logan?

She glared at Boswell. "Logan, stop and think about what you're doing. Shooting Wyatt won't save your father. It will only make things worse—a lot worse. You'll end up in juvenile detention, and I can promise you, that's not a place where you want to be."

Tears welled in Logan's eyes, but he didn't lower the gun.

Boswell sneered. "Don't listen to her. She's trying to trick you."

The truth rang clear. Boswell's only concern was for himself. He was willing to forfeit his son's future to save his own neck. Some people didn't deserve to be parents.

Wyatt asked Logan, "You know that we're TBI agents, right?"

Logan nodded.

"It's our job to uphold the law. But your father broke the law. So, we need to take him to the sheriff's department and get it all straightened out."

"No. You ain't taking him." Logan gritted his teeth. "I'll kill you."

Along with hate, Ashley could see fear in Logan's eyes. She knew that he didn't want to be separated from his father. But did he really have it in him to shoot Wyatt?

"You need to realize something," Wyatt said. "My bullet will be in your father's heart before your finger leaves the trigger."

They were harsh words, but maybe it was what Logan needed to hear. Maybe the child needed to be shocked into submission. But Ashley knew that even if Logan did pull the trigger, Wyatt wouldn't fire at Boswell. The suspect was still handcuffed. Helpless.

Tears streamed down Logan's face, but he didn't give in. He held the pistol steady.

"You're gonna kill my daddy anyway. So, I need to kill you too."

"No, I won't," Wyatt told him. "Just put down the gun, and everything will be okay."

It was apparent that Logan didn't believe him. The boy seemed terrified that Wyatt would shoot Boswell right in front of him.

"Cops lie. And you're a no-good, stinking cop."

"Whoever told you that cops lie doesn't know everything. They don't know me. I won't lie to you. If you'll give me the gun, I promise I won't hurt your father."

Boswell huffed. "He's lying to you right now, Logan. Can't you tell?"

Logan raised the pistol an inch, leveling it at Wyatt's chest.

"You know you don't really want to shoot," Wyatt told him. "You don't want to spend the rest of your life in prison."

"You're gonna put my daddy in jail."

Wyatt clenched his bottom lip between his teeth. Ashley knew that he was trying to think of the right words to say. He'd already told Logan that he wouldn't lie. He couldn't deny the statement the child had made. It was true. Boswell would be locked behind bars.

"Please, Logan," Wyatt finally said. "Give me the gun. We'll work everything out."

Boswell shouted, "Shoot him, Logan! Do it now."

Ashley's heart clenched. She could see Logan's mind spinning, his thoughts clear. Believing he should rescue his father, that he should obey Boswell's command, but at the same time, he agonized over the prospect of taking Wyatt's life.

She chanced a step toward the boy.

151

"Stop!" Logan yelled, swinging the pistol toward her.

That was what she'd wanted. To get his focus off of Wyatt.

Ashley needed to diffuse some of the tension that hung heavy in the air. To try and calm the child down. "You told me that your mother doesn't live here," she said. "Are you able to see her very often?"

The shift of subject seemed to confuse Logan, to redirect his thoughts. "Yeah. She gets me every other week."

Ashley smiled at him. "It's good that you can spend a lot of time with her," she said, keeping her voice steady and even. As though the two of them were just having a normal conversation.

Logan nodded. "Yeah."

Boswell interrupted. "Quit talking to my son. Our family ain't none of your business."

The outburst seemed to upset Logan. His bottom lip quivered.

Ashley ignored Boswell. "Let me tell you about someone I know whose name is Cole," she said.

Logan met her gaze. He took a deep breath. She could tell that he was listening, wondering what kind of story she was going to tell him.

"Cole and his mother are really close—probably the same way you and your mother are close. You love your mama a lot, don't you?"

The boy nodded again. "I know somebody named Cole."

Of course, he did. Cole had been to his house before. More than once.

"Shut up, Logan," Boswell warned.

Ashley threw the man a warning look of her own. "The Cole that you know is the same person I know," she said.

Logan appeared surprised. "Cole's nice."

The muzzle of the pistol sagged toward the floor, but just a tiny bit. Logan was probably getting tired of holding it.

"Yes, he is—very nice."

Although she'd never met the man, from what she'd gathered, the statement was most likely true. She continued, "Well, Cole's mother is really sad and upset right now."

"Why?"

"Because Cole never came home from work on Friday. The sheriff found his car parked beside the highway, but Cole was gone."

A look of concern flashed across Logan's face. "He's lost?"

Ashley nodded. "We think that somebody kidnapped him."

The news seemed to hit Logan hard. Fresh tears glistened in his eyes. Despite being raised by a selfish criminal, the young boy obviously had a soft heart.

"Cole's mother is really worried about him. But there's a chance that your daddy can help us bring Cole back home."

Logan locked his gaze on Ashley. "How?"

"We think that your daddy knows who took Cole, but we have to go down to the sheriff's department to find out."

Her plea to return Cole to his mother appeared to be eating away at Logan's resolve.

Boswell must have realized that his son was beginning to falter. "That's bull crap," he said. "I don't know nothing about Cole."

Logan's attention swerved to his father. "Cole works for you, Daddy."

"I told you to keep your mouth shut," Boswell spat out. "Or do you want me to shut it for you?"

Logan trembled, tightening his grip on the pistol.

Ashley clenched her fists. She couldn't stand the way Boswell treated his son. She wished she could punch the man in the face. Knock him out.

Instead, she breathed in deep and forced a soothing tone into her voice. "We both like Cole a lot, don't we?" she asked Logan.

"Yeah," he said, choking back the tears.

"If you got lost one day, do you think Cole would help us look for you?"

Logan nodded. His eyes revealed that he was starting to cave again.

"I do too. I don't think Cole would ever give up until we found you. Not until we brought you safely back home to your mama."

A sob escaped Logan's lips as tears spilled over his cheeks. The barrel of the gun drifted downward.

At that moment, Ashley knew that it was over. She stepped forward and wrapped her arms around Logan. The pistol fell to the floor. She held the boy tight, letting him cry.

Behind her, she heard Wyatt pull Boswell to his feet. She glanced over her shoulder as her partner marched the criminal out through the front door.

She continued to cradle Logan in her arms until he calmed down. She pulled a tissue from her pocket and wiped his face.

"Do you know your mother's phone number?" she asked him.

He blew his nose on one of the tissues she'd given him. "Yeah."

Ashley didn't want to contact child protective services. She wanted to handle things herself. She knew the state agency tended to move at a sluggish pace. And Logan needed to be reunited with his mother tonight. As soon as possible.

"Why don't you go put your shoes and coat on? We'll all ride over to the sheriff's department in Fergus County. I'll call your mother on the way, and she can meet us there."

"Okay."

Logan darted toward the hallway.

Ashley scooped the pistol up off of the floor and zipped it inside of an evidence bag. The TBI forensic techs and a DID team would conduct a thorough search of Boswell's house. The marijuana stash wasn't of concern to Ashley and Wyatt. They'd only wanted to find a reason to take the man into custody so they would be in a better position to grill him about the disappearances of Cole and Jerry.

Logan returned wearing sneakers and a dark blue jacket. Although Ashley could still see tears threatening his eyes, he appeared to be resigned to the fact that his father would spend time in jail.

"Are you ready to go?" she asked him.

"Yeah."

Draping her arm around Logan, she steered him out the door.

CHAPTER THIRTY FOUR

Ashley pushed through the door of the interrogation room at the Fergus County Sheriff's Department, her gaze sliding toward Boswell, slumped in a chair on the far side of the battered metal table. The urge to slap the smug expression from the man's face raged within her. But police brutality was frowned upon. So, she'd hold her peace.

At least she could celebrate one victory in regard to Boswell. The criminal would no longer be sharing custody of his son. Ashley had met Logan's mother, Sarah, earlier. Boswell's ex-wife seemed to be a good person who had just gotten mixed up with the wrong man. Ashley could relate. She'd been down that road herself. And Sarah appeared to be a loving and protective mother. Ashley had no qualms about leaving Logan in the woman's care.

A bald attorney in a navy suit sat to the left of Boswell. Ashley sank down into the chair opposite the attorney. Wyatt took the seat across from Boswell. She could tell by her partner's demeanor that he itched to punch the drug dealer as well.

Wyatt introduced himself and Ashley to the attorney, a man named Winslow.

Winslow had agreed that his client would answer a limited number of questions. The attorney had hinted to the sheriff that Boswell had information to trade. They wanted to make a deal.

"Let's cut to the chase," Winslow said, his attitude haughty. "No need to waste valuable time. Mr. Boswell has information you want, and you have the power to whittle down the charges. We can make an agreement here and now."

Wyatt and Ashley exchanged glances.

Wyatt folded his arms across his chest. "First, we need to find out what Boswell has to offer."

"It's big," Winslow stated as though he was handing Wyatt a winning lottery ticket. "My client is willing to turn over the name of his supplier. And that's just the half of it. He can also give you the location where the marijuana is grown. In exchange, you drop the charges down to simple possession. Deal?"

It was clear that the attorney thought he had the case won. The news that the Mansfields' farm had already been seized obviously hadn't yet trickled down to Boswell.

Before meeting Boswell, Ashley had thought he might have been the person who had hit her inside the grow house. But the man who had knocked her down possessed a heavier, and possibly more muscular, frame.

"No," Wyatt stated, simple and direct.

Winslow looked as though he'd been slapped. "I don't think I heard you right, detective."

"It's Special Agent. And I said there's no deal."

Along with his blatant arrogance, calling Wyatt by the wrong title hadn't earned the attorney any favors.

Anger shone in Boswell's face. "You told me—"

"Just calm down," Winslow interrupted. "Don't say anything."

The attorney stared at Wyatt. "What do you mean, there's no deal?"

"That's not the information we're looking for."

Boswell had been quick to sacrifice the Mansfields' weed cultivating operation. Ashley hoped that meant that he would be willing to lead them to Cole and Jerry.

Winslow sighed. "What is it that you want to know?"

Wyatt directed his attention toward Boswell. "Give us the location of Cole Gowen and Jerry Osborne."

Boswell appeared stunned. "You mean that horse-shit story you told my boy was true?"

Ashley heard conviction in Boswell's tone. A seed of doubt sprouted in her stomach. Had they guessed wrong again? Was Boswell just involved in trafficking the weed and nothing more?

Wyatt leaned toward the table. "Cole Gowen disappeared on Friday. Where were you that afternoon?"

Winslow said, "You don't have to answer that question."

Boswell glanced at his attorney and then looked at Wyatt. "No comment."

"I guess you'll also refuse to tell us where you were when Jerry Osborne disappeared."

"No comment."

Was Boswell holding back the information in order to negotiate a trade? Did he have an alibi? The criminal's body language didn't give her the answer.

Wyatt scooted his chair back from the table. "It looks like this interview is over."

Ashley glanced at the clock hanging on the wall. It was almost ten p.m.

Winslow stood. "You think about the deal we offered," he said. "You could get a promotion for a bust like that."

The attorney was obviously not very bright. He hadn't yet figured out that Wyatt and Ashley already knew the identity of Boswell's supplier.

Ashley pulled open the door of the interrogation room. Wyatt followed her out into the hallway. They headed toward the door leading out to the sheriff department's rear parking lot.

"Do you still think that Boswell could be the person who abducted Cole and Jerry?" she asked.

He hesitated a moment as though he was mulling over the facts of the case. "Yeah," he finally said. "It makes the most sense. And if Boswell had an alibi, he probably would have shouted it at the top of his lungs."

Wyatt had a point. It seemed unusual that Boswell hadn't defended himself. But an uneasy feeling nagged at Ashley. She knew that the man was guilty of drug trafficking, but she wasn't convinced that he was responsible for the disappearances.

As they exited the rear of the sheriff's department, Ashley's gaze swerved toward the SUV, parked in the corner of the lot. A dark figure lurked next to the vehicle's passenger door.

"Hey!" Ashley shouted.

Both she and Wyatt sprinted toward the SUV.

The figure ran.

"Stop!" Wyatt called out. "TBI!"

The figure kept going.

Based on the width of the figure's shoulders, Ashley felt certain that it was man. Her hiking boots pounded against the asphalt as they gave chase. But the man had a substantial head start. He disappeared around the corner of the neighboring building. A warehouse of some kind.

Wyatt passed Ashley as they sped toward the building.

Frantic thoughts raced through her mind. Who was this man? And why had he been prowling around the SUV? Was he Ashley's stalker?

She pushed herself harder, gaining on Wyatt.

As the pair circled around the end of the warehouse, they both skidded to a stop. The alley before them loomed dark and appeared empty. The man had vanished.

"Shit," Wyatt said. "That's probably the guy that's been following you."

"Yeah, I was thinking the same thing."

But Ashley knew that it would be foolish to venture into the alley. The man could be hiding in the shadows. He might have a gun. One of them could end up dead.

Wyatt must have been sharing her thoughts. "Let's head back to the motel," he said.

Side-by-side, they walked back toward the parking lot. As they approached the SUV from the opposite angle, Ashley saw what the man had done.

A wave of dread hit her. She looked at Wyatt.

"Shit," he said again.

CHAPTER THIRTY FIVE

Ashley sighed as she trudged across the parking lot of the Fergus County Sheriff's Department toward the SUV. Her shoulder still ached, and she had a painful catch in her jaw. She'd been running on full tilt since early that morning. It was now after ten o'clock, and she was exhausted.

And now this. It was the last thing she'd needed.

In the glow of the streetlight, she could see what the dark figure had been up to. He'd slashed the front tire on the driver's side of the SUV. They'd caught him before he could slash the one on the passenger's side.

Wyatt shook his head as if in disbelief.

"Shit," he said for the third time.

It seemed to have become his favorite word.

He clicked his key fob, and the cargo door sprang up.

He flipped open the panel covering the tire well and pulled out the spare. Ashley grabbed the jack and lug wrench. Due to the fact that her family owned an auto repair business, she'd learned to change a tire at a young age.

She followed Wyatt around to the front of the vehicle and watched as he loosened the lug nuts.

"I'm sorry you've gotten caught up in my ... drama."

Ashley didn't know what else to call it. She was referring to her stalker. They both believed the man who had slashed the tire was also the same person who'd stuffed dead frogs into her motel room bed.

"It's not your fault. And it's just a tire. Don't worry about it."

It wasn't the tire that concerned her. Ashley feared that the stalker might harm Wyatt. Either on purpose to torment Ashley, or by accident while trying to kill her. The tire was just an aggravation, a form of harassment meant to scare her. But what if the man had cut the brake line instead?

Wyatt slid the jack beneath the SUV's frame.

Ashley would never forgive herself if the stalker murdered Wyatt.

159

"I think the man's serious about killing me," she said. "Maybe we should switch back to sleeping in our original motel rooms. I don't want you to get hurt if he breaks in tonight."

Wyatt stopped what he was doing. He touched Ashley's arm. "Hey, listen to me. I'm not going to let this guy get anywhere near you. You're sleeping in my bed."

He must have realized that his words could be taken the wrong way.

He clarified, "I don't mean with me. You're sleeping by yourself, but in my room."

"I don't think that's a good idea. The man might see you in my old bed, think you're me, and kill you before you even wake up."

She knew that Wyatt had rigged up some kind of makeshift alarm on the door, but she didn't trust it. The stalker had already proven that he could get in and out of her apartment at will. He could do the same at the motel.

"That won't happen. And I'm lead agent on this case, so you have to do what I tell you."

A smile tugged at her lips. Ashley knew his pulling rank was an attempt to lighten the mood.

A realization hit her. She was learning how to read Wyatt. If he'd said the same thing just a few weeks earlier, it would have angered her. She would have believed that he was serious, that he was trying to throw his weight around. Maybe their partnership would work out after all.

Ashley still felt uneasy about allowing Wyatt to stay in her old room. But it seemed that he'd made up his mind, and she knew nothing she said would change it.

He returned to jacking up the SUV. In just a few minutes, he'd replaced the slashed tire with the spare.

She climbed into the passenger seat.

Wyatt steered the SUV onto the street and headed toward the motel. The tires hummed on the pavement. Like a lullaby, the steady sound threatened to lure her to sleep.

Glancing at the clock on the dashboard, she realized that she still hadn't spoken to Daniel. She'd texted him from the sheriff's department, just to check in, but he'd never responded.

Whenever she and Daniel were apart, even when they were working, they'd always talked to each other on the phone before they went to bed. Every night. Without fail.

160

Her heart sank. Was Daniel already asleep?

Wyatt pulled into the space directly across from her motel room and cut the engine.

"Good night," she said to him in a loud voice, just in case someone was watching and listening.

Unlocking the door to her original room, she went inside. She stopped and scanned the space around the beds. Then she checked the vanity area and bathroom. Nothing seemed disturbed. If the stalker had been in the room today, he'd left no trace behind.

She grabbed her toiletries, night gown, and the clothes she planned to wear the next morning. When she unlocked the connecting door between the two rooms, Wyatt was already standing there waiting for her.

He must have seen the sadness in her eyes and mistook it for worry. "We're going to catch the guy," he told her. "We always do. He got lucky tonight, but his luck will run out soon."

"I know," she said, passing by Wyatt as she crossed the threshold.

But right now, Ashley wasn't thinking about the stalker. She was thinking about Daniel. Wondering what could be going on. She knew that he'd been working a human trafficking case. Maybe the horrors of the investigation were weighing on him. She told herself that he was probably even more exhausted tonight than she was. Maybe that was the reason he'd forgotten to call. And yet …

"Good night," Wyatt told her, pushing his side of the connecting door closed.

Ashley dumped her belongings on the bed and pulled out her cell phone. She tapped out a text.

I missed talking to you tonight.

I hope you're okay.

Please call me when you can.

She stripped off her cargo jacket and grabbed her toothbrush. As she headed toward the vanity area, her cell phone rang. When she saw Daniel's name on the screen, her heart soared.

"Hi, Daniel," she said, overjoyed to finally speak with him.

"Hey."

His voice sounded flat. She wondered if he was still working. Maybe that was the reason he hadn't called until now. He could be on a stakeout.

"I've been thinking about you all day long."

161

He didn't answer. Had the connection dropped?

"Daniel?"

"I'm here," he finally said.

There was something strange in his tone. Something she couldn't pinpoint.

"Where are you?" she asked him.

"Home."

It wasn't the answer she'd expected. Maybe he'd just pulled into his driveway.

"Did you work late tonight?"

Again, he hesitated. "Ashley," he began. "I think we need to take a step back."

A step back?

Her stomach knotted.

"What do you mean?"

Daniel sighed. "Maybe we rushed into this too fast. I think we should take some time apart. Make sure it's what we both really want."

Ashley felt as though she'd been punched in the chest. That she'd had the wind knocked out of her. She wanted to ask him why. To make him tell her what had gone wrong. But she couldn't find her voice. She struggled to breathe.

Tears stung her eyes. She stood silent as they spilled down her cheeks.

"Ashley?"

She forced herself to speak, injecting a note of nonchalance into her tone. "Okay."

It was the only word she could get out. She knew her voice would fail her if she tried to say anything more.

"Be careful in Fergus County," he told her. "We can talk again when you get home."

And then Daniel ended the call.

Ashley dropped her toothbrush back into her toiletry bag. Still fully dressed, she climbed onto the bed and curled into a ball. Sobs racked her body. It felt as though the whole world was shattering around her.

Now more than ever, she knew that she'd fallen deeply in love with Daniel.

He was the man she wanted to marry. The man she wanted to raise children with. The man she wanted to grow old beside.

She couldn't imagine her future without Daniel in it.

But it was clear that he didn't feel the same.

A rapping noise cut through her sobs. She sat up. It was Wyatt knocking on the connecting door. She yanked a tissue from the box on the nightstand and wiped her face.

Taking a deep breath, she tried to calm herself down. She opened the door.

"I forgot my—" Worry took hold of Wyatt's face. "Ashley? What's wrong? What happened? Is your father okay?"

Although she fought hard to hold them back, fresh tears streamed down Ashley's cheeks.

Wyatt reached for her hands. He wrapped his fingers around hers.

"Talk to me," he said.

CHAPTER THIRTY SIX

Choking back a sob, Ashley pulled her hands from Wyatt's grasp and stepped away from the door connecting the two motel rooms. She realized that he'd only reached out in an attempt to comfort her, as any friend would. But somehow, letting him touch her in such a familiar way felt wrong. Especially now.

He followed her as she moved toward the sink in the vanity area. "Tell me what happened, Ashley," he said, his voice soft. "Let me help you."

She turned on the cold-water tap, grabbed a washcloth, and held it beneath the icy stream. She couldn't tell Wyatt about Daniel. Couldn't explain that her heart had been ripped to shreds.

Ashley struggled to find her voice. "I can't talk about it," she squeaked out, her gaze fixed on the washcloth. "Not now."

He inched closer to her. She hoped that he wouldn't touch her again. If he did, she knew the dam would break. A flood of tears would come rushing forth.

"Is it Daniel Lansing?"

Ashley pressed her eyes closed. Just hearing Daniel's name rocked her to her core.

What had gone wrong?

He'd seemed so happy while they were together. They'd connected on a level deeper than Ashley had believed possible. They'd complemented each other in so many ways and had so much in common. Her love for him was stronger than any she'd ever known.

It was a different kind of love. It was all encompassing. Physical, emotional, and spiritual.

She knew that she'd upset him when she'd mentioned Melody, reminding him of his ex-wife's affair. But she thought that they'd gotten past that. He hadn't brought the subject up again. Was he comparing the two relationships? Had he noticed something in Ashley that led him to believe that they could never be happy together? Did she and Melody share similar traits?

Caught up in the excitement of the way Daniel had made her feel, it was possible that Ashley had been ignoring the cold, hard truth. Had she projected her own wants and desires onto him? Believing that she saw something in his eyes that wasn't really there?

Maybe Daniel just didn't love her.

Maybe he'd realized that he never could.

She opened her eyes, allowing the tears to fall. "Yes, it's Daniel."

"Has he been hurt?"

Ashley could hear the concern in Wyatt's voice. He wasn't just asking to be polite.

Shaking her head, she met Wyatt's gaze in the mirror. "It's over," she stated, her voice faltering.

A sudden understanding crossed his face. Wyatt stepped even closer. "I'm sorry," he said.

It sounded as though he really meant it.

He placed his hand on her arm.

His touch seared her like a hot iron.

"No," Ashley said, backing away from him. "Please, don't."

She could tell by the look on Wyatt's face that the rebuff had hurt his feelings. She hadn't meant to seem so ungrateful. But the thought of allowing Wyatt to console her scared Ashley. She feared that if she opened up to him, he'd want to take things too far.

"I know you're just trying to support me right now," she told him. "And I appreciate it—I really do. But I need to be alone for a little while."

He nodded, his eyes filled with compassion. "If you need me … Well, you know where I am. Just wake me up. It doesn't matter what time it is."

He passed back through the connecting door into his own room.

Ashley pushed the door on her side closed and slid the deadbolt lock into place. She'd have to be more careful than ever around Wyatt now. She should never have let him know that she was single. But it was too late. She'd just have to face the consequences as they came.

If Wyatt decided to hit on her, she'd ask Brenda for a new partner.

She returned to the sink and washed her face. The cold water shocked her hot, swollen eyes. But it didn't do her any good. The second she wiped away her tears, new ones sprouted. She dropped the washcloth into the sink.

Her vision blurry, Ashley stumbled back toward the bed. Not bothering to change from her jeans into her nightgown, she fell onto the mattress and curled herself into a ball again. She pulled one of the pillows to her chest, burrowing deep into it, trying not to think about Daniel or what he'd said on the phone. But his words still echoed in her mind, replaying over and over again.

Maybe we rushed into this too fast.

We need to take a step back.

Maybe it's not what we really want.

A relationship with her might not be what Daniel wanted, but it was the only relationship Ashley ever cared about having. If she could no longer be with him, she didn't want to be with anyone. Not romantically. She'd devote her life to her work. Fulfill herself in other ways.

She knew deep in her heart that she could never love anyone as much as she loved Daniel.

It would be foolish for her to even try.

Ashley lay on her side, her tears soaking into the pillowcase.

Exhaustion overtook her, pulling her into a sleep filled with dreams of Daniel. Images of them building a home together, of babies bouncing on their knees, of them pledging to love each other forever.

A loud noise jerked her awake.

She glanced at the clock on the nightstand. 6:15 a.m.

The noise rang out again. It was Wyatt, knocking on the connecting door.

Stretching, she peeled herself from the bed. Her eyes felt swollen and grainy. Her throat ached. So did her head, her shoulder, and her jaw.

She shuffled to the door and pulled it open. Wyatt stood before her, his arms laden with brown paper bags.

"What is all this?" she asked.

He glided past her. "Breakfast."

He piled the bags on top of the scarred motel desk. Then he scooted the desk next to the bed. He began unloading the bags. He'd obviously visited the diner down the street.

"We've got pancakes, maple syrup, bacon, eggs, hash browns, biscuits, and southern gravy." He smiled at her. "Oh, I'll be right back."

Wyatt disappeared through the doorway. When he returned, he was carrying a tray stuffed with four large Styrofoam cups.

"Orange juice and coffee," he said.

Ashley couldn't believe that he'd gone to so much trouble. "Thank you."

She didn't really feel like eating. But she would force herself to take a bite or two just to let him know that she appreciated his effort.

He arranged Ashley's plate so that she could sit on the side of the bed to eat, while he sank down across from her in the desk chair.

He handed her a packet of plastic ware.

As she poked at her eggs, she heard Wyatt's cell phone ring.

He checked the screen. "It's Brenda."

"Clark," he said into the phone.

Ashley tried to make out the deputy director's words echoing across the line, but all she could hear was a muffled jumble of syllables.

Wyatt answered in the affirmative a couple of times, then he ended the call.

He met Ashley's gaze. "We've got a trace on the Taser," he said.

CHAPTER THIRTY SEVEN

Ashley shifted in the passenger seat of the SUV and yanked her phone from the cargo pocket of her jacket. Her heart sank as she checked the screen. No new messages. Phantom phone syndrome had struck her hard. Several times since they'd left the motel, she'd been certain that she felt her phone vibrating. When in actuality, it was her fierce desire to receive a text from Daniel that had sparked the sensation.

She wondered what he was doing. Was he thinking of her? Probably not. After all, he was the one who wanted to take a step back. She just hoped that he was taking care of himself and that he was safe.

With a sigh, she stuffed the phone back into her pocket and leaned her head against the side window. The scenery on the highway to Peck County whipped by in a blur. She and Wyatt were heading back to Boswell's house.

She heard a cell phone ring. This time it was real. It was Wyatt's phone.

"Clark," he answered.

She wondered whether it was Brenda. Or maybe it was Sheriff Hyland. Ashley jerked her gaze toward Wyatt, searching his face. She hoped that the sheriff's deputies hadn't found the bodies of Cole and Jerry. Wyatt's expression didn't give anything away.

"Got it," he said into the phone.

He met Ashley's gaze as he ended the call. "That was Brenda," he said. "The judge okayed the search warrant for Boswell's house."

The TBI forensic techs and the DID team wouldn't arrive in Peck County until the afternoon. But Ashley and Wyatt needed to get inside of Boswell's house now. It wasn't marijuana that they were hoping to find.

The TBI had run a trace on the Anti-felon ID tags shot from the Taser at Jerry's house. The serial number matched a shipment sent to the police academy in Peck County. The entire shipment had been reported stolen.

168

They'd learned that the police academy was located on the campus of the state university. And they already knew that Cole—and therefore Boswell—catered to the university students. It wasn't a huge leap to suspect that Boswell had stolen the Tasers. Or had paid someone to steal them for him.

The fact that a Taser had been used to disable Jerry, and that there was no evidence he'd been shot with a firearm, gave Ashley hope that he and Cole were still alive.

Open farmland gave way to forest as the SUV crested the hill and approached the road where Boswell lived. Wyatt glanced at Ashley as he eased into the turn.

He didn't say anything, but she knew what he was thinking. He was wondering how she was holding up. And whether or not her job performance would suffer due to her broken heart. In all honesty, she wasn't sure. It was more important to her than ever to find Cole and Jerry, but her thoughts kept swinging back to Daniel. She knew that she had to find a way to shake off her despondency and focus her attention back onto the investigation.

The ranch-style house with beige vinyl siding popped into view on her right. Wyatt piloted the SUV up the gravel driveway and killed the engine. An image of Logan, his eyes filled with a mixture of fear and hatred and his fingers tight around the pistol's grip, flashed in Ashley's mind. She wondered about the child's current emotional state. And how his father's criminal activity and incarceration would affect Logan in the long run. She prayed that he'd be able to put it all behind him and lead a productive and successful life.

"Sarah told me that the spare key is hanging from a nail on the maple tree next to the garage," Ashley said.

When Ashley had met Logan's mother at the sheriff's department the prior night, she'd told Sarah that the TBI would be conducting a search of the property. Sarah had volunteered the information regarding the key so the forensic techs wouldn't have to break inside.

"I'll get it," Wyatt told her. "Does it fit the front door or the back?"

"The front," she said as she strode toward the porch.

As she climbed the steps, Ashley could hear music from the television drifting through the panes of the front window. She'd forgotten to turn the TV off when she'd left with Logan the night before.

A minute later, Wyatt joined her. He unlocked the door.

As it had the prior evening, the odor of marijuana wafted toward her as Ashley crossed the threshold into the living room. She guessed some smells lingered in the air and clung to furniture longer than others. Or maybe she was just overly sensitive to it. It seemed to be the odors she hated that she noticed the most, even when they were faint. It was the same with tobacco smoke.

Ashley veered right and headed into the hallway. If Boswell had stashed the Tasers at his house, they'd most likely find the weapons in the master bedroom, the master-bedroom closet, or maybe the garage.

The first room she encountered was set up like an office. A metal desk with a glass top stood against the far wall. A soothing picture of a waterfall graced the screen of Boswell's computer resting on the desk. Ashley fished a pair of latex gloves from her pocket and pulled them on. She sank into the office chair and slid her finger across the laptop's touchpad. A password prompt popped up.

She felt Wyatt peering over her shoulder.

"No snooping today," he said, disappointment in his tone. "I'm going to check out the next room."

Ashley nodded.

They'd have to wait for the IT techs to find out what was contained in Boswell's computer files. Ashley noticed a black wire basket to the right of the laptop. Receipts in various colors and sizes spilled over the side of the basket. The paper on top caught her attention.

It was a receipt from Buc-ee's, a convenience store chain that featured a beaver as its mascot. She studied the black print. The receipt was for the purchase of gasoline and snacks at the location in Calhoun, Georgia.

A jolt of surprise struck her when she spotted the date. The purchases had been made the Friday Cole had disappeared. The timestamp read 3:24 p.m. If Boswell was the person who had made the purchases, he couldn't have abducted Cole.

Ashley snapped a photo of the receipt with her cell phone and then sealed the paper inside of an evidence bag.

She wandered farther down the hallway. The next room belonged to Logan. Decorated in blue, the room reflected the young boy's love of sports. Several pictures of Logan dressed in a baseball uniform hung on the walls. There was also a poster of the Tennessee Titan's logo and a poster featuring Smokey, the Bluetick hound that was the mascot for the Tennessee Vols.

170

After leaving Logan's room, she found Wyatt in the master bedroom.

He sat on the carpet next to the bed, an open cardboard box in front of him.

"Have you found anything interesting?" she asked him.

"Just a bunch of junk."

He replaced the lid on the box and slid it beneath the bed.

"I found something," she told Wyatt. "I think that Boswell was at the Buc-ee's in Calhoun, Georgia, buying gas at the same time Cole disappeared."

Wyatt shot her a frustrated look. "Another suspect down."

"We might still find the Tasers here. Just because Boswell was in Georgia doesn't mean he's not the mastermind behind the abductions."

Wyatt sighed as he stood up. "I'll check the closet."

"Okay, I'm going to head out to the garage."

As Ashley started to walk back out of the master bedroom, she heard Wyatt's cell phone ring. She stopped and turned around, but he'd already disappeared through the doorway to the master bathroom. She decided to continue her search. If the call was important, Wyatt would let her know.

Boswell's black Ford sedan sat parked in the two-car garage. She doubted that he'd hide the Tasers inside the vehicle, but she decided to check, nonetheless. The doors were locked. The only thing she could see inside the car was a black leather jacket draped across the rear seat.

A white chest-type freezer stood against the garage's far wall. Ashley feared opening it. Visions of the bodies of Cole and Jerry, their faces covered in ice, assaulted her mind. Her pulse quickened as she moved toward the freezer.

Taking a deep breath, Ashley lifted the lid.

Packages wrapped in white paper, labeled as beef and venison, crowded the space. No dead bodies. Relieved, she let the lid slam shut.

She didn't see any boxes located in the garage. Only a standing metal shelf lined with power tools.

Ashley jumped as she heard the door to the house creak open behind her.

Wyatt poked his head inside the garage.

A worried expression clouded his face. "Come on, Ashley," he said. "We have to hurry and get back to Fergus County."

Ashley's heart skipped a beat. Something had happened. Had the sheriff's deputies found Cole and Jerry—dead?

"Has someone else—"

"Yeah."

CHAPTER THIRTY EIGHT

The white southern colonial with stately columns standing at the top of the slope reminded Ashley of Tara from the movie, *Gone With the Wind*. As Wyatt steered his vehicle onto the home's long, gravel driveway, she spotted Sheriff Hyland's cruiser up ahead, parked next to a blue sedan. A dark gray sedan and a silver Toyota SUV were parked in front of the blue car.

Wyatt had received a call from Hyland while he and Ashley were searching Boswell's house. Another man had been reported missing. They didn't know many details yet. Only that Alden Rayburn was thirty-two years old and was a licensed CPA. His wife, Grace, had called in the report.

Acting on the side of caution, concerned that Alden might somehow be connected with Cole and Jerry, Hyland had requested Wyatt and Ashley's assistance.

"Do you think Alden could have been helping Jerry launder money through the dairy farm?" Ashley asked Wyatt.

"I'd say there's a good chance."

Too high of a profit on the dairy farm would likely prompt an audit from the IRS. It was no secret that the government agency flagged income that seemed outside the norm for a certain industry. Washing the funds from the marijuana operation would likely require more than a dash of creative accounting.

Wyatt braked his SUV to a halt, parking behind Hyland's cruiser.

As Ashley slid out of the passenger seat, she spotted the sheriff and Deputy Kelton as they emerged from behind the rear corner of the colonial.

Ashley and Wyatt shook the lawmen's hands in a greeting.

"This could go either way." Hyland stated. "No sign of a struggle, but something feels off. I don't think Alden just up and left on his own."

Wyatt nodded. "You were right to call us, sheriff. Three missing people in one county in just a few days … They almost have to be connected."

Hyland motioned toward the pasture at the rear of the property. "Kelton and I are gonna nose around the old barn. Grace and her sister, Faith, are waiting for y'all in the house."

Ashley strode up the brick pathway leading to the colonial's wide front porch with Wyatt close behind. A pretty blonde woman who appeared to be in her early thirties met them at the front door.

"I'm Faith," she said. "Come on inside."

Both Ashley and Wyatt donned protective shoe covers before stepping across the threshold.

A plastic drop cloth draped the floor of the home's foyer. A tall stepladder stood to Ashley's right. Paint cans and brushes surrounded the base of the ladder. It appeared as though restorations on the historic home were well underway.

Wyatt introduced himself and Ashley.

Faith steered them toward the dining room on the left. "There's something you should know," she said, her voice hushed. "Grace is in a fragile state right now. I realize you have to ask her certain questions. The wife is always the main suspect in these situations, right? But please be gentle. She's recovering from a miscarriage. And now with Alden gone, I think she's just about to reach her breaking point."

Ashley could understand how Grace felt. She'd suffered through two miscarriages of her own. The pain of the loss was difficult to fully explain to someone who hadn't experienced it themselves.

Wyatt said, "We'll keep that in mind."

Faith nodded and led them back through the foyer and then into a living room at the rear of the house. Grace, a younger version of her sister, rose up from a cranberry-upholstered, wingback chair as they entered the room. Although the woman was wearing makeup, her skin appeared pale, her eyes puffy.

Again, Wyatt made the introductions. "We're sorry about your husband's disappearance," he said.

"Thank you. I just don't understand what could have happened. Where he could have gone."

Grace directed Wyatt and Ashley to take a seat on the sofa. She resumed her perch on the chair. Instead of sitting, Faith slid in behind the wingback, standing guard over her younger sister.

174

Ashley noticed a family photo resting on top of an end table. A dark-haired man, who she assumed to be Alden, sat on what appeared to be a park bench. His arm draped Grace's shoulders, and they each held a toddler in their lap. Twin girls, dressed in matching yellow sundresses.

Wyatt asked, "When did you last see Alden?"

"It was on Saturday morning. Right before I left to go visit Faith in Nashville. Alden and I ate breakfast just before eight o'clock and then I left home with our twins around nine."

Sheriff Hyland had said that there were no apparent signs of a struggle inside the colonial. But with Grace in Nashville, it was possible that Alden could have been abducted from his home.

"And when did you speak last?"

A look of apprehension crossed Grace's face as though she had information that she would prefer not to share. "The truth is, Alden and I were arguing. He called me once on Saturday afternoon, but I didn't answer. I just let it go to voicemail. I was still angry, and I just didn't feel like talking to him. I guess you could say that I was giving him the silent treatment."

"Did he leave a message?"

Grace shook her head. "No."

If Grace hadn't heard from Alden since Saturday afternoon, then the man might have been missing for four days. A lot could have happened to him in that length of time.

Ashley glanced at Wyatt. "Do you mind telling us what you and Alden were arguing about?" she asked.

Grace sighed. "Money. Alden was upset that the repairs on the house had gone over budget. He just can't understand that we're building a future here. It's more than just a house. It's the place where our children will grow up. It represents love and security."

Due to his line of work, Ashley wasn't surprised to learn that the accountant's concerns over the financial investment of the repairs outweighed any emotional attachment he might have to the home. His job revolved around balance sheets and profit and loss reports.

"So, you didn't know that Alden was missing until you returned from Nashville this morning?"

Grace's gaze dropped to the floor. Ashley realized that something else was going on.

175

Faith interrupted, "You need to tell them everything, Grace. It's the only way that they can help you."

The woman sat silent for a moment as though she was waging a war in her mind. Struggling to find the right words to explain her situation.

Grace lifted her head and met Ashley's gaze.

A haunted look shone in her eyes.

Ashley had no idea what the woman was about to reveal.

CHAPTER THIRTY NINE

Perched on the sofa in the living room of the southern colonial, Ashley leaned toward Grace, studying the woman's eyes. Grace's haunted expression revealed that the argument she'd had with her missing husband concerning their finances wasn't the only thing weighing on her mind. It appeared as though she might be harboring a family secret.

Faith circled around to the side of the cranberry-colored wingback chair where Grace sat. She placed her hand on her sister's shoulder.

"Go ahead, Grace," she said. "Tell them."

The woman held her silence a few seconds longer.

Ashley and Wyatt exchanged glances. Did Grace know the identity of the person who had abducted Alden?

Grace inhaled deep, her breath audible as though she was steeling herself for the fallout from the information she was planning to share.

"I know I didn't call the sheriff's department until this morning," she began. "But I came home from Nashville yesterday and found out that Alden was gone."

Why had the woman waited so long to notify the authorities? There had to be a reason.

Faith prompted her sister, "Tell them why, honey."

Grace's bottom lip trembled. "I thought maybe Alden was done with me. With our family—our babies. I thought he had left with Suzette."

Ashley glanced at Wyatt again. "Suzette?"

"My husband had an affair last year. He swore to me that it was over, but that's the first thing that popped into my mind when I came home and realized that he wasn't here."

It made sense. It seemed natural for Grace to think Alden had left her of his own free will. Kidnappings of adults weren't all that common. Especially not in a small town like Arbuckle.

"What made you decide that there was foul play involved?"

"Well, for one thing, I searched Alden's study. He'd left his cell phone on the charger. And his car was still here, so I figured Suzette had picked him up. I had it in my head that they'd flown to Tahiti or somewhere. I looked through all of his desk drawers and through all of the files on his computer. I couldn't find any plane or hotel reservations. I checked our closet and none of his clothes were missing, but I was still sure he was with Suzette."

Grace paused for a moment as though sorting through her memories. She continued, "I called Shelton's Drug Store—Suzette's a pharmacist—and asked to speak to her. She wasn't there. And then, I let my emotions get the best of me. I acted like a crazy person."

Ashley wondered whether Grace had committed a crime of her own. Had she slashed Suzette's tires?

"What exactly did you do?"

"I took the twins over to my mother's and then I drove to Suzette's house. I sat in my car across the street until two o'clock this morning, waiting to see if she would come home. And she finally did. And she wasn't alone."

The details were starting to confuse Ashley. Grace had said that she'd last seen her husband on Saturday morning, but it was beginning to sound as though she'd caught Alden with Suzette last night.

"Who was she with?"

"Her best friend's husband. When I saw what they were doing, I knew that I'd been wrong about Alden. That's when I started to really worry. I stopped by the hospital emergency room and made sure that he wasn't there. And this morning, at first light, I started calling all of his family and friends. Finally, I realized that I had to get the sheriff involved."

Although Grace had wasted a lot of time—hours that could have been spent on a proper investigation—Ashley could empathize. She understood the woman's seemingly unhinged actions. She remembered how frantic she'd felt when she'd discovered her fiancé, Brett, was cheating on her.

"Did you notice anything odd about the house when you came home?"

Grace shook her head. "Just that it was empty. I mean, that Alden wasn't here. None of our valuables are missing or anything like that."

Ashley had something specific in mind. "Had your electricity been turned off?"

A shocked expression ran through Grace's eyes. "How did you know that? I didn't tell the sheriff. I didn't think that it was important."

"Was it switched off at the breaker box?"

She nodded. "We've had a lot of problems with the old wiring in the house. The breakers have tripped by themselves before. Are you telling me that you think someone turned the electricity off on purpose?"

They now had a solid piece of physical evidence linking Alden's disappearance with Jerry's. Whoever had abducted the men had used the darkness to their advantage. Ashley believed the culprit had likely worn night vision goggles to apprehend his victims.

"We think that it might be a possibility." Ashley didn't want to give away too much information. She realized that there might be other physical evidence in the house that had been overlooked. "Would it be all right with you if Wyatt and I took a tour of the house?"

"Of course."

"Do we have your permission to search through your husband's study?"

Ashley wanted to find out whether Jerry's name would appear in Alden's computer files.

"You can look at anything you want," Grace told her. "Anything that you think might help you find Alden. His computer password is our twins' birthday. November 30, with the month spelled out in letters."

"Okay, thank you," Ashley said. "And we'll leave everything exactly the way that we found it."

It was difficult enough to have a stranger paw through your belongings. She didn't want Grace to worry that they would leave a mess behind.

Grace nodded. "If the two of you don't mind, I think I'm going to go upstairs and lie down for a while. If you need something, just ask Faith."

Grace needed to rest. She'd been up the entire previous night.

Ashley rose from the sofa. Wyatt followed as she wandered out of the living room, crossed a rear hallway, and entered the adjacent kitchen. The renovations appeared to be complete here. New cabinets and marble countertops had been installed along with high-end stainless-steel appliances.

Circling the kitchen, she entered a short hallway with doors on each side. She pushed open the door to her right. The room housed a washer, dryer, and laundry sink. Nothing seemed out of place.

Wyatt's voice echoed behind her in the hallway.

"Ashley," he called out. "Come and look at this."

The door opposite the laundry room led into a large pantry. White candles littered the floor next to an empty cardboard box. Grace must not have cooked any meals since she'd been home. She probably hadn't ventured into the pantry.

After snapping photos of the scene with her cell phone, Ashley pulled a pair of latex gloves from her pocket and slipped them on. Using her fingertips, she picked up one of the candles. She noticed something was stuck to the wax on the underside.

Two pink dots. Mylar anti-felon ID tags shot from a Taser.

Her pulse quickened as she lifted the empty cardboard box. Several of the pink and yellow tags lay on the floor beneath it.

"There's no doubt about it now," she said. "The same person who kidnapped Jerry also took Alden."

Wyatt nodded. "I'll call Brenda and ask her to send the techs out."

Ashley moved past Wyatt and back out into the short hallway. She crossed through the dining room and then ended up back in the foyer. A pair of French doors stood open near the tall stepladder. She could see built-in bookcases inside. It must be Alden's study.

She eased across the threshold.

Alden's laptop computer rested on the surface of an antique cherry desk. Still wearing her latex gloves, Ashley sank down into the leather office chair. She clicked the external mouse plugged into the computer and a password prompt appeared on the screen.

She typed in the twins' birthday.

The photo of a sunlit beach dissolved, replaced by Alden's desktop. Ashley heard footsteps in the foyer. Wyatt strode thought the study's doorway. "Find anything yet?" he asked.

Ashley worked fast, but not that fast. "I just now started looking."

The icons on Alden's desktop had all been arranged alphabetically. A sense of déjà vu hit Ashley. Her ex-fiancé, Brett, organized his desktop the same way. And although he wasn't a CPA, Brett also worked in finance. She wondered whether Alden's shirts were arranged in his closet by color. Another quirk Brett possessed.

Pushing the thoughts of her past aside, Ashley clicked the icon for Alden's accounting app. When the password prompt popped up, she again entered the twins' birthday.

Invalid Password.

Maybe Ashley had hit a wrong key. She tried again, making sure that she entered the birthday exactly the way Grace had instructed.

Invalid Password.

Maybe Alden had only given Grace the computer's main password and not the key to his work data. It made sense that he would want to keep his clients' financial information confidential.

But Ashley wasn't ready to give up quite yet. She typed in the date using alternate formats. All numbers. All letters. The day first, and then the month. She entered every possible combination, but none of them worked.

Wyatt was peering over her shoulder at the screen. "Now what?"

A filing cabinet stood against the wall to the right of the desk. Did Alden keep a physical file on his clients? It seemed old-school for a modern accountant, but then Ashley reminded herself that Alden's personality appeared similar to Brett's. And Brett always kept a backup of everything. Just in case.

Swiveling the leather chair, Ashley stood and marched toward the cabinet. She grasped the handle of the top drawer. The cabinet was locked.

"If you were an ISTJ personality type, where would you hide your filing cabinet key?"

Wyatt shot her a blank look. "If I was a what?"

He obviously wasn't familiar with the Myers-Briggs Personality Test.

"The acronym stands for introverted, sensing, thinking, and judging. We're dealing with a person who is highly organized and makes most of their decisions based on logic and reason."

"Yeah. Now I see why you have a master's degree, and I don't."

She smiled. "Help me find the key."

Together, Ashley and Wyatt scoured the study. They searched through all of the drawers in the desk, checking underneath each one. They looked behind the filing cabinet, thinking the key might be taped to the back. It wasn't. They even searched through the bookshelf for a fake book. They couldn't find the key anywhere.

Wyatt finally said, "Why don't we just ask Grace?"

Ashley stared at him.

His lips curved into a grin. "Yeah, now we see who uses their logic skills."

Ashley mirrored his smile. And then she remembered something she'd seen in the kitchen.

"I think I might know where Alden keeps the key," she said.

She headed back out through the study door. Wyatt followed.

A small, framed blackboard hung on the kitchen wall near the refrigerator. A series of hooks lined the bottom. Two keyrings dangled from the hooks.

"Okay, Mr. Logic," Ashley said. "Which key ring belongs to Alden?"

"That's easy. Grace hauls the kids around. And I'll bet she does the grocery shopping. So the Toyota SUV belongs to her. Alden drives the sedan."

Ashley had already made the same determination. But she had an advantage. She'd seen the children's car seats strapped inside the SUV.

She grabbed Alden's key ring and headed back into the study. The second key she tried slid into the filing cabinet's lock.

The top drawer clicked open.

As she'd hoped, the cabinet was filled with hanging file folders, one for each of Alden's clients. She ran her hand toward the back. She paused at the last names beginning with the letter *M* first.

A wave of disappointment struck her. "There's no file in here for Tim and Vera Mansfield."

But that didn't necessarily mean anything. Alden might not be handling the Mansfields' personal finances. If Tim and Vera were running the proceeds from their weed growing operation through the dairy farm, then Alden should have a folder for Jerry and Marilyn Osborne instead. Ashley searched through all of the folders labeled with last names beginning with the letter *O*.

There was no folder for Jerry.

Had Ashley been wrong? Were they laundering the funds some other way? If so, then why was Jerry involved with the Mansfields? It didn't make sense. Maybe Jerry used another accountant. But if that was the case, then why had Alden been abducted?

Ashley sighed. Her head was beginning to ache along with her shoulder. What connection was she missing?

She rifled through the file folders one last time.

182

Ashley gasped when she spotted a familiar name. "Wyatt, we're finished here for now," she said. "There's someplace else that we need to go."

CHAPTER FORTY

The man shoved the toe of his boot into Scarlett's side.

"Wake up," he shouted.

She'd been sleeping a lot. He guessed that it was because she'd fallen and smacked her head on the corner of the laundry sink after he'd zapped her with the Taser. The gash on her forehead could use a couple of stitches. But it didn't matter. She wouldn't live long enough for the wound to heal.

He kicked her again, harder this time.

Scarlett's eyelids fluttered open.

She moaned, but the sound was softer than a whisper. Muffled by the gag in her mouth.

"What's that?" the man asked. "Can't hear ya."

He laughed as he peered down at her.

Lying on the cold, hardwood floor of his bedroom, Scarlett twisted her body, fighting against her restraints. She should know by now that she couldn't break free.

"You ain't got nobody to blame but yourself," he told her. "You started this. And now Toby is gonna finish it."

Scarlett moaned again.

The terror in her eyes sent a shiver of excitement coursing through the man's body.

He'd enjoyed every second of their time together since he'd kidnapped her the day before. Explaining in great detail exactly what was going to happen to her. He'd kept her next to his bed so that he could wake her several times during the night and remind her of her fate once again. And each time he told her what Toby was going to do, he felt the burden in his soul grow a little lighter.

"Jerry talked about you before he died. You wanna know what he told me? He said 'that whore ain't worth it.' That's what he thought of you. That you ain't nothing but a low-down, dirty whore. He never gave a shit about you."

Scarlett grunted as the man slammed his foot into her shoulder.

Tears ran down her cheeks. He wasn't sure whether they were spurred by pain or by fear. Probably both.

"You had it so good, but you gave it all up. You ain't nothing but a fool. And now, you're gonna pay. Did you really think I'd let you take what's mine?"

The man ripped the gag out of her mouth. He wanted to hear her beg again. Like she had last night, when she'd promised him everything under the sun, thinking she could make a deal.

"Please," Scarlett sobbed. "Let me go. I'll come back. We can work things out. Remember how it used to be? You and me can be happy again."

"You think I'm stupid? If I don't give you to Toby, you'll run straight to the cops."

He knew Scarlett would have him thrown into jail the first chance she got.

She shook her head. "I won't tell nobody. I promise."

"You lying whore."

Anger surged in his chest. He drew back his foot and kicked her in the ribs. Hard.

Scarlett screamed.

Kneeling down, he tightened the gag back around her mouth.

He wished that he could stay and torture Scarlett more, but the man had to leave. He had to get everything ready for Toby.

CHAPTER FORTY ONE

Ashley's thoughts raced as she climbed into the passenger seat of the SUV, struggling to fit all of the puzzle pieces together. The facts in the case seemed to center on the marijuana farm. Cole was connected to Boswell who worked as a middleman for Tim and Vera Mansfield.

Jerry was obviously linked to his neighbors' enterprise as well. Otherwise, Marilyn wouldn't have argued with the Mansfields about the delivery to Alabama, and she wouldn't have accused Tim of harming Jerry. It stood to reason that Jerry and Marilyn were laundering the proceeds from the weed growing operation through their dairy farm.

But how did Alden fit in?

Why would the accountant be abducted? There was nothing in his files linking him to Cole, or to Jerry, or to the Mansfields.

But he had a connection to someone else. A person also linked to Cole.

What if the dairy farm wasn't the only business the Mansfields used to launder their funds?

The SUV lurched as Wyatt pulled out onto the highway and slammed the accelerator.

Ashley glanced at her partner. "I really thought that there was a war being fought between the Mansfields and another weed grower," she said.

"Yeah, me too."

But now, it seemed that the real battle existed between the two parties cleaning the ill-gotten proceeds. Maybe one of them believed the pie wasn't big enough to be split.

Wyatt chewed his bottom lip. Ashley could see the gears in his mind turning.

"Tim and Vera probably divided the cash up fifty-fifty," he said. "Just so that they wouldn't have to worry about the IRS."

Ashley agreed with his assumption. If the dairy farm's income increased by too large of an amount, it would trigger an audit. The earnings from the Osbornes' farm had to remain in line with all of the other profitable dairies scattered throughout the United States.

A thought struck her. "I'll bet that the dairy farm wasn't the original place where the Mansfields funneled their money. It was likely added on as their weed business grew."

Wyatt nodded. "The money is the motive."

"Right," she said. "The Mansfields likely paid each business a percentage of the actual funds they laundered. That could mean a huge pay cut for the business that helped them start the whole thing."

It all made sense. The guilty party didn't want to shut down the Mansfields' marijuana cultivation farm. Instead, they wanted to eliminate Jerry's money laundering side of the organization. Their goal had been to increase their own profits, not to share the washing process with a newcomer to the game.

"Cole was the first to go," Wyatt reminded her. "Do you think he knew about the plan to take Jerry out?"

Ashley pondered the question for a moment. She guessed that it was possible that Cole had overheard something he shouldn't have. After learning of the plot, he could have threatened to alert Jerry and the Mansfields. But her instincts nagged at her. Her gut whispered that the motive for Cole's disappearance ran deeper.

"It wouldn't surprise me a bit if Cole's abduction ended up being about something a little more personal," she stated.

The SUV slowed as Wyatt veered into the next turn.

"What's your theory on Alden?" he asked her.

The thought had occurred to Ashley that it was possible the accountant wasn't actually involved in the money laundering scheme.

"I think Alden is probably really good at his job," she said. "And a big swing in the books wouldn't have gone unnoticed. Maybe the loss looked suspicious to him, and he started asking questions. Maybe Alden got a little too close to the truth about what was really going on."

But if Ashley's theory proved to be correct, then that would mean that she'd been right about something else as well. Since the beginning of the investigation, her instincts had told her that Cole was dead, but she'd refused to let herself believe it. She'd held out hope that she and Wyatt would find the man safe and would bring him back home to his mother. But now, she was forced to face the fact that the kidnapper had no motive to keep Cole alive.

Ahead on the left, the red-barn mailbox popped into view.

Wyatt steered the SUV onto the long, gravel driveway leading to the home of Jacob Stanley. Ashley didn't see the hog farmer out in the pasture, but his blue pickup rested at the end of the drive next to the white Appalachian farmhouse. The odds ranked high that Stanley was home.

Pulling in behind the pickup, Wyatt threw the transmission into park and cut the SUV's engine.

Overhead, the sky had morphed from crystal blue to drab, gunmetal gray. As the soles of Ashley's hiking boots hit gravel, a clap of thunder echoed through the dormant hardwood trees. A cold gust of wind whipped through the naked branches, tousling her long hair. She could tell that the rain wasn't far away.

Pulling her jacket tight around her, Ashley followed Wyatt up the dirt path leading to the farmhouse's long, narrow front porch. He knocked on the door.

"Mr. Stanley," he called out. "It's Wyatt Clark."

Ashley counted off the seconds, waiting to hear movement inside. The house stood silent.

Balling his fist, Wyatt pounded on the door a second time. "Mr. Stanley?"

Still, there was no answer.

They'd already paid a visit to Jacob Stanley once, to discuss the events that had led up to Cole's disappearance. At the time, Ashley and Wyatt had assumed that the hog farmer was an innocent bystander. They'd given the man no reason to believe that he was a suspect. Stanley had even invited them back, offering the sale of a country ham.

Did the man have a reason to avoid speaking with them now?

The news of the bust at the marijuana grow house had likely reached Stanley. Wyatt and Ashley still didn't know the identity of the person who'd knocked Ashley down. But it wasn't the hog farmer. Although Jacob Stanley stood shorter than five-nine, his girth was too wide for him to be the man who had fled the weed farm. But Ashley felt certain that the Mansfields' employee who had gotten away had spread the word.

Jacob Stanley might realize that he was now in the TBI's crosshairs.

Wyatt stepped back from the door. "You think Stanley's out tending to the animals?"

The idea that the hog farmer was hiding from them had obviously crossed Wyatt's mind as well. Ashley edged closer to the front window of the farmhouse. The blinds had been shut tight. She couldn't get a glimpse inside. Stanley could be standing right in front of her at that very moment and she wouldn't know it.

"I hope that's the reason he hasn't come to the door."

Ashley trotted back down the wooden porch steps. She scanned each window fronting the home, thinking she might catch a glimmer of movement. The house sat still.

She reminded herself that raising pigs was no easy feat. Caring for them required a lot of hard work. It was quite possible that Stanley hadn't heard Wyatt and Ashley arrive. He might be out mending fences or preoccupied with some other farming task.

"I guess there's a good chance that we might find Stanley in the barn," she said.

Wyatt looked at her. "Yeah, but which one?"

A gray, metal barn rested behind the pond and house on the left side of the property. Another larger, older barn—constructed of wood and painted red—stood quite a distance away, on a slope behind and to the right of the farmhouse.

Ashley shrugged. She guessed the odds were even.

Wyatt hopped down off of the porch. "You take the metal barn," he said. "I'll take the red one."

With a nod, Ashley headed around the left corner of the farmhouse.

CHAPTER FORTY TWO

Scarlett's eyes popped open. She'd heard a knocking sound. Someone was at the farmhouse door. A male voice called out, but the man's words were too muffled for her to decipher. If only there was some way that she could attract the person's attention.

She'd already learned that screaming would do no good. The gag in her mouth was too secure. Although she'd shouted at the top of her lungs, time and time again, her cries had been reduced to a whimper.

Desperate to free herself, she struggled against her restraints. Jacob had wrapped duct tape around her wrists so tight, she feared that it would cut off her circulation. He'd bound her ankles the same way. And then he'd hogtied her with another length of tape so that she couldn't stand all the way up. Her muscles had grown stiff from lying on the cold hardwood floor next to her ex-husband's bed.

The bed they used to share.

Before she'd realized that she had married a monster.

A second series of knocks echoed through the house. The man still stood at the front door. Were Ben and Daisy huddled on the porch of the farmhouse? Had they come looking for her?

The hope that her cousin had arrived to rescue Scarlett died in her chest almost as soon as it sparked in her mind. She hadn't met up with her cousin until after she'd already left Jacob. Daisy had no idea where to search for her. And Scarlett hadn't taken on the surname of Stanley when she'd married. Daisy only knew her by her maiden name.

Her cousin had no way to identify Jacob. His first name alone would get her nowhere.

Daisy would probably go to the police. But Scarlett was an adult, and by law, was free to disappear if she wanted to. The Bonner County Sheriff's Department would probably wait twenty-four hours before they even filed a report. By the time the deputies figured out what had happened, it would be too late.

Scarlett needed to rescue herself.

She had to find a way to make a noise. She had to alert the man on the porch to the fact that she was inside and needed help.

The door to the bedroom stood closed, so there was no way she could roll herself out into the hallway and into the living room. She'd have to create a ruckus here and hope that it would be loud enough to penetrate the walls.

A nightstand stood next to the bed. Scarlett scooted her body around, moving her feet toward the headboard. The gash in her forehead throbbed as she inched toward the table. She was pretty sure that the cut had become infected. And she suspected that she had a fever. She might end up dying from her injury. A part of her hoped that she would. A death from infection would prove sweet compared to what Jacob had planned.

When Scarlett thought she was close enough to the small table, within striking range, she stopped and drew her knees up to her chest.

Scarlett slammed her heels against the nightstand.

The table rocked, and the metal-based lamp resting on top crashed to the floor.

Had the noise reached the man's ears? Would he investigate? She prayed that he would. He was her last hope.

Jacob would come back soon. And then he would take her to Toby.

Fear sliced through Scarlett's heart as she remembered all the things Jacob had told her the night before. The way he'd described what had happened to Jerry made her blood run ice cold. Although the man was a criminal—a money launderer like Jacob—Jerry hadn't deserved to be murdered. Especially in such a horrific way.

Laundering the money from the sale of marijuana grown on Tim and Vera Mansfield's farm had been a dream come true for Jacob. He could never make that kind of a living raising hogs. But he hadn't saved any of his payout. Instead, he'd spent it foolishly. He'd even bought a brand-new, blue pickup truck.

When the Mansfields had recruited Jerry and Marilyn Osborne to launder half of the funds through their dairy farm, Jacob had become enraged. And with a huge chunk of his income gone, he'd fallen deep into debt. He'd sworn to shut down the dairy farm.

Scarlett had tried to warn Jerry. At the time, she'd thought Jacob planned to eliminate his competition using other means. She'd had no idea that Jerry's life was in danger. She'd reached out to the dairy farmer and had attempted to set up a meeting. But Jacob had overheard her on the phone. He'd accused Scarlett of having an affair. The beating she'd received from her ex-husband that night had been the last straw. She'd fled to a women's shelter and had filed for divorce.

And Scarlett had almost gotten away.

Almost.

Drawing her legs up to her chest, Scarlett kicked the nightstand again. Harder this time. The table bucked and then toppled to the floor. The impact of the nightstand against the hardwood had reverberated louder than the lighter-weight lamp.

Was it loud enough?

Did the man hear her plea for help?

Straining her ears, Scarlett listened and waited.

CHAPTER FORTY THREE

A bolt of lightning split the western sky as Ashley rounded the corner of Jacob Stanley's Appalachian farmhouse. A storm was brewing, both in the air and in her mind. Her instincts screamed that they'd finally uncovered the identity of the person responsible for the disappearances of Cole, Jerry, and Alden. But all she had was a gut feeling. There was no hard evidence. No physical proof.

Stanley fit the profile. He stood shorter than five-nine. He could have driven Cole's car to Rattler Ridge. And he'd already admitted to meeting Cole on Friday afternoon, just two hours before the process server had vanished.

The hog farmer's motivation to eliminate Jerry and Alden seemed clear. But why would Stanley abduct Cole? Was the theory that Cole had somehow discovered the plot against Jerry correct? Had he threatened to expose Stanley's plans?

Ashley wasn't so sure.

Marilyn had claimed that she didn't even know Cole. And from the woman's body language, Ashley had believed her. Furthermore, Cole's ex-girlfriend had never heard of the Mansfields. And being a grunt in the organization, it was probable that Cole had been kept in the dark regarding both the source of the weed and the methods used for the laundering of the money.

Dealers were often arrested. The Mansfields had employed Boswell as a middleman to shield their identity. They wouldn't divulge information to Cole that he didn't need to know. Information that he could trade to the police to avoid prosecution.

Ashley had realized earlier that Cole acted as a mere pawn in the marijuana trafficking operation. Boswell had likely recruited another dealer to replace him as soon as it became known that Cole was missing. And besides that fact, Cole's absence didn't harm Jerry's money laundering abilities one single bit.

And yet, Cole was gone. Why?

There had to be a logical explanation.

Stanley needed money. He was being sued for the repayment of a debt he owed. It was possible that the farmer had overextended himself when times were good and the money was flowing freely. But then Jerry entered the picture, and Stanley's income had been cut in half.

When Cole had delivered the summons for the lawsuit, it must have angered Stanley. Was it an instance of the proverbial shooting of the messenger? Had he taken out his fury on Cole? Ashley wasn't sure that was the correct answer either.

If Stanley had acted out of rage, wouldn't he have attacked Cole in the moment, at the hog farm? The idea that Stanley would wait, tracking Cole down later near Warwick's trailer, seemed implausible.

Ashley's thoughts continued to whirl as she wound around a maple and skirted the side of the farmhouse. As she neared a window, a loud thump echoed from the building. Ashley froze. Had they guessed wrong regarding Stanley's whereabouts? Was he really hiding inside the house?

She stared at the window, listening.

A gust of wind whipped around her.

Thump! Thump!

Ashley's gaze jerked upward. The naked branches of the maple behind her banged against the roof of the farmhouse. That must have been the noise she'd heard.

A clap of thunder jarred the ground. Ashley hurried toward the barn. She wanted to get inside the metal structure before the rain poured down. Unhooking the chain, she pulled open the steel gate and crossed into the pasture area running along the left side of the property.

Raindrops pelted Ashley's face as she refastened the chain. She raced for the barn. After trekking half of the distance, her boot hit a rut in the earth. Ashley fell forward, her body slamming into the dirt. The sudden jolt sent a shockwave through her shoulder. Her gunshot wound throbbed as she pushed herself up. Her left knee ached now as well.

She hobbled onward, moving as fast as she dared across the mangy pasture, pocked by the rooting of the pigs. By the time she reached the door of the barn, the shower had swelled to a deluge. Rain drenched her jacket and jeans, and fresh mud caked her boots.

Sliding the right door open, Ashley slipped into the barn.

With the storm clouds darkening the sky, shadows blanketed the interior of the metal building. Rain drummed the roof. Chilled from the downpour, she shivered. A foul odor filled her nostrils, but it was one she'd grown accustomed to. The smell transported her back to her childhood. To the farm where her uncle had raised his own hogs.

She inched inside, scanning the pens confining the sows and piglets, searching for Stanley. The animals grunted and squeaked as she made her way further into the gloom. She caught sight of a doorway up ahead to her right. It was probably the room where the farmer stored feed and supplies.

Out of caution, Ashley drew her Glock as she approached the door.

Stanley might be on the other side.

Easing the door open, she peered into the darkened room. She stood still for a moment, letting her eyes adjust. As she'd suspected, feed bins crowded the left side of the space. Shelves lined the walls, and a work bench sat to her right.

Stanley had told Ashley and Wyatt that he'd given Cole a tour of his barn. Had something happened between the two men during that time? Had they argued? Had Cole seen something the farmer wanted to keep hidden?

Ashley moved down the length of the work bench. Various hand tools—a hacksaw, a couple of hammers, files, and plyers—rested on the surface. Nearing the end of the bench, she stopped short. A helmet, equipped with night vision goggles, sat next to a small toolbox.

Although the possession of the device seemed damning, it wasn't the physical proof they needed. A large percentage of hunters used the goggles to go after raccoons and other nocturnal creatures. They needed something concrete. Something that couldn't be explained away.

With nothing more to see, Ashley wandered back out of the room and closed the door.

She strode deeper into the barn, keeping her eyes peeled for any signs of Stanley.

In a small pen, a sow lay nursing her piglets. Ashley knelt down and enjoyed the wholesome sight. Although they were close enough for her to touch, she knew not to try petting the piglets. She remembered how protective the mothers could be. And she didn't want to risk incurring the sow's wrath. Under the right circumstances, hogs could pose a danger to humans.

Ashley had decided to move on when something caught her attention. Squinting her eyes, she tried to determine what she was seeing. But the shadows here were too thick. She fished her Maglite from her pocket and switched it on.

Leaning over the side of the pen, she swept the flashlight's beam across the sow's stomach.

Her heart skipped a beat.

Pink and yellow dots clung to the skin of three of the ten piglets. With the piglets still too young to be let out into the pasture, the Mylar tags stuck to their bodies proved the Taser had been fired inside the barn.

Ashley grabbed her cell phone and shot photos of the dot-covered piglets.

She needed to call Wyatt and tell him what she'd found. Now.

As she stood up, she heard a noise behind her. She reached for her Glock as she spun around.

Pop!

Barbs from the Taser pierced the skin of her stomach and left leg. Agonizing pain gripped her body as each of her muscles contracted. With no control of her limbs, unable to move or to even utter a sound, she crashed to the floor of the barn.

Still pressing the Taser's trigger, Stanley stepped toward her, his face twisted with rage. She saw him raise the wooden club. Saw the blow coming. But there was nothing she could do to stop it.

Stanley slammed the club into the side of Ashley's head.

And then the world went dark.

CHAPTER FORTY FOUR

Jacob Stanley grinned as he wound the duct tape tight around the pretty TBI agent's wrists. What was her name? Ashley. That was it. Ashley shouldn't have broken into his barn. She shouldn't have been snooping around. Now, she'd have to pay the price.

He doubted the agent knew what was going on. Cops were usually a lot dumber than they looked. But it was possible that she'd found something. He had no idea how long she'd been there, or how much ground she'd covered. He couldn't risk letting her go.

Tearing off the strip of tape, Stanley switched to her ankles.

At least Toby would be happy. And it was fitting that this should all take place now. It was an anniversary of sorts. Today marked exactly six months since he and Toby had first met. Stanley had been angry that day. Jerry had come in and taken over, stealing his business. Stanley's income had been slashed to the point that he'd fallen behind on some of his payments.

But Toby had spoken to him. Had calmed him down.

Toby had told him what he should do.

At the beginning, Stanley had been reluctant. But things had gone downhill fast, and they'd just kept getting worse.

Stanley sold piglets to the agricultural department of the college over in Peck County. He'd seen Cole Gowen there dealing weed. It didn't take him long to figure out that the man was one of Boswell's lackeys.

And when Cole had shown up on his doorstep with the summons, Stanley had snapped. Being sued had pushed him over the edge. He'd killed Cole in a fit of rage. As he'd looked down at the man's body and realized what he'd done, he'd panicked a little.

But then he'd talked with Toby again. And together, they'd devised a plan.

It had been his intention to deal with Scarlett first. But he'd searched for her for weeks and couldn't find her. So, he'd made Alden his first priority. It was the accountant's fault that he'd gotten so far in debt in the first place. He'd paid the man to handle his finances. He should have been warned. And when the money had dried up, Alden had started asking all kinds of questions.

With the accountant out of the way, Stanley had focused on taking care of Jerry. The revenge had felt so sweet. So satisfying. Toby had been right all along. Stanley should have made his move sooner. Before the lawsuit.

Stanley ripped off a piece of tape, balled it up, and stuffed it inside of Ashley's mouth. Then he wrapped the duct tape around her head and sealed her lips shut. He wondered whether she'd driven out to the farm alone, or if the other agent had come with her. He seemed to recall that the man's name was Wyatt.

It didn't really matter. Stanley would take care of them one at a time. And if he ran into trouble, Toby would know what to do.

Stanley slipped the Taser into the pocket of his cargo pants.

Grabbing the wooden club, he headed toward the door of the barn. He was itching to finish his business with Scarlett. But first, Stanley needed to search for Wyatt.

CHAPTER FORTY FIVE

Drawing his Glock, Wyatt eased his way inside the old, red barn. He was soaked to the core. The torrential rain had plastered his hair to his head. Mud clung to his shoes and the bottom hem of his chinos. And now, the stench of pig dung assaulted his lungs.

He hoped that Ashley had fared better. That she'd made it inside the metal barn before the downpour had begun. She'd suffered through a lot during this case. She'd been shot, her bed had been filled with dead frogs, she'd been punched in the jaw and knocked off of her feet, and she'd had her heart broken. She needed to catch a break. And he knew that she'd be relieved when this investigation was over.

He wondered whether she'd find any evidence in the metal barn.

Wyatt had allowed her to venture into the newer barn alone because he didn't believe that Stanley had gone there. When he'd stood on the front porch of the farmhouse, he'd heard a noise inside. A soft thump. His gut had told him the sound had been made by a human. And according to Sheriff Hyland's notes, Stanley lived alone. The farmer was likely inside the house, hiding. Waiting for Wyatt and Ashley to leave his property.

Darkness filled the interior of the windowless, wooden barn. Wyatt pulled his Maglite from his inside jacket pocket and flipped it on. He braced himself for what he might find. He'd chosen to search the red building for a reason. He believed that Stanley had murdered Cole, Jerry, and Alden. And upon scanning the property, Wyatt figured the older barn might be the location where the bodies had been disposed of.

With the beam of his flashlight cutting through the gloom, Wyatt inched forward. He heard noises coming from up ahead. Grunts and snorts. He wondered how many hogs the space held. He hadn't seen any pens yet. Only bales of straw and hay. A tractor stood to his right along with the rusted-out hull of an old-model pickup.

As he passed by the tractor, a squeal split the air on his left.

Wyatt jerked his Maglite toward the noise. A huge pen housed a single hog. He didn't know much about pigs, but based on its massive size, he believed this one was a boar.

He moved closer.

The enclosure looked more like a large dog kennel than a hog pen. The metal fence-type walls stretched around eight feet in height. A green plastic kiddie pool rested in one corner of the pen. There was a padlock on the gate, and a carved wooden plaque had been mounted to the top of the gate's frame.

The plaque read: Toby.

The boar grunted and then charged full speed toward the gate.

Wyatt jumped backward, his pulse racing. He got the unsettling feeling that the hog would tear him limb from limb if given the chance.

"You're the one, aren't you, Toby?" he said in a hushed voice.

Edging as close to the pen as he dared, Wyatt swept the beam of his flashlight across the floor inside, covered with fresh straw. The bedding made it impossible to tell whether there was anything of significance left in the kennel.

Sighing, he headed further into the barn.

Wyatt discovered two more boars, but neither of their pens looked anything like Toby's. And the boars in the rear of the building lacked name plaques.

He scoured the old barn as well as he could. Wyatt didn't find any evidence of the crimes he believed had been committed on the farm, but if his suspicions were correct, the TBI forensic techs should find plenty of DNA. It was the one thing Stanley couldn't get rid of.

Wyatt made his way back toward the wooden barn's sliding door. He poked his head out. The driving rain pricked his face like needles. It was a long trek to the metal barn where Ashley had gone. One he didn't look forward to.

Steeling himself for the rain's onslaught, Wyatt ran across the pasture.

CHAPTER FORTY SIX

Ashley forced her eyes open. Pain throbbed in the side of her head from the blow from Stanley's club. A foul-tasting wad of something— she wasn't sure what—had been stuffed into her mouth, crowding her tongue. She lay on her side, her wrists bound behind her. Duct tape circled her ankles, holding them tight.

How long had she been unconscious?

And where was Wyatt? Was he okay?

She shivered as the cold radiated from the hard, concrete floor of the hog barn and seeped through her rain-dampened jeans. Stanley had caught her by surprise, appearing out of nowhere. She hadn't had time to draw her Glock. And now, she feared that Wyatt was in danger. Ashley had to get up. She had to find him.

A wave of dizziness struck her as she raised her head. Her vision blurred. Was she going to pass out again? She choked back the urge to vomit, her stomach reeling. Easing her head back down, Ashley pressed her eyes closed and willed the world to stop spinning.

Every muscle in her body felt drained as though she'd suffered through a full-body charley horse. Which actually, she had. When the Taser's barbs had pierced her skin, fifty-thousand volts of electricity had shot through her body. As her muscles contracted, the pain had been excruciating, feeling more like fifty-thousand hornets, all stinging her at once.

The sow grunted as she nursed her piglets in the pen next to where Ashley lay. Overhead, rain pelted the metal roof, sounding almost like kernels exploding in a popcorn popper.

Taking a deep breath, Ashley attempted to sit up again. Once more, nausea threatened her. She leaned against the steel hog pen. The sow took notice and squeaked at her. Ashley realized that the response was a gentle warning for her to keep her distance from the piglets.

It's okay, mama hog.

The sow seemed to read her thought, settling back down. For the first time, Ashley realized that the hog resembled its owner. Jacob Stanley's face—his plump rosy cheeks—flashed in her mind.

And then a memory hit her, jiggled loose from her subconscious.

Ashley finally knew what had been bothering her about Warwick. It was something the man had said. At the time, the remark had sailed through her ears unnoticed. But the words had been captured in the deep recesses of her mind. They'd been nibbling away at her for days.

When she'd confronted Warwick about being the last person to see Cole alive, Warwick had responded, "*I don't give a rat's ass about some fat server.*"

A *fat* process server?

Ashley had seen photographs. Cole was a younger copy of his uncle, Sheriff Hyland. Tall and slim. What could have possessed Warwick to use that term? Considering the modest salary earned by process servers, he couldn't have been using *fat* to describe wealthy. He had to have been remembering a physical characteristic.

And then, all at once, everything clicked in Ashley's mind. All of the pieces of the puzzle had finally snapped together.

The Mylar AFID tags stuck to the bellies of the three little piglets bore witness to what had taken place inside of the metal hog barn. Ashley's instincts had led her to believe that Stanley had killed Cole out of rage. But Warwick's subpoena had been delivered two hours later than Stanley's summons. Ashley couldn't understand why the farmer would wait until after Cole had left his property to strike.

But the truth now rang clear. Stanley didn't wait. He'd killed Cole here in the barn. Near the very spot where Ashley now sat.

In order to throw off law enforcement and avoid suspicion, Stanley had pretended to be Cole. He'd driven the process server's car to Warwick's trailer and had delivered the subpoena himself. And then he'd abandoned the car on Rattler Ridge.

Jacob Stanley was the fat server.

Cole must be buried somewhere on the farm.

Terror rocked Ashley's body as another realization hit her. Stanley didn't have to bury Cole. The farmer was the owner of an all-natural disposal system.

When Ashley was a child, she'd had an elderly neighbor. One morning the man had gone out to feed his pigs. He'd slipped and fallen into the pen. The hogs had attacked. The only thing they didn't eat was the elderly man's dentures.

Jerry and Alden must have suffered the same fate. Ashley just prayed that the kidnapped men hadn't been fed to the hogs while still alive.

Ashley jerked her arms, struggling to free her wrists. It was no use. The duct tape was wound too tight. She needed her bound hands in front of her, rather than behind her back. Then at least she could see exactly what she was dealing with.

Curling into a ball, she attempted to slide her arms down over her hips, so that she could slip her feet through and bring her hands around. But it didn't work. The duct tape had been wrapped too high on her forearms.

Tears of frustration stung her eyes. She knew that she had to hurry. It was possible that Wyatt had been attacked as well. He could be unconscious. Bound and gagged up in the old, red barn. Ashley hadn't seen any boars here in the metal barn. Only sows and piglets. The boars were probably kept in the older barn.

And Ashley knew that boars were larger and more aggressive than sows.

It seemed likely that the boars had disposed of the murdered men's bodies.

She needed to get up onto her feet. She had to break out of her bonds. She couldn't allow Stanley to kill Wyatt.

Determined to fight through the vertigo, Ashley pushed herself back up into a sitting position. As she'd feared, the room spun in front of her. Closing her eyes, she inhaled and counted to ten. Although her wooziness didn't completely pass, it wasn't quite as severe.

I can do this.

Ashley swung herself up onto her knees, rocked back onto her feet, and then stood. Her stomach somersaulted in protest. But she couldn't stop. She had to keep going. She hopped forward.

With her balance out of kilter, Ashley's body swayed to the right and she almost fell, face-first onto the concrete floor. Steadying herself, she pressed her eyes shut and hopped again. And then again.

She made her way across the barn to the feed storage room.

Pushing her back against the door, she turned the knob. The cloud-ridden sky outside had grown darker and the shadows in the barn heavier. She rubbed her arm against the wall, felt a light switch, and flipped it on with her elbow. The hanging florescent tube hummed as it sparked to life.

Ashley hopped to the workbench. She located the hacksaw she'd seen earlier and dragged it to the corner of the benchtop. Bracing the saw's handle with her hip, she pushed the duct tape binding her wrists against the blade.

After a few seconds of sawing, Ashley's hands broke free.

Strands of her hair ripped from her scalp as she pulled the tape from her mouth and head. She grabbed the hacksaw and sliced through the bonds around her ankles. Her head still throbbed, and her balance still felt off, but the nausea had subsided.

Stanley had stolen her Glock and her phone. Ashley scoured the workbench. Anything she thought she might be able to use as a weapon—a screwdriver, a file, a wrench—she stuffed inside the cargo pockets of her jacket. She found a folding knife in one of the workbench drawers.

The blade proved short—two inches—but it would get the job done.

And then her eyes caught sight of something else. A small sledgehammer. It wouldn't fit inside any of her pockets like the other tools would, but under the current circumstances, she didn't mind carrying it in her hand.

As she scanned the benchtop one last time, her heart skipped a beat. Something was missing. The night vision goggles she'd seen earlier were no longer there. Stanley had taken them too. Why? Although the rain had dimmed the sky, it wasn't completely dark out yet.

Did the old red barn lack electricity?

Is that where Stanley had gone?

Ashley had been holding her Maglite when she'd been shot with the Taser. She hoped that it was still lying on the floor of the barn. Hoped that Stanley hadn't stolen the flashlight from her as well. She'd noticed that the old barn didn't contain any windows. She didn't want to brave the darkness knowing that there were boars inside.

Thunder juddered the metal building as Ashley ran back to the area of the barn where she'd been tased. She searched the concrete floor but couldn't find the flashlight. She was about to give up, convinced it was gone, when she spotted something black sticking out from beneath the straw inside the sow's pen.

The Maglite rested next to one of the piglets.

Ashley inched closer to the pen.

Should she reach her hand inside, nice and slow? Or should she strike fast? She chose the latter. As Ashley jerked the flashlight out from beneath the bedding, the sow squealed and jumped up from the floor. The pig rushed toward the side of the pen, nipping at the air.

Ashley had yanked her hand back just in time.

Shoving her Maglite into the pocket that held the knife, she flew toward the entrance of the barn. Lightning danced across the sky as she slid back the door. She jumped, her heart pounding as the wind slammed a broken tree branch against the metal siding. She swung her attention across the pasture toward the top of the slope.

Wyatt was out there somewhere. But so was Stanley.

Gathering her courage, Ashley raced out into the storm.

CHAPTER FORTY SEVEN

Mud splattered Ashley's hiking boots and the legs of her jeans as she barreled across the pasture heading toward the old, red barn. Rain stung her eyes, making it difficult for her to see. Lightning streaked through the clouds followed by a jarring clap of thunder. She skidded to a stop as she reached the barn's sliding doors.

Was Wyatt still inside?

Had he run into Jacob Stanley?

Ashley hadn't heard any gunfire. She hoped that was a good sign. But then she realized that Stanley wasn't carrying a pistol or rifle. He didn't need one. He'd managed to catch her by surprise, shooting her with the Taser and knocking her unconscious with his wooden club. He could have done the same thing to her partner.

She just prayed that Wyatt was keeping his guard up.

Darkness swallowed Ashley as she eased across the threshold into the barn. She switched on her Maglite, carrying it in her left hand. She raised the small sledgehammer in her right, ready to strike.

Her pulse raced as she inched farther into the gloom. If Stanley was hiding in the barn, he would see her before she saw him. He had the night vision goggles. Stacks of hay and straw bales flanked Ashley as she swept her flashlight beam across the floor. Rain hammered the tin roof; the noise was so loud that it was the only thing she could hear.

An eerie feeling rippled through her. The feeling that she was not alone.

She stopped. Stood still. Strained her ears.

Beneath the din of the hard-driven downpour, faint grunts echoed through the old wooden structure. The boars. She wondered how many there were. How secure were their pens?

A chill danced down her back, her rain-drenched clothing only half the culprit. She thought about Cole, Jerry, and Alden. Images of an attack—the men's faces twisted with fear, the boars' teeth glistening—assaulted her mind.

Her nausea returned. Only this time, it wasn't from the blow to her head. Her stomach cramped from the vision of the horrific way the men must have died.

Ashley needed to find Wyatt. Fast.

The urge to shout out to him pricked at her heart. But if Stanley was in the barn, and if he didn't yet know that Ashley was inside, then her call would alert him. She had to stay quiet. But then she realized that Stanley would see the glow from her flashlight from a long distance away.

Bracing herself for the sudden rush of darkness, Ashley switched off the Maglite.

Her heart pounded as she waited for her eyes to adjust. Gradually, shapes began to form in the black gulf that yawned before her. She took a hesitant step forward. And then another.

The toe of Ashley's hiking boot struck against something hard.

A pitchfork that had been leaning against a hay bale clanked to the floor at her feet.

A squeal split the air on her left. The clamor had upset one of the boars. Had Stanley heard the noise? Was he here? Was he preparing to shoot her with the Taser again?

Tightening her grip on the sledgehammer, Ashley veered left, toward the direction from which the boar's cry had come. She rounded a stack of hay bales.

The snorts and grunts grew louder.

The dark silhouette of a pen rose before her. But with the wire fence taller than Ashley, it was like no hog pen she'd ever seen before. But then the reason for the wall height dawned on her.

Fear tugged at her heart.

The pen had a dual purpose. It wasn't just built to keep the boar inside. It was constructed to prevent the boar's victims from climbing out.

Would she find evidence of the murders inside the pen? She knew that boars could eat an entire human, even the bones. The only thing she remembered hearing that hogs couldn't digest was hair and teeth.

Horrified, she stepped closer to the pen.

"Ashley."

The voice startled her, and she jumped. It was Wyatt's voice.

She grabbed her Maglite and flipped it on, bouncing the beam around the barn, searching for him.

"Wyatt, where are you?"

"In the pen."

Terror squeezed Ashley's soul.

She swung the flashlight's beam back to the left. She saw the boar, dark and enormous, its menacing eyes glinting. But she didn't see Wyatt.

Choking back tears, she imagined him curled into a ball on the pen's floor. Torn and bleeding.

She edged up next to the fence, still looking for him. "Are you hurt?"

"Not bad," he said. "Not yet."

A tiny bit of relief flowed through her. "I don't know where you are—I can't see you anywhere."

"I'm in the corner."

Ashley directed the flashlight's beam toward the right rear of the pen. She caught sight of a green, hard-plastic kiddie pool leaning against the corner. He must be hiding behind the pool, using it as a shield to ward off the boar's attack.

With her heart hammering, Ashley raced around to the back side of the pen.

Wyatt's fingers gripped one edge of the swimming pool, the bottom edge clamped beneath his feet. His back pressed the fence. His wrists were still bound, but he'd managed to get his hands in front of him. He'd peeled the duct tape from his mouth and ripped it from his ankles.

Although she could tell Wyatt was attempting to show her a brave face, she could see a hint of fear in his eyes. She couldn't blame him. Given his situation, he should be terrified.

Ashley pulled the folding knife from her pocket and flipped it open. "Can you put your hands next to the fence?"

His expression let her know that he didn't want to let go of the pool. That he worried it would fall and the boar would charge. But what choice did he have?

Wyatt released his grip. The pool shuddered as he slid his hands toward her. Ashley heard the boar moving as she sliced through the tape that bound Wyatt's wrists.

"Thanks," he said, grabbing the edge of the pool again.

"We have to find a way to get you out of there."

Wyatt sighed. "The gate's padlocked."

Ashley rushed back around to the front of the hog pen. Stanley had wrapped a chain around the fence and the gate's frame, securing it with the lock. She didn't remember coming across any bolt cutters in the feed supply room. How was she going to get the gate open?

"Did you happen to see what Stanley did with the key?"

"Yeah. It's in his pocket."

Tears of frustration welled in Ashley's eyes. If she couldn't figure out a way to rescue Wyatt, if he died here, she would never forgive herself.

And then she remembered the police radio and Wyatt's rifle stashed in the SUV. She could call for help. Armed, she could come back and stand guard over Wyatt until the deputies arrived.

"Give me your key fob," she said, hope clear in her voice.

"Stanley took it."

The news hit Ashley like a punch to her gut. She had no idea how she could get Wyatt out of the pen. She fell silent as she skirted the side of the fence, studying the way the mesh was joined to the posts. She'd pull the whole structure apart if she could figure out how to do it.

Wyatt interrupted her thoughts. "Stanley's unhinged," her partner stated. "He thinks Toby talks to him. Tells him what to do."

"Toby?"

"The boar."

The fact that the farmer suffered from hallucinations made him even more dangerous.

And then Ashley thought about the word Wyatt had used to describe Stanley. *Unhinged.*

An idea struck her. Her gaze flew around to the side of the gate. She couldn't cut the chain or the lock, but maybe she could open the gate from the other side.

Take off the hinges.

She shined the flashlight on the screws fastening the hinges to the gate's frame. They had Phillips-type screw heads. The only screwdriver Ashley had found on the workbench was now in her pocket. But it featured a single flat blade, designed to be used on a screw with a straight slot carved into the head.

She'd just have to make it work.

The boar squealed.

Ashley's attention jerked toward the hog. Toby trotted toward the back corner of the pen. He butted the swimming pool with his snout.

Wyatt shouted, "No! Get back!"

Ashley's heart leapt to her throat. Wyatt needed some kind of weapon. Something to help fend off the boar. She picked up the small sledgehammer and ran around to the back side of the pen.

Standing on her tiptoes, she draped the hammer over the side of the fence.

"Here, take this."

Wyatt grabbed the sledgehammer.

Toby charged again, ramming his snout into the kiddie pool.

Wyatt swung the hammer into the boar's shoulder. Toby squealed. Maybe from the pain. But instead of lunging forward for a fight, he backed up. The hog snorted as though he was rethinking his plan. Trying to come up with a better angle of attack.

With Wyatt safe for the moment, Ashley returned to the gate.

Aiming the flashlight, she placed the screwdriver on the head of one of the screws holding the bottom gate hinge. She applied pressure and rotated the screwdriver. It didn't catch in the Phillips-type slot. She thought the blade might be too big. She tried again. The screw still wouldn't turn. She realized that the screwdriver's flat blade was stripping out the screw's head.

Exasperation burned in her chest.

Now what?

The gaps between the wires of the fence were far too small for Wyatt to get his foot into. With no room to get a toe hold, there was no way he could climb out.

"Did you search through the whole barn?" she asked him.

"Yeah. There are two more boars in the back. But they're not like Toby."

Ashley guessed that hogs as massive as Toby would prove rare.

"Did you see a stepladder anywhere?"

"No."

Maybe she could find a box or something he could stand on. Then maybe he could swing himself over the fence. And then it hit her.

"I just figured out a way to get you out of there," she said, excitement in her tone.

Ashley sprinted back toward the entrance of the barn. The two-string bales of straw, stacked in rows, each stood about fourteen inches tall. Although straw was lighter than hay, the bales weighed around forty pounds.

Wrapping her fingers around the twine, Ashley pulled a bale from the top of the stack. She dragged the straw to the back side of Toby's pen.

"I think two of these bales will get you up high enough to climb over the fence," she told Wyatt.

"Yeah, you're right," he said.

He sounded as though a huge weight had just been lifted off of his chest.

Ashley went back for a second bale. This time, she grabbed the pitchfork. Although the pitchfork's tines appeared dull, maybe too dull to pierce the boar's thick hide, they might provide just enough pain to keep the animal at bay.

"I brought you something that might work better against Toby," she said.

Standing on her tiptoes again, Ashley lifted the pitchfork over the fence first.

Wyatt let go of the pool's edge and grabbed the pitchfork's handle.

Toby grunted when he saw the kiddie pool move. He sprang forward, his teeth bared.

The boar slammed his weight into the side of the plastic pool.

Wyatt's feet held down the pool's inside bottom edge. When Toby rammed the pool, Wyatt lost his balance. His feet slipped. The plastic pool flew to the side.

Ashley screamed.

Wyatt fell to the floor, the shield protecting him from Toby gone.

CHAPTER FORTY EIGHT

Panic sliced through Ashley's soul as she watched Wyatt fall to the straw-covered floor of Toby's hog pen. The boar had knocked the plastic swimming pool from her partner's grasp, sending Wyatt's feet flying out from under him. The defensive barrier tumbled to the side, out of Wyatt's reach. There was no longer anything protecting him from the boar's attacks. He was completely vulnerable. And Ashley felt powerless to save him.

Now, Toby would kill Wyatt.

Once the attack began, with the boar's razor-sharp teeth, Wyatt would be dead in a matter of moments.

"No!" Ashley cried out. She picked up one of the bales of straw and hoisted it over her head. She had to get Wyatt out of the pen.

Toby squealed, trotted in a circle, and then rushed toward Wyatt.

The pitchfork still in his hand, Wyatt dodged the attack, rolling toward the front of the pen. He struggled to get to his feet. The boar snorted and circled around again.

Ashley heaved the straw bale up over the top of the fence. It landed on the other side with a thud. Toby squeaked, ran to the bale, and sniffed it. Then the boar loped to the far end of his pen. He snorted and pawed at the floor; his attention now focused back on Wyatt.

It seemed as though Toby was playing a game. As if he was hunting Wyatt for sport.

Wyatt pushed himself to his knees.

Toby charged.

The tines of the pitchfork glanced off of the thick skin of the boar's shoulder. Toby squealed. He nipped at the air and then retreated.

Ashley hurled the second bale of straw over the fence.

As Wyatt attempted to stand, Toby raced toward him again. Wyatt raised the pitchfork. The boar rammed against the side of the tool, knocking Wyatt back to his knees.

Ashley had to do something. Now.

Although she'd thrown the straw inside the pen, Wyatt couldn't take his eyes off of Toby long enough to stack the bales and climb out. He was too busy playing defense.

Ashley raced back toward the barn's entrance. She grabbed the twines of two straw bales, one with each hand. As fast as she could go, she dragged the bales toward Toby's pen.

Wyatt stood in the front left corner of the enclosure, his back against the fence, the pitchfork gripped tight in his hands. Toby pranced in a circle as if gearing up for another strike.

Ashley stacked the straw bales, one on top of the other, against the outside of the fence.

"No, Ashley," Wyatt said, his voice firm. "You're not climbing into the pen."

She didn't have a choice. One of them would have to fend off Toby while the other one stacked the bales that lay on the inside of the fence. It was the only way Wyatt would be able to get out.

She refused to let him die. "I don't think you're in the position to stop me," she said.

"Ashley," Wyatt began, his voice strained. "You don't understand. Toby killed Jerry and Alden. Maybe Cole too. This boar has tasted human blood. He craves it now. If you get inside the pen, he'll kill you."

Wyatt wasn't telling her anything that she didn't already know.

But before Ashley jumped over the top of the fence, she should find a longer weapon. She'd have to allow Toby to get close to her before she could use the sledgehammer.

Too close.

"Just hold on," she told Wyatt. "I'll be right back."

Ashley sprinted to the location where she'd found the pitchfork. A garden hoe leaned against one of the bales of hay. She snatched it up. And then she saw something else. A braided nylon rope lying on top of the hay.

Grabbing the rope, she looped the end around, tying it in a slipknot. Then she hurried back to Toby's pen.

The boar grunted. He cantered toward Wyatt.

Ready with the pitchfork, Wyatt poked Toby's snout. Squealing, the boar turned back and trotted toward the rear of the enclosure.

Armed with the hoe and the rope, Ashley climbed on top of the straw bales.

"I told you not to come in here," Wyatt said, almost sounding angry.

She knew that he feared what would happen to her. Believed that she was going to die right in front of him. She understood his anguish. Ashley felt the same way. She couldn't stand back and watch Toby tear Wyatt limb from limb. She had to intervene. Even if it meant that she'd be injured in the process.

"Just be ready," she stated. "I might not land on my feet."

Lifting the hoe over her head, she hooked the blade on the fence, the handle trailing down on the inside of the enclosure. She slipped the rope over the crook of her arm. She needed her hands free.

Taking a deep breath, Ashley vaulted over the top of the fence.

CHAPTER FORTY NINE

Ashley's heart hammered in her chest as she climbed over the wire-fence wall of Toby's hog pen, the rope hooked around her left arm. She knew that she was risking her life. That the boar would rip her to shreds if given the chance. But she had no choice. If she didn't venture into the enclosure, if she didn't help Wyatt escape, Toby would kill him.

As the soles of her hiking boots hit the straw bedding below, she heard the boar snort. Heard his hooves scratching the floor.

Wyatt yelled, "Get back!"

Ashley knew her partner's words were directed at Toby.

Grabbing the hoe hanging on the inside of the fence, she twirled around.

Wyatt stood in between Ashley and the boar, the pitchfork raised in defense. Toby veered to the left, trying to get around Wyatt. Now that Ashley was inside the pen, the boar had a new target. She guessed Toby had decided to attack the smallest person first.

The easiest prey.

Wyatt jumped to the side, cutting the boar off, and poked his snout with the pitchfork.

Toby squealed. He backed up, and then turned and trotted toward the opposite side of the enclosure.

"I have an idea," Ashley said. "There's a slipknot tied into this rope. I'll put it on the floor, and you can lure Toby toward it. As soon as I see his hoof step inside the loop, I'll put it tight."

Wyatt nodded. "Be careful."

She just hoped that her plan would work. That they could maneuver Toby into the trap.

Wielding the hoe in one hand, Ashley inched toward the opposite side of the pen where Toby now stood. The boar eyed her. She could tell that he was gearing up to attack.

Wyatt moved with Ashley, staying in front of her, threatening Toby with the pitchfork.

She dropped the rope on the floor.

Toby grunted.

Ashley could almost swear that the boar knew what they were doing. Could sense that they were trying to catch him. She walked backward, the end of the rope tight in her grip.

"I'm ready whenever you are," she said.

"Okay." Wyatt stepped to the side. "Get as far away as you can."

Following his advice, with the rope wrapped around her hand and wrist, Ashley continued to move backward.

Wyatt edged behind the loop. "Come on, Toby," he said. "Come and get me."

But the boar seemed much more interested in Ashley now.

Toby snorted and darted to the side of the loop, away from Wyatt and toward her.

"Dammit!" Wyatt yelled. He jumped in front of Ashley and stabbed Toby's neck with the pitchfork.

Seeming full of fury, the boar turned and charged at Wyatt.

Toby's rear foot fell inside the loop.

Ashley yanked the rope taut. Toby squealed. Realizing that he had been caught, the boar jerked his back leg and lunged toward the rear of the enclosure. At five times Ashley's weight, she couldn't hold Toby still. The momentum sent her flying forward.

Ashley crashed to the floor. The hoe slipped from her fingers.

With the rope still wrapped around her wrist, Toby dragged her through the straw.

She heard Wyatt cursing and Toby squeal. Wyatt must have stabbed the boar again.

Ashley felt Wyatt grab the rope.

"Let go!" he shouted.

It took her a couple of seconds to untangle the rope from her hand. As she pushed herself to her feet, she caught sight of Toby.

The boar rushed toward her, his teeth bared.

Terrified, Ashley screamed.

His snout inches from her, Toby stopped short. He squealed and squeaked.

Wyatt had tied the rope to one of the fence posts. Set in concrete, the post held Toby back.

Ashley realized that she was trembling. She met Wyatt's gaze. If he hadn't grabbed the rope when he did, if he hadn't secured it to the post …

216

As if he was reading her thoughts, Wyatt pulled Ashley into his arms. He held her tight. It wasn't a romantic embrace. It was a hug that meant they were both thankful to be alive.

After a few seconds, they let each other go. Wyatt stacked the straw bales against the fence. He motioned for Ashley to climb out of the enclosure first.

Still feeling shaky, she topped the fence and dropped to the floor on the other side.

Toby continued to squeal. Wyatt tossed the pitchfork, the hoe, and the sledgehammer over the fence. Then he climbed out of the pen.

Ashley picked up the pitchfork.

Wyatt grabbed the sledgehammer.

"Let's go find Stanley," he said. "We've got a score to settle."

Side-by-side, they headed back toward the sliding doors of the old, red barn.

CHAPTER FIFTY

Hit by a gust of biting wind, Ashley shivered as she stepped out through the doorway of the old, wooden barn with Wyatt close behind. The rain had dwindled to a drizzle. But the prior deluge, riding a cold front, had dropped the temperature near freezing.

Her gaze swung down the slope toward Stanley's farmhouse. Smoke drifted from the chimney. The farmer was likely tucked inside, nice and warm. And he probably believed that Wyatt was dead. Ashley wondered whether Stanley had discovered that she'd escaped from the metal barn. Maybe he had.

Instead of being huddled in the farmhouse, it was possible that Stanley was out looking for her.

She glanced back at Wyatt. He slid the barn doors closed. "You ready?" he asked, steel determination in his eyes.

Ashley nodded. She'd never felt more eager to arrest a criminal than she did right now.

With the pitchfork clasped tight in her grip, and Wyatt armed with the sledgehammer, they jogged across the pasture. Although they didn't yet have physical evidence to prove Stanley had killed Cole, Jerry, and Alden, they had grounds to arrest the farmer for assaulting Ashley and attempting to murder Wyatt. If Stanley was inside the farmhouse, under the current circumstances, they had the authority to do anything necessary to take him into custody.

Wyatt pulled the steel gate open, and they crossed from the pasture into the home's rear yard.

A light burned in the back room of the farmhouse. Ashley crept toward the rear porch. Careful not to make a sound, she mounted the steps. Hanging back in the shadows, hoping she wouldn't be seen, she peered through the glass panes in the back door.

Ashley's pulse quickened as the urge to knock the door down surged through her.

Inside the living room, a dark-haired woman sat bound to a wooden rocking chair. A gag covered her mouth. With Ashley's view limited to a narrow swath, she didn't see Stanley anywhere.

She eased back down off of the porch.

"Stanley kidnapped another victim—a woman," she whispered to Wyatt. "I couldn't see all the way into the room, so I don't know whether or not he's in there with her."

Wyatt sighed. She could tell that he was pondering their predicament. They had to do whatever it took to rescue the woman. But Wyatt probably feared that if they busted into the house, Stanley would kill his newest victim, quick. Just to be done with her.

After a moment of silent deliberation, Wyatt's eyes settled on Ashley. "We need to sneak inside," he said. "If Stanley finds out that we're still alive, he might grab a gun. He could shoot the woman. And then us."

Ashley agreed. They couldn't do anything that would put the woman's life in jeopardy.

"I wonder if Stanley left the front door unlocked."

"It's worth a shot."

The thought of breaking into Wyatt's SUV crossed Ashley's mind. But she realized that the break-in would set off the car alarm. And they couldn't call for backup anyway. The police radio wouldn't work without the vehicle's battery switched on.

They skulked around the corner of the farmhouse into the front yard.

The rooms on this side of the house sat dark. Not even the porch light glowed. Wyatt followed Ashley as she climbed the steps.

She paused at the front door, stood still, and listened. "I don't hear anything," she whispered. "Stanley's probably in the living room with the woman."

Ashley's fingers closed around the doorknob.

She looked at Wyatt and shook her head. "It's locked."

"We'll have to find another way in."

She knew that they couldn't afford to waste time. Stanley might be planning to take the woman to Toby's pen. He could march her out the back door of the farmhouse before Ashley and Wyatt realized what was going on.

"The door seemed to give a little when I pressed against it. I don't think the deadbolt's locked. Do you have a credit card on you?"

"Stanley took my wallet."

The farmer had emptied all of Ashley's pockets as well.

She sighed, racking her brain, trying to come up with a solution. It would likely take too long to run to the metal barn and search the workbench for a tool to pick the lock. By the time they returned, the woman could be dead. They had to break in now.

And then she saw it. Something that just might do the trick. A dried-up, dead plant rested in a flimsy plastic flowerpot at the top of the porch steps. Wyatt threw Ashley a puzzled look as she grabbed the pot, turned it upside down, and banged it against the porch rail. After a few jolts, the plant and dirt tumbled out onto the ground.

"I think this plastic will be flexible enough to use like a credit card. We just need to cut it to the right size."

Wyatt smiled. "Good thinking. Give me your pocketknife."

She handed him the knife and watched as Wyatt split the side of the pot and carved out a rectangle of plastic.

"Keep your fingers crossed," he said.

Wyatt stuck the piece of plastic between the door and the frame and then slid it down to the lock. The door popped open.

A feeling of triumph rippled through Ashley. She picked up the pitchfork, and Wyatt grabbed the sledgehammer.

With a nod, he eased the door the rest of the way open. Ashley's pulse raced as they crept across the threshold into a narrow foyer. A staircase rose on their right. In the room on the left, she could see the silhouette of a dining table and chairs. They both stood still. Listening.

Faint voices drifted toward them. And then music. It seemed as though the sounds were coming from a television somewhere in the rear of the house. Probably the living room where the woman was being held.

They moved forward. A dark hallway was behind the staircase. A light glowed through a doorway on the left side of the hall. They would have to burst into the living room and take Stanley by surprise. But what if he had his Taser handy? He'd likely shoot the first person who jumped through the doorway. Ashley didn't want that person to be Wyatt. Although she could hold her own in a fight, with her partner being physically stronger, he stood the best chance at overcoming Stanley.

Ashley motioned for Wyatt to let her go first.

He hesitated a moment as though he was considering their options. She guessed that he'd probably reached the same conclusion she had. But he seemed reluctant to let her take the fall. He shook his head no.

Deciding not to give in this time, Ashley pushed past Wyatt and entered the hallway.

A floorboard creaked beneath her feet.

She froze. The noise had reverberated through the house. Stanley must have heard it.

Goosebumps broke out on her skin as she stood still, counting off the seconds, expecting the farmer to appear at the living room doorway. But Stanley failed to materialize. She struggled to return her breathing to normal. She glanced back at Wyatt and nodded, letting him know that she planned to keep going.

Ashley's heart pounded as she slinked toward the door. Tightening her grip on the handle of the pitchfork, she braced herself for the sting of the Taser's barbs. She glanced back at Wyatt one last time. Then she took a deep breath and peeked around the doorframe.

The back side of the rocking chair faced Ashley. She couldn't tell whether or not the woman bound to the chair was still alive. But she had a view of the entire room now. Stanley wasn't there. At least not at that moment.

On the living room's far side stood another doorway. A light shone from the adjacent room. It was possible that was where Stanley had gone.

Gesturing to Wyatt that their path was clear for now, she stole into the living room.

The woman's eyes widened when she spotted Ashley.

"Everything's going to be okay," Ashley whispered. "My name is Ashley, and that's my partner, Wyatt. We're special agents with the TBI."

The woman nodded, tears springing to her eyes.

Ashley noticed that the woman had a gash on her forehead, covered with dried blood and a touch of yellow pus. The area appeared swollen as well. She feared that the cut had become infected. The woman needed antibiotics as soon as possible. Otherwise, sepsis could set in.

Wyatt flew to the other side of the room and stood next to the second doorway, his back pressed against the wall. Ashley knew that he was waiting for Stanley to walk through the door from the adjacent room. And if he did, Wyatt would hit the farmer with the sledgehammer.

Pulling the folding knife from her pocket, she sliced through the duct tape binding the woman's arms to the chair. The woman peeled the tape from her mouth as Ashley freed her ankles.

"What's your name?" Ashley asked her.

"Scarlett. Jacob's my ex-husband."

Ashley wondered whether Scarlett was involved in the money laundering scheme. She realized that it was possible the woman had been targeted simply due to the couple's failed love affair. But those questions could wait. They had more important things to worry about.

"Do you know where Jacob is right now?"

"I think he went to the barn," Scarlett said, standing on shaky legs. "The metal one. He said he had a woman tied up out there."

Ashley exchanged glances with Wyatt. "That would be me," she told Scarlett.

"I'm real glad you got away. He was planning to ..."

Scarlett didn't have to finish the sentence. Both Ashley and Wyatt were aware of Stanley's plans for all three of them. And rescuing Scarlett was their number one priority.

"Is there a phone in the house? A landline?"

They could call for backup and an ambulance and then barricade themselves inside a safe room in the farmhouse.

"No. Jacob uses a cell phone."

Ashley sighed. "We need to get you out of here—right this minute," she said. "You need to go to the hospital and have a doctor look at the wound on your head. Do you know if Jacob has an extra truck key around here somewhere?"

"He keeps a spare in the kitchen."

Afraid they couldn't trust the stroke of luck, she wondered what they would do if the key was no longer there.

"Wyatt and I will walk you out to the pickup. I want you to drive straight to the emergency room, okay?"

"Okay."

"And you can ask them to call the police when you get there."

"I will."

Ashley just prayed that she and Wyatt could find Stanley and take him into custody before Scarlett made it into town. Because if Stanley saw Ashley and Wyatt first, and managed to subdue them with the Taser, the sheriff's deputies would likely arrive too late to save them.

"Which way is the kitchen?"

They followed Scarlett back down the hallway. To Ashley's relief, the woman located the extra key fob in one of the cabinet drawers. Then they doubled back to the foyer.

Ashley inched the front door open and peeked outside.

Fear sparked in her chest.

Stanley stood next to the pickup truck.

CHAPTER FIFTY ONE

Ashley trembled as she pushed the front door of the farmhouse closed. How were they going to sneak Scarlett out of here? The woman needed to see a doctor. And fast. Ashley was convinced that the wound on Scarlett's forehead had grown infected. She'd checked the woman's vitals. Had touched her skin. Scarlett definitely had a fever. Having studied emergency first aid at the policy academy, Ashley knew that sepsis could set in quickly.

Scarlett might die if she didn't get to a hospital.

Ashley met Wyatt's gaze. "Stanley is standing right beside the pickup truck," she said.

Wyatt sighed. "Does your ex have guns in the house?" he asked Scarlett.

Why hadn't Ashley thought of that? Armed, they'd be able to take Stanley into custody. Unless he was carrying another weapon besides his Taser.

"Yeah. But they're all locked in a gun cabinet. He keeps that key in his pocket."

Anxiety flowed through Ashley. "Do you know whether or not Stanley has a gun on him now?"

Scarlett shook her head. "I'm not sure."

Ashley looked at Wyatt again. She could tell that he was weighing their odds.

"We'll just have to go for it," he stated. "We'll leave Scarlett here behind the door. You and I will rush Stanley. One of us will get hit by the Taser. But the other has a shot at taking him down."

Ashley agreed. It was the only thing they could do. Scarlett had to get medical attention before it was too late.

"I'll go first," she said.

"No," Wyatt stated, his voice firm. "Not this time."

By her partner's tone, she knew that there was no changing his mind. And she could tell it wasn't the Taser he was worried about. Like Ashley, Wyatt feared Stanley had a gun.

Wyatt moved past her. He eased the door open and peered out into the front yard.

"Stanley's gone," he said, surprise in his voice. "I don't see him anywhere."

At first, Ashley felt relief. But then she realized that it could be a trap. Stanley had to have realized that both she and Wyatt had escaped. He likely figured they'd gone inside of the farmhouse looking for him.

Was Stanley hiding? Lying in wait for them to come out?

Wyatt must have shared her thoughts.

"Both of you stay here," he said. "I'm going to make sure Stanley is really gone. And Ashley, don't come out until I tell you it's safe. I mean it."

Although she felt a strong urge to argue the point, to force Wyatt to let her go with him, Ashley nodded instead. She realized that she needed to stay with Scarlett. Just in case Stanley came back inside the house through the rear door.

"Be careful," she said, worried that he might not come back.

"Always."

Wyatt squeezed through the front door.

Keeping the door open a crack, Ashley watched him cross the front yard. He searched the area next to the pickup and then disappeared around the corner of the house.

What would she do if Stanley killed Wyatt?

Ashley refused to let herself even consider the thought. She had to focus on saving Scarlett.

The seconds ticked by, seeming like hours. Finally, Ashley saw Wyatt heading back toward the front porch.

"Come on," he told her. "We need to hurry."

Ashley steered Scarlett out of the door. With the woman shielded between herself and Wyatt, they rushed to the pickup. The truck dinged as the woman pressed the button on the key fob, unlocking the doors. The noise might not have been loud enough for Stanley to hear. But he likely wouldn't miss the sound of the engine starting.

"I don't know how to thank you," Scarlett stated as she climbed into the driver's seat. "Please come with me." Tears choked her voice. "We can all get away."

Wyatt said, "We can't go. If we don't catch Stanley, he'll kill again. I'm sure of it. And you can thank us by getting to the hospital in one piece." He slammed the pickup's door.

225

Gunning the engine, Scarlett made a U-turn and sped off down the driveway. Ashley hoped that the woman would be okay. That she'd heal. Both physically and emotionally.

"Do you think that Stanley went back up to the metal barn?"

"Maybe. Let's find out."

They raced across the yard to the side pasture. As Wyatt unlatched the gate, Ashley scanned the property. An eerie feeling pricked at her soul. She wondered whether Stanley was watching them through his night vision goggles.

Slipping through the gate, they headed up to the barn.

Ashley covered Wyatt, ready to strike with the pitchfork, as he slid the barn door open. He peeked inside.

"I don't see Stanley."

Although their eyes were adjusted to the darkness, she knew that Wyatt was judging by the black silhouettes of the hog pens crowding the barn's interior. Stanley could still be crouched inside. Waiting for them.

With Wyatt entering first, they crept over the threshold.

A sow and her piglets uttered soft grunts as Ashley stole past their hog pen. Nearing the supply room, she noticed that the door gaped open, and the light burned inside. A chill raced down her spine.

Stanley was likely in the room.

Readying their weapons, they approached the door. Wyatt mouthed the words, *one, two, three*. Then he swung around the doorframe.

"Empty," he said.

Ashley let go of the breath she'd been holding. Wyatt made a beeline for the workbench. She guessed that he wanted to see if he could find any additional tools they could use against Stanley. As she prepared to join him in the quest, Ashley thought she heard a noise.

A thump radiating from deep within the barn.

Was it just one of the hogs?

Ashley eased back away from the supply room. Her heart racing, she inched further into the barn. The hogs had mostly settled down for the evening. Only a few grunts could be heard as she ventured toward the rear of the building.

Tightening her grip on the pitchfork, she rounded the pen where she'd been attacked earlier. She'd never been past this point before. She padded ahead.

Through the gloom, Ashley spotted a white door on her left in the darkest recess of the barn.

Apprehension wormed its way into her stomach as Ashley grasped the doorknob with her left hand. With her right hand clamped around the handle of the pitchfork, down close to the tines, she pushed the door open.

A black void yawned before her. She couldn't see anything.

She reached her hand inside the doorway and felt a switch on the wall. She flipped it on. The sudden burst of light stung her eyes. The room proved small. Shelves filled with veterinary and farming supplies lined the walls.

Switching off the light, Ashley headed back toward the entrance of the barn.

As she grew nearer to the room that contained the workbench, she spotted Wyatt up ahead in the doorway.

Pop!

Fear ripped through Ashley's heart as the familiar sound of the Taser echoed toward her.

She stifled a scream as she watched Wyatt fall to the floor.

CHAPTER FIFTY TWO

Ashley's heart leapt to her throat as she watched Wyatt crash to the floor of the metal barn, shot by Stanley's Taser. Dodging the hog pens, she raced through the shadows toward the supply room. She had to stop Stanley. If the farmer managed to subdue them, this time, she knew that he wouldn't fail. He'd feed them both to Toby.

Her gut told her that Stanley would stay by the boar's side until he was certain that Wyatt and Ashley were dead.

And then he'd escape. He'd likely keep on killing.

Ashley couldn't let him carry out his plans.

As she rounded the last pen, her fingers tightened around the handle of the pitchfork. She spotted Stanley crouched beside Wyatt. The farmer raised his wooden club.

No! Ashley's mind screamed.

The club slammed against the side of Wyatt's head.

Ashley felt sure that her partner was now unconscious.

The rapid footfalls of her hiking boots on the concrete floor seemed to alert Stanley. His gaze flew toward her. He tried to scramble away, but it was too late.

Ashley swung the pitchfork like a baseball bat. The tool smacked the farmer's shoulder.

The blow knocked Stanley to the floor.

Although she could have pierced the farmer's heart with the pitchfork's tines, she didn't want to kill Stanley. She wanted him alive to stand trial for his crimes.

She lunged toward the man. With no handcuffs or any way to restrain him, she'd have to knock the farmer unconscious. Keep him out long enough to find his duct tape.

Struggling to get to his knees, Stanley's hand flew to his jacket pocket. He pulled out something black.

Fear sliced through Ashley's heart.

Did Stanley have a pistol?

And then the weapon snapped into focus. It was a second Taser.

The TBI had learned that a shipment, meant to last through a full two years, had been stolen from the police academy in Peck County. Stanley could be in possession of dozens of the Taser guns and thousands of the cartridges.

The farmer jerked the Taser up, aiming toward Ashley.

Before he could squeeze the trigger, she kicked her right leg forward. The toe of her hiking boot struck Stanley's hand. The Taser sailed into the air and then skidded across the concrete floor behind him.

But Stanley still held the wooden club firm in his other hand.

He swatted the club, hitting Ashley's right knee. The hard lick knocked her off balance. Flung to the right, she crashed to the concrete. The pitchfork slipped from her grasp, clanking against the floor.

Digging in her heels, she scooted backward, trying to escape the farmer's reach.

Back up on his knees, Stanley grabbed her left ankle.

With all of her strength, Ashley bashed her right boot into the farmer's face. The bones of his nose cracked, and he cried out in pain. Stanley let go of her ankle, blood streaming down his chin.

Ashley clambered to her feet. She rushed toward the Taser lying on the floor behind the farmer.

Stanley pushed himself up. As he stood, he slung his arm out. His club sliced the air again.

This time, Ashley dodged the blow. She scooped the Taser from the floor, swirled around, aimed, and fired.

The probes exploded from the gun, trailing their wires behind them.

Like fiery darts, the barbs shot toward Stanley. Penetrating his clothing, they pierced the farmer's skin. One hit his chest. The other stabbed his right leg. Fifty thousand volts of electricity surged through his body.

Stanley stiffened as his muscles contracted. Then he fell, his body slamming against the concrete.

Ashley marched toward the farmer, her finger still pressing the Taser's trigger.

There was only one thing left that she had to do.

Although she knew that Stanley had murdered Cole, Jerry, and Alden in the most horrific way, she dreaded taking the next step. Inflicting pain on a fellow human being, no matter how evil he was, went against everything Ashley believed. Everything she stood for. It stung her in her very core.

But she had no choice.

If she didn't follow through, Stanley would escape. He would be free to kill again.

As soon as her finger left the trigger of the Taser, the flow of electricity would stop. Stanley would be able to attack her. Or run away. She couldn't let either one of those things happen.

Ashley picked up Stanley's wooden club and struck him on the side of his head, just hard enough to render him unconscious.

Dropping the Taser on the floor, she searched through the pockets of Stanley's jacket. She found a small roll of duct tape and his cell phone. She wrapped the tape around his wrists and ankles, hog tying him so that he couldn't stand.

She flew to Wyatt's side. Ashley checked her partner's vitals and then gave him a gentle shake.

"Wyatt?"

Relief flooded her heart as Wyatt's eyes fluttered open.

A weak smile tugged at his lips. "Hi," he choked out.

In that moment, she knew that he would recover from his injury.

But the comfort she experienced was short lived. The horror of everything that had happened hit her all at once. They hadn't been able to save Cole, or Jerry, or Alden. She suspected the grief-stricken face of Cole's mother would haunt her for many years to come.

She was just thankful that they'd been able to stop Stanley. Even though it didn't feel like enough.

Ashley dug the farmer's cell phone out of her pocket and dialed 9-1-1.

CHAPTER 53

Two Weeks Later

Ashley scanned the crowded parking lot of Wheldon's Food Market in Briarwood as she shoved her empty shopping cart into the return corral. All around her, people were smiling, laughing, and reveling in the joy of the holiday. Numb to the decorations and the festive music, she felt like an outsider. Someone who didn't belong.

It was the morning of Christmas Eve. Tomorrow, her family—including her uncle, aunt, and cousins—would be gathering together for a feast. And for the first time in her life, Ashley didn't care.

Of course, it would be nice to spend the day with her father and brothers. And she would enjoy seeing her other relatives, but Ashley dreaded making the trip to Laurel County. She didn't feel like celebrating. She was still too caught up in her own pain. Mourning the death of her relationship with Daniel.

If she hadn't promised to roast a turkey and cook her famous cornbread dressing for her family's Christmas meal, Ashley would have stayed at home today. The turkey had been defrosted and brined and was ready to go into the oven. But she'd needed cornmeal and celery and a few other necessary ingredients. So, she'd braved the throngs of shoppers.

And risked being followed by her stalker.

But there was one thing for which she was thankful. She hadn't received any threats since she'd returned from Fergus County. She hoped that meant the stalker had tired of the game. That he'd decided to leave her in peace.

As she climbed into the driver's seat of her sedan, Ashley's cell phone rang.

The first thought that popped into her mind: Daniel.

But she knew that it wasn't her ex-boyfriend calling. She hadn't spoken to him since he'd told her that they needed to take a step back. Which she felt was code for the old cliché: *I'm just not that into you.*

She fished the phone from her pocket and checked the screen. It was Wyatt.

Although she and her partner were technically *"on call,"* they'd been given some time off work. Not for the holidays. They'd been granted hiatus due to the fact that an internal investigation was being conducted regarding the shooting of Tim Mansfield. The marijuana grower would recover from his injury—a relief to Wyatt and Ashley. However, the investigation was part of the TBI's normal protocol.

"Hey, Wyatt."

She hoped that her partner would tell her that they had an urgent case to solve. That they had to leave town. Begin work today. It would give her an excuse to skip the holiday meal and avoid all of the questions she knew she'd face at her father's house. Questions about Daniel. She hadn't yet told her family about the breakup. And she still wasn't ready to share the news.

Plus, a new case would provide her troubled mind a much-needed diversion.

"I just wanted to tell you that Brenda called," Wyatt said. "The DNA results are back. The teeth found in Toby's pen are a match. Cole, Jerry, and Alden. All three of them were … disposed of."

The information didn't surprise her. One look at the boar and she'd known.

And if Wyatt and Ashley had arrived at Stanley's farmhouse just a little bit later, his ex-wife, Scarlett, would have been murdered as well. But now, the woman was safe.

"Thanks for keeping me updated," Ashley said.

Wyatt paused, as though he was pondering what he planned to say next. "How're you doing?" he finally asked.

She knew that he was referring to her emotional state. Wondering whether or not she was still brooding over Daniel. Although she was beginning to consider Wyatt a friend, she couldn't talk to him about her failed relationship.

But she wouldn't lie and say that she was fine. She'd just redirect the subject.

"I'm heading to my father's house for the holiday," she stated, forcing a cheery note into her voice. "I'm in charge of cooking the turkey."

"That's good."

She knew Wyatt had plans to spend Christmas with Kaylee. They'd discussed his itinerary on the drive back from Fergus County. At the time, Ashley suspected that Wyatt was just trying to keep her talking. To keep her mind off of Daniel. She'd appreciated his effort, but it hadn't worked.

"Well, I guess I'll talk to you later then," she stated, feeling awkward that she didn't know anything else to say.

"Merry Christmas, Ashley."

"The same to you."

Tears stung Ashley's eyes as she circled the parking lot and then wheeled her sedan out onto the street. She'd never felt this way before. Not even when she'd found out her ex-fiancé, Brett, was cheating on her. Her relationship with Daniel had been different from any she'd ever experienced. Deeper. More real.

And now, it was over.

As she coasted the sedan into her garage, Ashley realized that she didn't remember the drive home. She'd been on autopilot. Lost in her thoughts.

Her breath fogged in the frigid air as she carried her grocery bags up the flight of stairs to her apartment. The weather forecast had included a chance of snow. They might have a white Christmas this year. An unusual occurrence in middle Tennessee.

Ashley unlocked her door, hesitating at the threshold.

Every time she came home, she always wondered if someone had been inside her apartment. She stood still and listened. Trying to sense whether or not she was alone.

Telling herself not to worry, that it had been two weeks since anything had happened, she locked the door behind her. She strode into the kitchen and dumped her bags on the counter.

And then an eerie feeling crept up her spine.

Ashley drew her Glock and inched toward the short hallway off of the living room. She checked the bathroom first. Since the stalking had begun, she'd made it a habit to keep her shower curtain pulled back, so that she could see inside. The room was empty.

She moved into the bedroom. Peered underneath the bed and checked the closet. She found nothing out of place. No one was there.

After slipping off her jacket and shoes, and removing her holster and Glock, she headed back to the kitchen.

Her mind drifted again as she put away the groceries. Daniel had said that they would talk once she returned home from Fergus County. She had no idea what kind of timeframe he had in mind. Although her heart begged her to call him, to ask him to explain the reason he'd pulled away, she wouldn't do it.

If Daniel didn't love her, nothing she could say would change it.

As she placed the milk inside the refrigerator, she heard a faint noise behind her. She spun around.

Her pantry door flew open.

Ashley screamed as a man in a black ski mask lunged toward her. He clamped his arms around her like a vice. She struggled to break free.

She felt a prick on her shoulder. Like a needle.

The room began to spin as Ashley's vision blurred. Her arms and legs tingled.

And then darkness overtook her.

NOW AVAILABLE!

LET ME ESCAPE
(An Ashley Hope Suspense Thriller—Book 6)

Ashley Hope is an average Southern woman, happily engaged—until dark secrets from her past tear her life apart. Now a member of Tennessee's State Police's Violent Crimes Division, Ashley is assigned a frightening new case: victims of a new serial killer are being found deep in rural country, a terrain that Ashley knows all too well—and to which she vowed to never return.

"Phenomenal debut with a huge creep factor… So many twists and turns, you'll have no idea who the next victim will be. If you love a thriller that will keep you awake well into the night, this book is for you."
—Reader review for Let Me Go

LET ME ESCAPE is book #6 in a new series from #1 bestselling mystery and suspense author Kate Bold, which begins with LET ME GO (Book #1).

A dark crime thriller full of mystery and suspense, the ASHLEY HOPE mystery series is rife with twists and jaw-dropping secrets as it unfolds into a riveting psychological thriller. Join this brilliant new female protagonist as she hunts down a serial killer, keeping you spellbound and turning pages late into the night. Fans of Rachel Caine, Teresa Driscoll and Robert Dugoni are sure to fall in love.

Future books in the series will be available soon!

"I really enjoyed this book… It draws you in right away and keeps you turning the pages right up to the end. I am really anticipating the next book."
—Reader review for Let Me Go

"A really good read. The story went quickly and the characters were interesting. I'm looking forward to the next book in this series!"
—Reader review for Let Me Go

"Good read with good plot, plenty of action, and great character development. A thriller that will keep you awake into the night."
—Reader review for Let Me Go

"Excellent start to a new series… Get this book and read it, you will love it!"
—Reader review for Let Me Go

Kate Bold

Bestselling author Kate Bold is author of the ALEXA CHASE SUSPENSE THRILLER series, comprising six books (and counting); the ASHLEY HOPE SUSPENSE THRILLER series, comprising six books (and counting); the CAMILLE GRACE FBI SUSPENSE THRILLER series, comprising eight books (and counting); the HARLEY COLE FBI SUSPENSE THRILLER series, comprising seven books (and counting); and the KAYLIE BROOKS PSYCHOLOGICAL SUSPENSE THRILLER series, comprising five books (and counting).

An avid reader and lifelong fan of the mystery and thriller genres, Kate loves to hear from you, so please feel free to visit www.kateboldauthor.com to learn more and stay in touch.

BOOKS BY KATE BOLD

ALEXA CHASE SUSPENSE THRILLER
THE KILLING GAME (Book #1)
THE KILLING TIDE (Book #2)
THE KILLING HOUR (Book #3)
THE KILLING POINT (Book #4)
THE KILLING FOG (Book #5)
THE KILLING PLACE (Book #6)

ASHLEY HOPE SUSPENSE THRILLER
LET ME GO (Book #1)
LET ME OUT (Book #2)
LET ME LIVE (Book #3)
LET ME BREATHE (Book #4)
LET ME FORGET (Book #5)
LET ME ESCAPE (Book #6)

CAMILLE GRACE FBI SUSPENSE THRILLER
NOT ME (Book #1)
NOT NOW (Book #2)
NOT WELL (Book #3)
NOT HER (Book #4)
NOT NORMAL (Book #5)
NOT AGAIN (Book #6)
NOT SAFE (Book #7)
NOT TODAY (Book #8)

HARLEY COLE FBI SUSPENSE THRILLER
NOWHERE SAFE (Book #1)
NOWHERE LEFT (Book #2)
NOWHERE TO RUN (Book #3)
NOWHERE LIKE THIS (Book #4)
NOWHERE GIRL (Book #5)
NOWHERE TO HIDE (Book #6)
NOWHERE CERTAIN (Book #7)

KAYLIE BROOKS PYSCHOLOGICAL SUSPENSE THRILLER

Made in the USA
Columbia, SC
27 March 2023

14376633R00145